D0868175

"Joern intricately weaves together a compelling family saga and a beautifully rendered paean to the land her characters love and are struggling to preserve. . . . Joern's lyrical and painterly descriptions of the vast Sandhills are the perfect backdrop for this subtle drama." —*Booklist*

"Joern is particularly skilled at depicting contemporary small-town life and the issues rural communities face: the difficulty small farmers and ranchers have staying afloat financially and the decision of younger generations either to leave for urban areas or to endure directionless lives. She packs a lot of story into 250 pages." —*Library Journal*

"Joern's characters are as stern as the land, and the world of her debut novel is sturdy and memorable." —*Publishers Weekly*

"[Joern] is a fearless teller of hard truth. Set in the Sandhills of Nebraska, *The Floor of the Sky* is a tale of quiet heroics, a story of tenacity and courage, an intimate glimpse into the lives of independent ranchers determined to survive. A powerful portrayal of family, land, and loyalty. We are the wiser for having read it." —Sheila O'Connor, author of *Where No Gods Came* and *Tokens of Grace*

"[Joern's] characters are sensible, endearing, and deeply haunted, and there's enough story and intrigue for ten novels. Secrets, old and new, keep the past constantly bumping into the present, making for a mesmerizing family saga." —Timothy Schaffert, author of *The Singing and Dancing Daughters of God*

"Pamela Carter Joern writes with compassion and a wry sense of humor, in a direct and true style that takes in the vivid details of the world of the Nebraska Sandhills and the complexities and nuances of her characters' inner lives. Her work may bring to mind the novels of Kent Haruf and Larry McMurtry—though, like the fiercely independent women that populate her novel, Joern is clearly an original!"—Dan Chaon, author of *You Remind Me of Me*

"A testimony to the power of family secrets and the enduring legacy of the land."—Mary Clearman Blew, author of *Balsamroot: A Memoir*

"[An] emotionally rich first novel about an unwed pregnant teen spending the summer with her grandmother in the hardscrabble Nebraska Sandhills. . . . Her visit stirs up long-simmering tensions for Toby, Toby's bitter sister Gertie, and George, who has worked on the farm for more than fifty years. . . . [George's] unspoken love makes for irresistible reading. . . . Think Paul Newman with Joanne Woodward. . . . A resonant love story, whatever the age of the lovers."—*Kirkus Reviews*

TOBY'S LAST RESORT

FLYOVER FICTION

Series editor: Ron Hansen

TOBY'S
LAST RESORT

PAMELA CARTER JOERN

UNIVERSITY OF NEBRASKA PRESS | LINCOLN

© 2023 by Pamela Carter Joern

All rights reserved

The University of Nebraska Press is part
of a land-grant institution with campuses
and programs on the past, present, and
future homelands of the Pawnee, Ponca,
Otoe-Missouria, Omaha, Dakota, Lakota,
Kaw, Cheyenne, and Arapaho Peoples,
as well as those of the relocated Ho-
Chunk, Sac and Fox, and Iowa Peoples.

Library of Congress Cataloging-
in-Publication Data
Names: Joern, Pamela Carter, 1948–
author. | Hansen, Ron, editor.
Title: Toby's last resort / Pamela Carter
Joern; series editor, Ron Hansen.
Description: Lincoln: University of Nebraska
Press, [2023] | Series: Flyover fiction
Identifiers: LCCN 2022031517
ISBN 9781496232694 (paperback)
ISBN 9781496235268 (epub)
ISBN 9781496235275 (pdf)
Subjects: BISAC: FICTION /
Literary | LCGFT: Novels.
Classification: LCC PS3610.O25 T63 2023 |
DDC 824/.82—dc24/eng/20220708
LC record available at https://
lccn.loc.gov/2022031517

Set in Minion by Mikala R. Kolander.
Designed by N. Putens.

For Nadine, Elijah, Henry, Tyson

Rust, thistles, silence, sky.
—"Polish Sleepers" by Seamus Heaney, twentieth-century poet

There are hundreds of way to kneel and kiss the ground.
—"The Ground" by Rumi, thirteenth-century poet

AUTHOR'S NOTE

I GREW UP IN THE PANHANDLE OF WESTERN NEBRASKA, A PART OF THE Great Plains drenched in history and barren to the unpracticed eye. I remember big sky and space, and I spent many afternoons after school trudging across fields or pastureland while spinning tales in my head.

Many years later, from my city desk, I wrote my first novel, *The Floor of the Sky*. I borrowed the title from a Willa Cather quote: "Elsewhere the sky is the roof of the world; but here the earth was the floor of the sky." I wrote that story partly out of homesickness. Immersing myself in the world of the Bolden family, set in the Nebraska Sandhills on the Bluestem Ranch, was a way to visit a landscape that I miss and to honor the people whose lives are forged by devotion to it.

The Floor of the Sky is a story of family secrets that impinge on the present: of Lila, a pregnant, teenaged granddaughter who seeks a home for her unborn child; of George, the hired hand who carries a quiet love; of Gertie, embittered and wronged; and of Toby, a widowed grandmother who is the center pin, holding the family history and the deed to the ranch.

When I entertained questions at readings, I was often asked, "What about Nola Jean?" Nola Jean, the offstage mother of Lila, nearly estranged daughter of Toby. I responded, "She's not the subject of this book." But I didn't forget the question. Nola Jean has tugged at my consciousness for years until finally, due to the pandemic, I found the time to sit down and listen to her.

I reentered Toby's world with a sense of relief and coming home. I found Toby still had much to teach me as I threaded my way through Nola Jean's story and discovered new characters. This story takes place ten years after *The Floor of the Sky*. Nola Jean and Toby are older, and so am I. What to do about aging is one of the questions that concerned me, and I amused myself by thinking of this story as Toby's Last Resort long before the idea for her actual resort took place. I had a good time sitting again at Toby's kitchen table; I hope you will too. If you are new to the table, welcome.

TOBY'S LAST RESORT

Toby

THE LAST TIME WE SAW TOBY, SHE WAS SITTING ON GEORGE'S FRONT porch, facing east toward the promise of daybreak while the sun squatted in the western sky. Hear that? The lilting strain of a meadowlark, a solo piccolo. Toby follows the worn path from the front porch of George's house over the rise to the family cemetery. Late afternoon in early summer. Prairie grass rolls across the hills, verdant from spring rains, dotted here and there by a lonesome tree. A breeze tickles the sage, rattles the leaves in the cottonwoods. The air smells as brisk and green as freshly scythed hay. Toby stops at the top of the rise, lets her gaze follow the sweep of land, turns to take in all four directions. She owns this property as far as the horizon, homesteaded by her grandfather not long after the Civil War. She's the last Bolden likely to live here, and she's grown old. What will happen to this land when she's gone? For now, Toby finds solace standing on the ground she's known all her life, covered by a canopy of sky tucked to the four corners of the earth.

She slips the looped wire off a post to open the gate to the family plot. Grama grass and a few yuccas entwine with the barbed wire fence, six old boots atop fenceposts, toes pointing home. Toby stops briefly to pay homage to her mother, Rosemary. Her father, Luther, is buried here too. She's too old now to spit on his grave, though he was a mean-spirited man who, one way or another, wounded all three of his children.

Her husband, Walter, is buried here. Her sister, Gertie, and her brother, John, both claimed ten years ago by the fire that burnt the ranch house—a Sears kit house named the Alhambra after a Spanish fortress—that had been her father's pride. Gertie's husband, Howard, died in a nursing home soon after. He now lies beside Gertie in this place of nothing but rest.

Toby heads to the corner of the cemetery where Luther consented to let George Bates bury his wife, Ella, and later his younger brother,

David. Luther would never have gone so far as to consider a hired hand family, but Rosemary had loved Ella and insisted she belonged in the family graveyard. Then, Luther had enough guilt over David's death that he could not deny Toby's petitions. Toby and David, teenagers in love, had tried to run away, but Luther followed after them with a loaded shotgun. He had Rosemary in the car, pulled up alongside David, the gun went off and the two cars collided. Ruled an accident, David died from the shotgun blast and Rosemary from injuries caused by the crash. Luther lived out the rest of his days in a wheelchair, but he never lost his stranglehold on the family. Later, when Toby realized she was pregnant, Luther bullied her into giving her baby up for adoption. George found a home for her son with a distant cousin of Ella's, and when the boy was twelve, Toby helped nurse him while he lay dying of leukemia.

Standing now by David's grave, Toby thinks how this constellation of trauma shaped all their lives, hers and Gertie's and George's. Sorrow comes in waves, she thinks, as she moves past these graves to the stone she's come to tend. George lies here.

"We had so little time," she says, as she squats to pull grass away from the stone. She'd known George nearly all her life. First, as the older brother of the boy she loved. Then an advocate against her controlling father and bitter sister. A friend to her husband, Walter. After Walter died, she slowly came to realize that George loved her, long before she recognized her love for him. Even then, they did not speak of it. After the fire, she moved into George's house, and still, they did not name the bond between them. Sitting on the porch one evening, George stood and held his hand out to her. She took his hand, looked into his eyes and nodded, and only then, he led her to his bed. They made love the way older people do, slow and tender, hands lingering on scars or bony hips or loosened skin, paying their respects to the ravages of time. Afterward, she lay silent while George held her, overcome with relief and joy and regret. If she were a different sort of woman, she would have wept. Only weeks later, she found George sprawled on the floor of the barn, stone cold. She sat for a long time with his head in her lap before she called the county sheriff.

She'd plummeted after that. Too much loss in too short a time. The Alhambra was gone. She had money, more than she could have imagined, thanks to George's foresight in investing and the conditions of his will, but now what? For the first time in her life Toby was alone, too young for the old folks' home, too old to start over somewhere else, and she didn't know what to do.

She remembers precisely when the idea for Toby's Last Resort came to her. She'd stood looking out the window of George's house on a brilliant January day, the sun luminous in a cloudless sky, the hills dusted white like a powdered sugar doughnut. She held a mug of coffee, hankering for a splash of whiskey she was trying to avoid. She looked around the living room, the threadbare couch, the worn braided rug on the bare board floor. Ran her fingers over the back of the rocking chair, picked up an afghan and held it to her nose to capture his scent. "What now, George? You were my last resort," she whispered.

She swears that she heard George laughing. "Not something I'd want on my tombstone," he seemed to say. "You're not ready to quit on life, are you?"

She'd gone straight to the phone and called Tom Edwards, a local contractor, and asked for an appointment. Then she went to see Malcolm Lord, the banker. They tried to talk her out of it, but by the end of the next summer, there were three one-room cabins built on her land. Working out the logistics of where to put them and how to make sure each had running water and electricity occupied her for months. She wanted none on the site of the burned house. None would be visible from the porch of George's house. The people she had in mind as guests would need privacy. It meant additional wells, miles of electrical wiring, newly graded roads, but finally, by October she had completed the first step of her vision.

She asked Dorothy Kincaid, a local watercolor artist, to help her furnish the cabins: a good bed with a nightstand, dresser, loveseat and chair, desk, kitchen table with two straight-backed chairs. Decent lamps. Cookware and implements for the small kitchens, towels for the bathrooms, bedding, and tucked in the back hallways, stacking washers and dryers. Dorothy chose wall paint that emulated the prairie: sage, sandstone, wheat. Toby insisted that each cabin have a front porch with two wicker rocking chairs. It was Dorothy's idea to name the cabins after Nebraska wildflowers: Goldenrod, Primrose, and Larkspur. Goldenrod and Primrose were near a couple ponds, sheltered by cottonwoods and thorny Russian olive trees; Larkspur, in a little draw nestled by sage, with a lone cottonwood and a towering windmill that stood like sentinels. For years, she'd leased her pastures to Royce and Julia, a neighboring couple striving to ranch in a sustainable way, but with extra fencing and careful timing, their pasture rotation was not disturbed.

The whole town thought she was crazy. No one will come, they all said. Who in the world would spend time way out here? Plus, Toby, what if something happens to you? You're not getting any younger. Toby scoffed and tossed her head, but at night, alone and awake, the same fears crouched in the corners of her mind. She consoled herself thinking that all her critics would be silenced if she went on a cruise or bought an expensive house in town. It was her money, by god, and she'd waste it any way she saw fit.

Dr. Penny Sadler helped her advertise in medical magazines, on the radio, local newspapers. She put a big ad in the *Nebraska Life* magazine, complete with pictures.

TOBY'S LAST RESORT:

A place for the wounded, brokenhearted, misfits, and dreamers! Time and space to think, to heal, to breathe.

She promised no program, no therapy, no structure of any kind—just a safe haven. Each applicant had to state their reasons for coming to Toby's Last Resort, and because no daughter of Luther Bolden could assume that all people are innocuous, they had to submit to a background check. Toby charged a reasonable rate and offered her fully furnished cabins for time periods of one to three months.

The first summer, she had only two guests, each for one month: a university professor writing a book about grasshoppers and a bronc rider with a broken leg who needed a place to recuperate. After that, word spread, and people began to come from surrounding states as well as Nebraska: a man awaiting a divorce, a wildlife artist, professors on sabbatical, a couple who'd lost a son to drugs, a young woman fleeing an abusive husband.

The third summer she hired Anita and Luis Lopez. When Luis retired early from his job as a mechanic for John Deere, Anita sold her fabric store. They travel to New Mexico in the winter to be near their son and his family, but summers they pull their trailer onto the old homestead site of Toby's Bluestem Ranch. Anita helps with the gardening and housekeeping chores, while Luis mends fences and manages the two horses, Cream and Sugar. Royce and Julia board her horses during the winter in exchange for a better rate on the pastureland they lease.

All in all, it's a good scheme, but Toby turned eighty-two in February. Her wiry hair is white as a bald eagle's head. At her last checkup, Dr. Penny said everything looked fine, but Toby knows she is slowing down, mentally and physically. Mornings, she hobbles to the kitchen for that first cup of coffee. She falls asleep in a chair with an open book on her lap. She misplaces things. Her mind wanders down long passageways of time, as it has now, squatting by George's grave, forgetting what it was she'd walked out here to tell him. A mourning dove pitches its hollow who-oo-who into the still air as she grips the top of the stone, uses it to help her stand. "Well, old man," she says, her hand lingering on the stone. "Have a restful night."

She laughs at her little joke and walks back over the same path. Once over the rise, she sees an unfamiliar car parked next to George's white picket fence. She porches her hand over her eyes but can't make out the license plate. As she nears, a figure rises from the rocker and moves toward her. A woman. Tall, bottle blonde, a slight floozy air about her. She's out here, on a ranch, wearing city shoes and a too short something that might be called a skirt. The woman stops and waits for Toby, arms crossed, one hip cocked.

"What the hell are you doing here?" Toby says.

Nola Jean

NOLA JEAN ARRIVED IN LATE AFTERNOON AFTER A LONG DAY OF DRIVING. She had decided to drive straight through from Minneapolis, armed with books on tape. Across South Dakota on I-90 through Chamberlain, south at Kadoka to Highway 20, thread through the Sandhills, stay awake by counting windmills. Take the shortcut at Hay Springs to Alliance, then meander east and south on country roads until arriving at the Bluestem. Congratulate yourself on remembering how to find this needle in a haystack. She's thinking this while standing on Toby's front porch, peering in through the screen door. Miffed that Toby isn't inside, she walks back to her car to pick up her cell phone. No service. Not a surprise.

Toby's car is here. She can't be far. Could be out riding. Nola Jean bites her lip. She decides to wait for Toby on the porch and sits in one of the rockers. Maybe this was a bad idea. She didn't tell Toby she was coming, didn't want to get into her reasons on the phone. Now that she's here in this godforsaken place, nothing but dust and grass for miles, the old uneasiness settles in. She's stiletto heels in this land of boots and spurs. Nothing matters out here but grind and hard work.

Tired, hot, thirsty, and conflicted, she watches Toby appear from over the rise to the cemetery. She should have known that's where she might be. More friends among the dead than the living. She stands and walks forward. Stops and waits, arms folded. Toby's gait is slower. Definitely older. Nola Jean doesn't wave, wondering if Toby will recognize her and wave first. Or if she will call out.

Is Nola Jean smiling? Probably not. But then, Toby doesn't smile either. Not even when she says, "What the hell are you doing here?"

"Hello, Mother," Nola Jean says.

Toby

NOLA JEAN SITS AT THE KITCHEN TABLE, WHILE TOBY WAITS ON HER: leftover fried chicken, green salad, a boiled potato each. If Nola Jean had bothered to let her mother know she was coming, Toby could have done better. She's never gotten used to seeing Nola Jean in George's house. She knows the house is technically hers now, but in her mind, it will always be George's place.

Finally, Toby sits to eat. "Lila settling in all right?"

"I think so," Nola Jean says. "Takes time. She's only been there a week."

Toby chews silently. Thinking about that summer when her grand-daughter stayed with her, sixteen and pregnant. Now, doing postgraduate work in Germany.

"I'm proud of her," Toby says. "She's moved on."

Nola Jean's fork stops midair. "Meaning I haven't?" she says.

For god's sake, Toby wants to say. Instead, she gives her head a slight shake, says nothing. They eat in silence until their plates are empty of all but a few chicken bones. Toby stands to dish up dessert. While her back is turned, Nola Jean speaks.

"How many this summer?"

Toby takes her time slicing the pie she'd made that morning. Blueberry. No ice cream. She's of a mind that ice cream ruins a good piece of pie. She sets a piece in front of Nola Jean. Runs her hands down the front of the apron she donned before supper. She despises fidgety people, but Nola Jean unsettles her. Her own daughter has always turned her into something she doesn't want to be. She fetches herself a piece of pie and sits down before she speaks.

"Why do you care?"

Nola Jean looks past her, out the window. There's not much to see out there. Plus, the kitchen faces west so the sun is in her face. "Could we not do this?"

Toby is chastened by the sorrow in Nola Jean's voice. She purses her mouth, waits a few moments, not wanting to look like she's giving in too easy.

"Two," she says. "But both are staying longer than two months."

"Are they here yet?"

"One tomorrow. The other in a couple days."

"I saw Anita and Luis's trailer when I drove in."

Toby nods. "Been here about a week. Getting ready."

Nola Jean tucks into her pie. Four bites, then she says, "You always could make a fine pie."

Even this compliment, Toby finds suspect. Along with other things her sister, Gertie, resented, Gertie's husband, Howard, preferred Toby's pies to hers. Toby wonders sometimes if Gertie poisoned Nola Jean with her accusations and accumulated insults. She listens hard for a critical edge but finding none murmurs, "Thanks."

"I thought I might like to stay a couple of weeks," Nola Jean says, still chasing blueberries round her plate. "Maybe more."

Toby raises an eyebrow. She could count on her fingers the number of days Nola Jean has spent out here in the last ten years. "Don't you have to fly somewhere?"

Nola Jean looks up. "I took a leave. I might not go back."

"That's a surprise." Nola Jean has thrived in her job as a flight attendant, flying off to Paris and London and Copenhagen, bringing Toby expensive bracelets and clothing she'd never dare to wear.

"I got tired. That's all."

"What now, then?" Toby knows Nola Jean needs to keep earning. Her ex-husband, an itinerant musician, can barely keep himself. He's of no use to her, never was.

"I have a few possibilities," Nola Jean says.

She doesn't offer specifics on what those possibilities might be, and Toby won't ask. She hopes Nola Jean has better sense than to pin her hopes on finding some man with a lucrative career. With Nola Jean's track record in choosing men, that's bound to be a disaster.

"Guess you can stay in Larkspur," she says. There are two bedrooms in George's house, but she and Nola Jean do better with some space between them.

"You want me to pay rent?"

Toby flinches. "I thought you might like some space. That's all."

Nola Jean studies her for a moment. Toby has no idea what she might be thinking. She can't read her own daughter. Never could.

"Is it ready?" Nola Jean asks.

Toby nods. She and Anita have prepared Primrose and Larkspur. They hadn't counted on needing to open all three cabins. They have tomorrow to get Goldenrod up and running. Her mind is on a detour, planning where she'll place her two guests. The man, a Methodist pastor from Wisconsin, is on sabbatical. He collects crosses, of all things, and has hired a local cowhand to take him around the countryside looking for folk art. The other is a woman poet, recovering from a sour medical diagnosis. She'll put her in Primrose, since it's closest to Nola Jean. Best to keep the reverend as far from the two women as possible.

Later, she follows behind Nola Jean's Honda in her Chevy sedan to help her get settled. Nola Jean's seen these cabins before, but she stands a good while scanning the spare room.

"No TV, I see."

"No internet, either. If you walk to the top of the hill, you can get some service on your cell phone. Otherwise, come on up to George's to use the landline." There's a TV at George's too. Small antennae, she only gets the basic channels. Uses it for news mostly. She doesn't see much point in mentioning it.

Toby pauses. She's never known Nola Jean to fill her time with anything peaceful or quiet. "You going to be all right?"

"I have some things to do," Nola Jean says. "I may be gone a few days."

Toby waits for more explanation. Nola Jean tosses one suitcase on the bed and springs it open.

"Well, good night," Toby says.

Nola Jean nods but keeps moving clothes into the small chest.

Toby turns in the doorway. "Come on up to George's for breakfast. If you want."

Nola Jean looks up then. Toby's not sure, but she thinks something softens in Nola Jean's face.

"Okay," she says. "I'll go into town tomorrow for some groceries."

"That's good, then," Toby says.

"You can come with me. If you want," Nola Jean says.

Toby considers. She knows they'll have some dancing to do to figure out how this is going to work. Neither of them is going to want too much togetherness.

"Let's just see how the morning goes," she says.

Nola Jean

NOLA JEAN TAKES HER TIME UNPACKING. SHE HAS PREPARED FOR THE
isolation of this place. Books, a pile. Fiction and biographies. One
nonfiction book titled *Motherless Daughters* that the therapist she's been
seeing for a year recommended. Magazines, fashion and decorating.
She piles all these on the desk, careful to place the latest *Elle* on top.
Her fingers linger on the cover while she takes a deep breath.

She fishes bottles of wine out of the hatchback of her CRV. She sets
the whole carton on the floor of the kitchen. From a knapsack she
withdraws several maps, including a detailed Nebraska state atlas. She
knows it's easy to get lost on these Sandhills roads. She piles these on
the floor next to the desk. As an afterthought, she drags over one of
the kitchen chairs, places it next to the desk and settles the maps there.

No closet, though there are hooks along the wall by the bed. Nola
Jean hangs her jacket and a light cardigan. She finishes unpacking her
other clothes into the small dresser. She leaves her jewelry tucked in a
travel case and slips it into the top drawer.

She wanders into the bathroom, relieved to see there's a medicine
cabinet. She unloads a few toiletries, no prescription medications, lots
of sunscreen and lotion. There's no vanity. She arranges her makeup
on top of the small dresser, though there's no mirror above it. Christ.
How does anybody manage in these places for months?

That about does it, and it's 7:45. Not even close to dark. She doesn't
plan to spend her days sitting in this cabin, but what the hell is she going
to do in the evenings? She could drive twenty miles into Elmyra, hang
out at one of the town's bars. She could knock on Royce and Julia's door,
but they're not exactly kindred spirits, their entire life consumed by
ranching and cows. Clearly, she's not going to be sitting on her mother's
front porch, the two of them sharing intimate stories into the night.
Nola Jean had been shocked to learn of Toby's past ten years ago when

Lila spent the summer here. She'd no idea that Toby had given a child up for adoption. Why had Toby kept this from her?

Motherless Daughters talked about the lifelong effects on women who lose their mothers early. The author, Hope Edelman, said motherless daughters may unconsciously expect their own daughters to supply the nurturing they missed out on. Or they opt for distance, fostering independence because they don't want to burden their daughters. Either way, the relationship is fraught with tension.

Nola Jean sees the truth in this theory. There's a Bolden family cycle of missing mothers and adoptions: Toby's father lost his mother young and was a miserable man; Toby's mother died when Toby was a teenager; Toby gave a child up for adoption; Toby and Walter adopted Nola Jean; and ten years ago, Lila gave up her daughter for adoption. A crazy legacy.

Toby doesn't know her. Correction. Maybe she does but just doesn't like her. Other people tape their child's drawings to the refrigerator with pride, but hers were barely glimpsed. Not even shoved in a drawer. She created imaginary siblings, cut them from paper, named them, and talked to them for hours. She left them lying atop her dresser one morning in a rush to get to school and later rescued them from the trash can. When she confronted her mother, Toby shrugged and said, "I thought you were done with that foolishness." By the time Nola Jean was in high school, she didn't bother to tell her parents if she was in a school play. She saved the money she made working as a carhop, bought clothes she kept in town at a friend's house where she stayed much of the time. Her subterfuge brought her less ridicule, but in the end, she felt like an imposter around her parents. Even now, in this place, she disappears, and the woman who shows up costumed as her is someone she doesn't recognize.

Nola Jean shakes her head, stops a moment to consider which would be worse—does her mother not see her? Or does she see her and just not like what she sees? That's the question that drove her to therapy in the first place. That, and the train wreck of her marriage.

She walks into the kitchen and pulls a bottle of red wine from her stash. She brought a bottle opener with her, though knowing Toby's penchant for alcohol, there might be one here. Curious, she opens the top kitchen drawer. Silverware. But the next drawer: a spatula, wooden spoon, and sure enough, a bottle opener. A can opener too.

No wine glasses, but she pours a modest amount into a small tumbler. Picking up the *Elle* magazine, she decides to sit on her porch. When she steps outside, she's aware that the sky behind the cabin is ablaze with a fiery sunset, so widespread that she can see vestiges of pink and turquoise from her perch even though the cabin faces east. All the cabins face east. George's place too. Toby has a thing about it. Says she likes to wake up to the morning light. The house Nola Jean grew up in, the big Alhambra that Toby's father built, faced east. That was a lovely palace compared to this, and Nola Jean is surprised to find she misses it. Even though she couldn't wait to escape.

An owl hoots. Crickets are striking up the band. She takes a sip of wine and removes a letter and an envelope from within the pages of the magazine. She's read the letter dozens of times. It's why she's out here. Plus, she's bent on talking Toby into moving into town over the winter. It's ridiculous that Toby stays on out here. At her age.

Midlife work, her therapist says. Nola Jean is fifty years old, and she wants to know more. More about Toby. More about herself. More about the woman whose return address is listed on the envelope she's hidden inside the covers of *Elle* magazine.

Josie

JOSIE IS AWAKE, ELBOWS PROPPED ON HER DINING ROOM TABLE. HER second mug of coffee, cold and bitter. An open book in front of her. She's sat like this since 4:00 a.m. when she woke with the dreads. Her days have started like this lately, stirring to the feeling that something's horribly wrong, impending doom. Instinctively she stretches an arm and feels for Dan's sleeping body, notes the rise and fall of his breath. He's not dead then. She's not a widow, in spite of the scare they'd had with his small stroke. She runs through her mental list of family. Both sons, okay. Sam, wasting his education and intellect on the ski slopes, but that's not new. Chad, married, a pharmacist. One daughter-in-law (not her favorite person, but that's not new either), two adorable grandchildren, all fine. Her mother—well, what can you expect at age ninety-four? Then, as her mind gropes to the surface, hidden and waiting to spring at her, Cecile! Oh god, oh god.

She knows then she won't go back to sleep. She rises quietly, grabs a hooded sweatshirt off the closet doorknob, slips her feet into terrycloth mules, and heads downstairs. Coffee. And a library book. She can't focus on the pages. She reads the same paragraph over and over.

She doesn't believe in karma. Or divine punishment. But now, at this age, when she and Dan are comfortably retired, living near their sons and grandchildren for the first time in years, when they should be able to travel and enjoy the fruits of Dan's labor as an aerospace engineer, and long, long after she ceased being haunted, out of the mist comes Cecile. Oh god, oh god.

She has to get a grip. She knows it. She's burning on a cross of indecision, wanting to tell Dan all of it, afraid to speak a word. And her mother! How can she unveil this now, after lying for half a century? What will her sons think of her if they find out? What about Becky, her sanctimonious daughter-in-law? Would she decide Josie was not a fit moral influence for little Ryan and Mindy? She couldn't bear it. She couldn't. She can't tell a soul.

When it happened, she nearly went mad with the need to tell somebody. Anybody. Against all her training as the daughter of a Church of the Light minister, she sought out a Catholic Church, a big one in downtown Lincoln, because she knew, mostly from novels and television, that priests were honor bound not to reveal things said in the confessional. She knelt in a pew for a long time, screwing up her courage. She remembers the pungent incense, the flicker of candles, the worn kneeling pad. The cloying darkness of the sanctuary, the few rays of light through stained glass. Opulent, by the standards of the house churches she grew up in. She believed in hell then, (not sure she doesn't now, only the location has changed to this present world), and she'd been told that Catholics were suspect because they worshipped Mary. And the Pope. The sharpest admonition of her upbringing was "Don't marry a Catholic," and yet, here she was, in the worst moment of her life, thinking of baring her innermost secrets to the enemy. She couldn't do it. Not even when a kindly priest, in long black robes, approached her. She looked into his face, saw nothing but concern and compassion, and she fled. Sobbed and fled. And she's been fleeing ever since.

"Josie?"

She starts when Dan speaks from behind her. She pastes a smile on her face, turns to him.

"You all right, Love?"

Look at him. This man. The love of her life. Her stalwart, ethical, fair-minded husband. He loves her. The version of her that he knows. Their forty-fifth anniversary coming up, and she needs his love like she needs air to breathe.

She raises a hand to straighten her hair, realizing she didn't comb it. Her hand trembles, and Dan catches it midair, holds it to his chest.

"What is it?" he asks.

She rises and brushes past him. Wills herself to be the wife he counts on.

"How about steel-cut oats?" she says.

Anita

ANITA AND TOBY SIT OVER CUPS OF COFFEE WAITING FOR NOLA JEAN
to appear for breakfast. She's late, by western Nebraska standards. Anita
ate her breakfast hours ago with Luis in their trailer. She and Toby have
work to do to get that last cabin up and running, but here they sit. Idle.
Neither is patient. They make small talk and drink too much coffee.
Anita wonders why Toby doesn't just leave that stack of cold French
toast on the counter and let them get to work. So typical of Nola Jean.

"Is Gabe coming out today?" Toby asks.

Anita nods. "He and Luis are mending fence in that south pasture."

Anita reaches up and pats her thick hair. She takes pride in it. She's
a short, rounded woman with a quick tongue, a big heart, and a fierce
loyalty to those she loves. Toby's on that list, as is Luis. Their kids and
grandkids. And Gabe.

"Gabe did a great job with the team this year," Toby says.

Anita nods. She knows Toby could care less about the high school
boys' basketball team. She's filling the air to buy time. Still, Anita's proud
of her little brother. She nearly raised him after their mother died when
Gabe was only a year old. She was fifteen at the time.

"How long's Nola Jean staying?" Anita asks. She tries not to make
it sound like she's anxious. Though she is. Nola Jean unsettles Toby.
Anyone can see how Toby caters to her. Anita has never understood
why. Toby acts like she's scared of Nola Jean. Or maybe, guilty. But as
far as she knows, Toby and Walter never did anything to that girl but
give her a good home.

Toby stands to stretch her back. Pours more coffee. "A week or two.
Not sure."

Toby waves the coffee pot at Anita to ask if she wants more. Anita
shakes her head, then has second thoughts and holds out her cup. Toby

pours, then sits again. Her hand travels across the tabletop, absently searching for crumbs.

"Weren't Nola Jean and Gabe in the same grade?" Toby asks.

"Yeah," Anita says. She peers down into her cup.

"Be nice if those two could be friends," Toby says.

Anita stands abruptly. Plants her empty cup on the counter. "I'm going to head on up to Goldenrod. Get started."

"Okay," Toby says.

Anita turns before she's through the door. "Gabe's busy. He's got summer camp for the boys and helping out here." She notes the puzzled look on Toby's face. She's said too much. Again. Luis is forever telling her to stay out of things.

She shoulders her bag and thumps out to her car. She slams the door and rests her head on the steering wheel. She's mad. But who is she mad at? Herself, for blabbing? Toby, for being naïve? Gabe, for being—well, a man? Nola Jean, for being a selfish sexpot whore?

That's it, she decides, and laughs to herself. Let it go, old woman, she says to the rearview mirror. But all the way to Goldenrod, she's plotting how she can keep Gabe from finding out Nola Jean is anywhere near the Bluestem Ranch.

Nola Jean

NOLA JEAN WAITS IN DR. PENNY SADLER'S OFFICE. SHE DOESN'T HAVE an appointment, but she asked Dr. Penny if she could take her out for coffee after her morning schedule. She couldn't phone ahead until she knew for sure that Toby wouldn't want to come to town with her. She should have known she wouldn't. Nola Jean wolfed down two pieces of cold French toast while her mother stood at the counter, clearly anxious to get rid of her.

"Did you want to go to town?" Nola Jean asked, swishing Toby's weak coffee around her mouth. What she'd give for a Starbucks!

Toby shook her head. "I got work to do. Anita's waiting down at Goldenrod."

Nola Jean heard the recrimination. She set her cup down, picked up her plate, washed it off in the sink, and shouldered her purse. She was already dressed for town. Stylish jeans, a fitted chambray shirt. Boots.

"You going to be here for supper?" Toby asked.

"How about if I cook?"

She watched her mother weigh this idea. She doubts Toby even knows that she can cook. She's never spent much time at Nola Jean's house.

"Fine by me," Toby said. "There's still pie."

"You need anything else?"

"Salad stuff, if you want that. I got canned beans."

All the way to town, Nola Jean had considered her menu. Stir-fry? Curry, if she could find coconut milk. In the end, she settled for pork chops, a head of cabbage for slaw. She hopes her mother will approve and wishes she didn't care.

Finally, Dr. Penny steps into the waiting room. Slides into a light jacket.

"Best place is the bakery," Dr. Penny says. She's younger than Nola Jean, slight build, glasses. She exudes warmth and confidence. She's popular here, and it's not hard to see why. A lot of young doctors come out to these small towns, part of their contract to work off medical school loans, but most don't stay long. Dr. Penny's been here fifteen years or more. She's got a husband who runs a small insurance office and kids in the local schools.

In the bakery, they each select a poppyseed kolache, one of the perks of this area that attracted Czech immigrants a century ago. Everybody in the place knows Dr. Penny, so it takes a while for them to get situated at a small table as far from listening ears as they can get. Nobody recognizes Nola Jean. At the next table, a German shepherd hunches on the floor next to a man dressed in overalls.

"What's on your mind?" Dr. Penny asks. "I assume this isn't entirely social."

"No, but it's nice to see you."

"How's Lila doing?"

"Great. Working on a PhD in Germany."

Dr. Penny raises her eyebrows, silent applause. Neither of them mentions Lila's baby that Dr. Penny delivered.

"Toby, then," Dr. Penny says. She's direct. Nola Jean likes that about her. In fact, she thinks she and Dr. Penny could be friends if they had a chance. She nods her head.

"I see. Are you concerned about something in particular?"

"She respects you."

Dr. Penny smiles. "Well. I like her too."

"I want you to help me convince her to spend her winters in town."

"You think that's a good idea?"

"She'll listen to you more than me."

"No, I mean, do you think it's a good idea to move her into town?"

"She's eighty-two. She still rides. Did you know that?"

Dr. Penny sighs. Sits back in her chair. "I admit I've considered it," she says. "She's remarkably fit, for a woman her age. Royce and Julia look in on her, make sure her drive is plowed so she can get out. Or someone else can get in."

"Something could happen, and it would be days before anyone found her."

"That ranch is her lifeblood."

"I know. I'm not saying she should give it up completely. Though I do think she should quit running her hard-luck resort."

"That's what you call it?"

Nola Jean looks away. The man with the dog rests his hand on the dog's head, a tender gesture that raises a lump in Nola Jean's throat. She could say that every effort was made throughout her childhood to harden her off against adversity. The Boldens were the epitome of the by-your-bootstraps theory. She could mention that Peg, her therapist, has pointed out that she sometimes makes comments that are sure to raise hackles, as if being in charge of raising them is safer than showing vulnerability and being betrayed. She could apologize and admit that she's jealous of her mother's compassion for strangers.

Instead, she tries to make her tone innocent. "Isn't that what it is?" she says.

Dr. Penny takes a sip of her coffee. Grimaces. Nola Jean likes her even better for recognizing a bad cup of coffee. She forces herself not to say anything, wondering if Dr. Penny will scold her for being snotty about her mother's rehabilitation project.

"How long are you here?"

Nola Jean shrugs. "Couple of weeks. Maybe more. Depends."

"Let's do this. Let's meet again after a couple of weeks. After you've had a chance to assess how your mom is doing. I won't do anything behind her back."

"You know, I've never called her that. Mom."

"What do you call her?"

"Toby, mostly. Sometimes Mother."

"Why is that?"

"She was never the warm, fuzzy type."

"No, I wouldn't think so." Dr. Penny's tone softens.

"My dad—Walter," Nola Jean pauses, horrified that her voice is clogged. She takes a breath to compose herself. "He was kind," she says, her glance falling again on the man with the dog. His overalls. The elbows of his shirt worn through. He slips his dog a bite of his doughnut, then rises to leave. Nola Jean watches them go out the door, the man and the dog, while Dr. Penny gathers her stuff and stands.

"Irwin Lund," Dr. Penny says.

"What?" Nola Jean stands too.

Dr. Penny nods toward the door. "That man. Irwin Lund. He lives alone. Kind of a recluse. Diabetic. He shouldn't be eating doughnuts. He takes that dog everywhere."

Nola Jean nods. She's trying to maneuver Toby into doing something she will not want to do, while every fiber of her being salutes Irwin Lund for asserting his independence. Which makes her, among other things, a complete hypocrite.

Anita

"YOU SHOULD TELL GABE. OTHERWISE, HE'LL RUN INTO HER. BETTER if he's prepared."

Anita lays down her knitting. She made a mistake in the last row. Knit when she should have purled. "Damn," she says.

"You know I'm right." Luis, talking again.

"Aren't you tired?" she says.

Luis chuckles. "You mean, why don't I stop telling you what you already know?"

"I'm counting," she says, studying the stitches while she backs the row off one needle onto the other. The yarn is red, her grandson's favorite color. She's knitting a sweater for him, and with any luck—if Luis stops talking—she'll have it done by winter.

"We got that fence mended. Next, Toby wants us to haul that dead cottonwood branch out of the Larkspur draw."

She's found it. The errant stitch. Now, to make sure the yarn lays properly on the needle. Tricky, in this knit two, purl two ribbing.

"I said we'll be working down by Larkspur next."

"I heard you. I'm not deaf."

"All right, then."

His voice is tender. When they were younger, that voice made her weak in the knees. Even now, her blood vibrates like a strummed guitar.

"Humph," she grunts, wanting him to know she's heard. Wanting him to be still.

They sit in silence. Their trailer doesn't have much space, but they've never minded. Luis sits on the small couch, feet propped on a footstool; Anita in a worn recliner with a lamp over her shoulder. A small TV and DVD player top a rickety table. They get no television coverage out here, but they own twenty-five movies stashed in the bedroom closet. They grew up on movies and like nothing better than snuggling on the couch with a bowl of popcorn and a favorite film. They've watched them so many times that it's like visiting old friends. One end of the sitting room evolves into a galley kitchen, round table and two chairs. Bathroom with a shower off the hallway, small bedroom in the back. The colors are muted, grays and blues. They got a good deal on this trailer, bought it secondhand from a woman who was suddenly widowed. They saw the ad in the paper, drove to Torrington the next day to look it over, and bought it on the spot. The only real change they made after purchasing it was to replace the dingy carpet with good quality linoleum. Anita likes a floor she can scrub. Photos of their family hang on the wall at various angles. Some are taped to the wood paneling with masking tape. The open windows let in an evening breeze and the coarse rasp of crickets.

When enough time has gone by, Anita broaches a new subject. "That poet moved into Primrose today."

"I saw her car. Little bitty thing."

"So's she. Fragile, kind of. Thin."

"Toby say anything about her?"

Anita shakes her head. "You know Toby. She never does."

"No, I wouldn't think so."

Luis and Anita share many things. A long history. A marital bed. Abiding love. Appreciation of hard work. Respect for Toby.

More silence. Anita counts her stitches and also the ways Luis has graced her life. She's known him since she was fifteen, the year her mother died. Their families lived just blocks apart, and one day Luis showed up at the house with a bouquet of flowers. Small and wiry, a mere shadow of the stocky, tough man he would become. He held the flowers out to her. Roses bought at the floral shop. She took them. He walked away. Not one word, but she's been his ever since.

She lays her knitting aside. Slips off her reading glasses.

"Ready?" she says.

He stands. Pulls her to her feet. Slides his arm around her shoulder. They each go through their nighttime rituals. Once they are in bed, her head against his shoulder, Luis says, "You want me to tell him?"

"I'll do it. Tomorrow."

Toby

TOBY'S MIND IS ON HER GUESTS. THE WOMAN WHO ARRIVED YESTERDAY, Isabel—Isabel Lee? No, not that. Isabel, Isabel, dammit. She shuffles through papers sprawled across the kitchen table until she finds the poet's application. Isabel LaCrosse. Now, that's a name she ought to remember. A poet's name. She wonders if it's Isabel's given name. Odd phrase, that, given name. Like most women—women her age—she took Walter's name when she married him. Was Jenkins a given name? She felt like a Bolden, would always be a Bolden, for good and for ill, and yet, the name she was given at birth is not her name now. She supposes her given name is Gwendolyn, though she's always been called Toby, after the family dog at her own insistence.

She wrestles her mind back to her guest. Some days she finds it hard to focus. She knows this is a normal part of aging, except when it becomes extreme. Gertie's husband descended into Alzheimer's, a horror she is determined to head off, should she recognize it coming. She snorts and thinks, Ay, there's the rub, and though she can remember *Hamlet* from eons ago, she wonders now how such a young man could speak so eloquently of the dilemmas of aging. Why not King Lear? She should look at that again. Lord, how cluttered the mind, at age eighty-two, the years stacked up like boxes on a lazy Susan that spins out of control and some things just fall off. What was that she was thinking? What was that poet's name again? LaCrosse. Isn't there a town somewhere named that? One of those north places, Minnesota or Wisconsin. It's a game too. LaCrosse. Something with a ball and sticks.

She sighs. Names are one thing, but she full well remembers why she chose Isabel. She needs space and time to heal from months of chemo-therapy. She wants to write about the struggle to live with uncertainty. We all live with uncertainty, but Isabel has knowledge of uncertainty she can't deny. Toby had been taken with her photo, unabashed bald head, direct gaze. Isabel had chosen to send an unadorned photo of herself in this present time. Toby admires the kind of courage that looks mud in the eye.

Her other guest will arrive today. The minister who collects crosses. That's odd. A kind of fetish. Look at her, remembering a word like fetish. She chose him out of brazen curiosity. Matthew O'Connor. Matthew, good name for a Methodist minister. O'Connor, possibly Irish? She hasn't had much use for church or churchiness in these past years, though she's capable of awe at a full moon or the reliable turn of seasons. She's moved by the beautiful and terrible plight of humanity, there's that. The cry for love alongside the pervasive inability to manage it. Don't know it when we see it, half the time. The other half, we offer it to the undeserving or in such an incognito manner that it's a wonder any two people ever connect.

She knows she's avoiding the inevitable with all this ruminating. Trying not to wonder what Nola Jean wants to talk to her about. Last night, Nola Jean had cooked a fine meal, pork chops and coleslaw, and they passed the time pleasant enough. After pie, they'd sat on the front porch. Nola Jean seemed nervous, darting from subject to subject. They covered the weather, Lila's apartment in Germany, what goes into making a good pie. Nothing about Nola Jean's future plans or why she's out here.

Finally, when night was gathering and bugs clustered around the porchlight, Nola Jean leaned forward in her chair. Toby could see she had something on her mind.

"Um . . . I was wondering, do you have some time tomorrow? There's something . . . something I want to talk to you about."

Toby caught a breath. They'd had all evening. "Oh?"

"It's not . . . I mean, I don't need anything. I'm not asking to borrow money or . . ." Nola Jean laughed. A nervous laugh. What the hell?

They had settled on ten o'clock in the morning. Toby didn't sleep much. Now, it's nine o'clock. Finally. She'd better get dressed. What could be so important—or so devastating—that Nola Jean needs an appointment?

Anita

TOBY TOLD HER SHE WOULDN'T NEED HER HELP THIS MORNING. SAID she had something personal to tend to. Anita plans to spiff up the trailer, make a pot of stew, knit a few more rows. She can't do any of that until Luis leaves, and Luis won't leave until Gabe shows up. She and Luis are early risers. They've had breakfast, washed up the dishes. He's leafing through a *National Geographic*; Anita fusses with the throw pillows on the couch, wipes the kitchen table for the third time.

"Looks like a beautiful day," Luis says.

"Uh-huh."

"Why don't you sit down?"

"Am I bothering you?"

"Yeah. You are. You're bothering me."

He's put his magazine down and peers at her over the top of his reading glasses. His eyes are kind. Laughing. She recognizes the line, straight out of *My Cousin Vinny*, but she's in no mood for playfulness.

"Is that so?"

Luis cocks his head to one side. She knows that gaze; she's seen him use it on nervous horses. She lifts her arm to throw the wet dishrag at him.

"I wouldn't," he says. As if she's of no more consequence than a fly.

Just when she's considering whether to laugh with him or turn this into a real fight, she hears Gabe's truck pull up outside.

"There he is," she says, already halfway out the door. She hears Luis mumble something along the lines of thank the Lord, which could only be said in sarcasm, since he has nothing but a grudging respect for her ardent Catholicism, but she's got no energy to waste on correcting him.

She stands on the stoop to their trailer and watches Gabe unwind himself from the driver's seat. Tall, lanky, a shock of black hair laced with enough gray to belie his athletic build. Good looking, always has been. He's had plenty of women in his life. They come and go. No one seems to stick. In clear-eyed moments, she recognizes that he's the common denominator, but it's hard for her to admit the possibility of a flaw in Gabe.

She walks out to meet him. He bends to give her a peck on the cheek. He smells of soap, a hint of lavender. She grabs his shirtsleeve.

"Gabe, wait."

"Something wrong?"

She looks past him, over his shoulder. She feels foolish now, making something of this.

"Nola Jean's here," she says. She glances at him, notes the surprise on his face, looks quickly away.

"That right?" he says.

"She's in Larkspur. Plans to stay a while."

"That'll be a first," he says, moving toward the trailer. "Luis inside?"

"I thought you should know," she says. She's still looking away from him. Taking in the pot of geraniums by their outside chairs, the sun glinting off the morning dew. A few clouds in the sky, low on the horizon like billowing bedsheets.

He turns back to her. His voice low. "That was all a long time ago," he says.

He moves off then. But she hears the quiver in his voice. Not long enough, she thinks.

Nola Jean

NOLA JEAN AVOIDS STEPPING IN A GOPHER HOLE AND KEEPS AN EYE out for rattlesnakes when she notices that her new neighbor is sitting outside on her porch. She'd been walking the path around the pond not far from the Primrose cabin. She remembers catching good-sized bass in these ranch ponds, as incongruous as that seems. Nobody ever stocked them, as far as she knew. She wonders if anyone fishes them anymore. She waves at her neighbor, not wanting to intrude on her privacy. That's what people come here for, apparently.

"Hello," the woman calls.

Nola Jean decides to walk over and say hi. She can leave in a hurry if she needs to.

"Don't you look the picture of health?" the woman says. She's thin. Tiny, though hard to gauge since she's sitting down. Her hair is super short and curly. Brown and gray. She's wearing sweatpants and a sweatshirt, even though the sun is warm. Nola Jean's in jeans, a long-sleeved shirt to ward off the sun and bugs, boots, a red wide-brimmed hat.

"I'm a walker," Nola Jean says. "Always have been."

"Sit down." The woman nods to the other rocker. Then, quickly adds, "If you care to." She smiles, and suddenly she's lovely. Her whole face lights up, overcoming the dark circles under her eyes. Nola Jean takes her up on her offer.

"I'm Nola Jean."

"Isabel." She sighs heavily. "I like to walk too."

Nola Jean nods, not sure what to say.

"Have you been here before?"

"Oh, well. I'm Toby's daughter. Adopted daughter." Why the hell did she add that qualifier? What next? A scarlet "A" emblazoned on her shirt?

"So, you grew up here?"

"Since I was two."

"That must have been heavenly."

"You think?"

"So much beauty."

"Isolated, though."

Isabel looks at her. Piercing gaze, hazel eyes. Nola Jean shifts in her chair.

"I suppose that matters a lot to a child," Isabel says.

"It mattered to me." Then, to change the subject, Nola Jean adds, "How about you? Where are you from?"

"Iowa City."

"You're a long way from home."

"I suppose. I grew up in Milwaukee. What about you? Do you still live here?"

"Here? Oh, no," Nola Jean laughs. "I live in Minneapolis. I'm a flight attendant. Was. Well, maybe I still am." She's revealing too much. Something about this woman, her directness, her stillness. There's music in her voice too. She'd make a helluva bedtime story reader.

"That sounds interesting," Isabel says.

Nola Jean pushes a lock of hair out of her face. Blonde. Not natural, though it used to be. Now her hair is mouse brown threaded with gray if she lets it go. Which she doesn't.

"Not so much," Nola Jean says. "Mostly waiting on passengers. People can be real ass—well, jerks."

Isabel laughs. "They sure can. I call it assholian behavior."

Nola Jean laughs too. Relieved to discover this odd little woman is not a saint. "That's a good phrase," she says.

"Isn't it?" Isabel pauses, then adds quietly, "I suppose we're all ass-holian from time to time."

Nola Jean nods. Hard to argue with that.

"I have seen some beautiful places," Nola Jean adds. "I fly internationally."

"I hope to do more of that," Isabel says.

They sit quietly for a few moments. Nola Jean isn't sure what she can ask and what's off limits. Finally, she says, "How about you? What's in Iowa City?"

"I teach at the university. Writing, mostly."

"They're famous for that, aren't they?"

Isabel shrugs. "That's the graduate program. I teach undergrads. Freshman comp mostly. I'm a poet."

"Oh." Nola Jean has never known an actual poet. Oh sure, people who scrawl verses on the backs of envelopes or send haiku into the newspaper, but a person who identifies as a poet? Never.

"Is that why you're here? To write poetry?"

"Partly. Are you a writer?"

"Oh, no. But I am a reader. You know, long flights. I majored in English literature."

"A walker and a reader. That's two things we have in common."

Isabel smiles again. This woman exudes compassion, without even trying. Nola Jean has no idea how she does that, but she'd like to spend the day here.

"Do you have family there? In Iowa City?"

"Nope. No husband. No kids. I have a couple siblings back East. My mom still lives in Milwaukee. You?"

"Divorced. One daughter who's working on a PhD in psychology. She's studying in Germany."

"How about siblings?"

"No. Just me. I am Toby's one and only."

Isabel looks at her again, that piercing gaze. "Well, Nola Jean, I'm going in to rest now, but I hope to see more of you."

Dismissed, Nola Jean stands to leave. She's well on her way back to Larkspur before she realizes that Isabel never divulged why else she's in this lonesome place. Partly, to write poetry. But what's the other part?

Nola Jean and her friends make a game of inventing lives for their passengers. She's become an astute observer over the years. She can spot someone recovering from a breakup, a workaholic, a neurotic traveler. She doesn't know what to make of Isabel. She's calming to be around. Comforting. Somehow at ease in this world, a quality Nola Jean envies.

Toby

FOR ONCE, NOLA JEAN SHOWS UP ON TIME. TOBY MOTIONS HER TO THE kitchen table. She's got coffee on, but Nola Jean refuses her offer. After they're sat down, Toby thinks it might have been a mistake, putting this table between them. What kind of signal does that send?

"Guess I'll have a cup," she says, standing to pour herself coffee.

"Maybe some water," Nola Jean says.

Toby busies herself opening a cupboard, filling a glass. When they are both sat at the table, she waits for Nola Jean.

Nola Jean knots her hands atop the table. Removes them to her lap.

"Oh, for god's sake," Toby bursts. "What is it? You're not dying, are you?"

Toby realizes, only after she says this—her attempt at a joke—that this is precisely what has been gnawing at her. She's scared to death that Nola Jean is sick.

"No, nothing like that." Nola Jean takes a deep breath. "I've been seeing a therapist. For about a year."

Toby nods, thinking, Oh lord, here it comes. All the things she's done wrong. Recriminations over actions she can do nothing about. She's seen enough TV to know this is how psychology works. She's highly suspect of it. Even though Lila, her only grandchild, is pursuing a PhD in psychology. Toby was raised to think of mind-drilling as pseudo-science. At best, unnecessary. Potentially harmful. Some things are better left unsaid. She was guided by that tenet most of her life, and that, too, turned out to be wildly off the mark, as she found out the summer of the fire. Really, at eighty-two, she has no idea how she's supposed to live. By what rules. It's hard work to look past her own fear, but there's such anxiety on Nola Jean's face that she decides to try to put her at ease.

She says, "I see. Has it helped?"

Nola Jean lets out a gust of air. Reassured? Who can say?

"I think so," Nola Jean says. "My marriage." She shrugs as she offers this up. "And I wanted to know more. About myself."

Toby nods. She can't trust herself to say the right thing, so she opts for silence.

Nola Jean rushes ahead. Toby realizes, as she listens, that Nola Jean has rehearsed this speech. Sad, that own daughter is afraid to talk to her. But also, she's aware that Nola Jean is couching this tenderly. She's touched, and that's the last thing she expected.

"We've never talked about my adoption. What you remember. Or even, what you were told about my birth parents."

"It was different in those days," Toby says. "Nothing was in the open. We weren't encouraged to tell you much. Adoption carried a stigma back then. Some people never told their kids that they were adopted."

"But you told me," Nola Jean says.

"Yes. We thought we should since you weren't an infant. We figured you probably wouldn't remember your parents, but if you did, we didn't want you to be confused. Mostly, we didn't want you to hear it from someone else."

She's wondered, over the years, if telling Nola Jean was a mistake. If she got teased at school. If she told her friends. She has never asked Nola Jean, and for all the stars in the Milky Way, she has no idea why at this moment.

"Was that hard for you?" She steels herself for the answer she's sure is coming. Tries not to hold her breath while waiting for it.

Nola Jean bites her lip, a habit she's had since childhood. "Sometimes," Nola Jean says. Her voice, very quiet. "Other kids, you know."

"You told your friends?"

"I told Sharon. In fourth grade. She said something about me taking after you, looking just like you, and I said that wasn't likely and then I had to tell her why. After that, everybody knew."

Toby nods. No way would Nola Jean want to look like her. Or have anybody think that she did.

"Sometimes—" Nola Jean starts and stops this sentence three times. "Sometimes I thought you told me because you were ashamed of me."

Toby reaches her hand across the table. Pulls it back. "No. We were never ashamed."

"I was different. I knew I was different."

"From us, you mean?"

Nola Jean looks away, out those west-facing windows. Toby waits. She's thinking of the people she knows whose children have moved on to lives far afield of their upbringing. It's not that unusual. Small towns and country life are dying across the Midwest. Sustainability is a problem, and the lure of culture can't be denied. She's prepping herself to say all of this when Nola Jean finally speaks.

"I didn't know anyone else who was adopted."

"Oh," Toby says. Oddly relieved, in a way she's not proud of. Maybe this isn't going to be as bad as she thought.

"I guess that's why I wanted to know more about my parents."

"The only thing we were told is that your parents both died in a tragic car accident. There was no other family, and that's how you landed in the orphanage."

Toby pauses, peering into the past. She's not sure, even now, how much to tell Nola Jean. How wounded she had been, how raw, after the death of the son she'd given up. How she and Walter had driven to Omaha to the orphanage. How frightened she was at the prospect of caring for an infant, when she still had Luther home in a wheelchair. She'd had to talk Walter into adopting an older child. Walter was set against it because he thought older orphans could be scarred from loss and deprivation, and neither he nor Toby were equipped to handle a child with out-sized emotional needs. He agreed to look at the prospects, which made Toby uncomfortable, like judging horses at an auction, their gait, their temperament, but a child?

They drove all day, stayed the night in a hotel, ate a big breakfast, and then went to the St. James Orphanage. Big brick building. A nun, Sister Margaret, met them at the door. She was dressed like a nurse, not in a habit. She took them to a large room, multiple windows, children playing with blocks or dolls. Some sat at low half-moon tables with a nun seated in the middle holding out a picture book or overseeing an art project. The room smelled like a damp dog. Except for a few crying children, it was eerily quiet. Even now, Toby remembers thinking it felt like the day before a storm, when the air is uncommonly still and suffocating.

"I know it can seem overwhelming," Sister Margaret said.

Toby wanted to run from the room. Walter took hold of her hand.

"You said you wanted a boy, is that right?"

They both nodded, unable to speak. They had talked about a boy. Their world was tough. Plus, Walter hoped he could turn a boy into a competent ranch hand.

Sister Margaret told them about different boys, a five-year-old named Ralph, one who liked stories about horses. Though making an effort to listen, Toby's attention was drawn to one small girl standing at a table all by herself in a corner of the room. The child built a stack of blocks, three high, then knocked it over. Next, a stack four high, knocked it over. Toby watched her go through this ritual five times, until she finally attempted a stack of eight blocks that wouldn't stand alone. In fury, she swept her arm across the table, scattering all the blocks to the floor. She did not cry or make a sound. She surveyed the aftermath, then knelt and picked the blocks up again. Here was a child who could take care of herself. She wouldn't require too much of them. Toby wanted that little girl.

Walter was surprised, of course, when Toby asked about the girl. She'd only been in the orphanage three months. Her parents had been out to a movie when their car was hit by a drunk driver. The babysitter, a local schoolgirl, told the police the child was two years old. She knew because she and her parents had been invited to a birthday party in April; she couldn't remember the date. The police interviewed the babysitter's mother who confirmed her daughter's account. She also told the police that there was no other family. The couple were young, just getting started, the father a salesman. The neighbor doubted if there was much of an estate. The house and estate were turned over to the courts, and the police brought the girl to the orphanage.

Walter had been hard to persuade away from wanting a boy, but that night in the hotel room, Toby stressed that this girl had come recently from a loving home. She did not tell Walter her belief that the child had composure that other kids did not have or that her self-sufficiency had prompted Toby to see herself as this girl's mother.

The next day, they went back to the orphanage, and Sister Margaret brought the little girl to them in a private room. Walter fell in love with the girl's beauty: curly yellow hair, ivory skin, sapphire-blue eyes. Her name was Nola Jean, and they took her home. Only later, after hysterical nights, after her refusals to eat, her body stiffening when they tried to hug her or help her into a bath, only then did Toby realize that what she had witnessed had been less about self-sufficiency and more about trauma. She and Walter had chosen a child they thought would be easy, and instead, they'd gotten a confused, feral creature.

If they were wrong about Nola Jean, they weren't wrong about themselves. Sure, Walter knew what to do with a motherless calf. Toby had coaxed countless calves and foals to thrive on a makeshift bottle. Both exhibited patience and basic kindness with critters whose needs they understood, but with a willful, unhappy human child, they were lost. Exhausted and without resources, they didn't know what to do, except to give her what they would have wanted. Time and space. Plenty of space.

Toby realizes Nola Jean is talking. She's been so lost in her reverie that she has no idea what has been said.

"I'm sorry." She's muttering. Dammit. "What did you say?"

"I said, are you all right?"

Toby rubs her brow with her hand. "I was remembering that day we first saw you," she says. "You were wearing a red dress. Your hair floated like a cloud. Your father, Walter—well, both of us, thought you were beautiful." She smiles. Or tries to. She worries that the smile looks forced. Tight.

"I hired a private investigator," Nola Jean says. Biting her lip again. She looks thirteen and like she's been caught in the haymow with a pilfered bottle of beer.

"Oh. I see," Toby manages.

"I don't mean any disrespect," she says in a rush. "You gave me everything you could."

Toby nearly snorts at this, noticing Nola Jean doesn't say she was happy. Or that what they gave her was enough.

"I wanted to know more about my birth parents. I might have inherited medical conditions, for instance."

Toby thinks it's more than that. Much more. She's well aware that she and her only daughter hold few interests in common. Nola Jean never took to ranch life. The first day when she got out of the car, she vomited, and though she was a toddler and it had been a long car ride, Toby has always taken that moment as a sign. Walter tried to teach her to ride, but Nola Jean clenched in fear. She wanted nice clothes when Toby and Walter were content with denim and flannel. She hated the isolation of the ranch. After much pleading, they had allowed her to stay often with a friend in town during her high school years.

"The thing is . . ." Nola Jean takes a deep breath. "I found out that the people who died in the car accident weren't my birth parents. They had also adopted me."

"What?" There's a lag in Toby's comprehension. Like a skipped record.

"The people who died. They had adopted me," Nola Jean repeats.

"How . . . how could that happen? The orphanage—the one we went to—had a birth certificate with their names on it. Doug and Susan Scranton."

"You know how it worked. The state issued a new birth certificate with adoptive parents' names as parents. They adopted me when I was three months old from St. Thomas Orphanage in Lincoln. Before that, I was in a foster home. They named me Nola Jean, after a beloved great-aunt."

"They named you?"

"I don't know what—if anything—my birth mother named me. My birth date is the same. At least I didn't find out, after all this time, that I'm not really an Aries."

Nola Jean attempts a laugh, but it comes out brittle and hollow.

"How did you—your investigator find out?"

"He located a distant cousin. She knew that my first adoptive mother couldn't have children. Something about a childhood illness. So then he started checking with orphanages in the area."

"Oh," Toby says. That feral two-year-old. Oh lord, they'd had no idea. "What about . . . did you find out anything about your birth parents?"

"Nothing about my father. But my mother's name was Josephine Taylor. She's still alive. And married. Her name now is Josephine Klingman, and she lives in Fort Collins."

"You've been in touch." Toby understands, now, why the long visit.

"I wrote to her. I wrote five letters before I got brave enough to send one. I didn't want to disrupt her life, if . . . well, you know. Anyway, I waited a long time, and then she wrote back. She agreed to meet me at a restaurant."

"I see," Toby says.

"I know this is all a shock. It was to me too."

"Yes. Well, I don't . . . a shock? Yes."

"I wanted you to know."

Toby nods. Her mind is pitching down multiple alleys, all of them dark. "When?" Her voice sounds strained, forced through a colander.

"Next week. Tuesday."

Toby's hand flutters to the collar of her shirt. Up over her brow. The damn thing seems to have a mind of its own. She doesn't know what to say. She doesn't even know what to think.

"Well, then," she finally mutters.

Nola Jean stands. Waits by her chair for a moment. "Guess I'll go now," she says.

"Okay," Toby manages. She doesn't walk Nola Jean to the door. She doesn't move from where she's sitting. She's wandering down dark alleys and unfamiliar roads. She's still sitting there when Matthew O'Connor knocks on her door.

Christ, Toby thinks. She stands on wobbly knees to meet a cross-collecting Methodist minister.

Anita

ANITA IS AT THE GOLDENROD CABIN, MAKING SURE IT'S READY FOR occupancy, when Matthew O'Connor shows up. She has just gathered her supplies, a bucket filled with cleaners, a mop, feather duster for reaching cobwebs. She hadn't needed any of them because she and Toby had readied the cabin the day before, but she takes pride in her work and wanted to make sure an errant critter hadn't moved in overnight. Plus, she's itchy today and needed something to occupy her hands, if not her thoughts. She's on the front porch when a red Ford Escort pulls up. From the driver's side, a man steps out. Bearded. Glasses. Stocky build. Wearing a T-shirt and jeans. From the other side—she might have known—Nola Jean. How does she do it? Does she lie in wait, like a black widow spider?

Matthew steps forward with his hand outstretched. "Here," he says. "Let me take that for you."

It takes Anita a beat to realize he's talking about her bucket. Before she can reply, he's wrested it from her. "I'm Matthew," he says.

Nola Jean has reached the porch by now. Wearing a long-sleeved shirt, jeans, boots. Carrying a red hat. "Hey, Anita," she says. "I was walking back from my meeting with Mother. Matthew offered me a ride if I'd show him the way to his cabin."

To Anita this sounds like a guilty recitation. Why should she care? And what kind of meeting with her mother? Who uses the word meeting when they talk to their mother? Neither of her kids or five grandchildren would use that term. Meeting, indeed.

"Can I put this in your truck for you?" Matthew asks.

He seems friendly. Polite. But Anita also wonders if he's hurrying her away so he can be alone with Nola Jean.

"How about I show you around the cabin first?"

"Great." Then, to Nola Jean. "C'mon in."

To her credit, Nola Jean hesitates. But of course, she comes.

Anita points out the obvious in the small one-bedroom cabin: here's your kitchen, here the bathroom, here your linens. She feels like a damn fool. Nola Jean stands and looks out the window onto the prairie.

To keep the conversation going, Anita says, "I hear you collect crosses."

Matthew laughs. Brown eyes that crinkle at the corners. Anita can see that he's easy to be around. "I do," he says. "It all started when a couple parishioners brought crosses to me from their travels."

"How many do you have?" Anita asks. She's thinking maybe a dozen.

"I'd say 150." He must register the surprise on Anita's face, because he quickly adds, "Some of them are very small. Meant to be necklaces. But yeah, I probably have 100 hanging on my study walls at my church. My favorites are the folk art crosses. You'd be amazed. I have crosses made of chicken wire, toothpicks. Many are beautiful. Some are fancy, of course."

"Huh," Anita says. "In my church, we have crucifixes."

He laughs again. "Yeah. I'm a Methodist, so no crucifixes. Just empty crosses."

"Why is that?" she asks. "What do you have against crucifixes?"

He stops, then. His chatter has been open. A newbie wanting to please. But now he rubs his hand over his beard. "I don't think we need to get into a long theological discussion, do you?"

All this time Nola Jean has not said a word. Or turned away from looking out the window. Now, she pivots and says, "I should go."

Anita adds, "I'll walk out with you."

The reverend walks them to the door. Says he hopes to see more of them. Anita knows he's eager to get unpacked, get his bearings.

"You want a ride?" Anita asks Nola Jean.

"No. I like the walk," she says.

"Suit yourself," Anita says.

She watches Nola Jean walk away. Nola Jean seems lost in thought, inhabiting another planet. Anita can't help wondering what she and Toby discussed. And it's not lost on her that Nola Jean didn't bother to ask about Gabe.

Josie

JOSIE KNOWS SHE CAN'T GO ON LIKE THIS. SHE MISSED THE TURN TO her mother's assisted living place. Circled the block, missed it again. She can't keep her mind on anything.

Her mother is waiting for her in her room. Though small, it's neatly furnished: twin bed with a blue quilted spread, small stand for framed photos, a TV on a shelf unit, a blue chair, and a blue tweed gliding rocker. There's no kitchen in this room; her mother takes all her meals in the dining room. There is a small refrigerator for snacks, a cupboard. Her mother's dresser fits inside the sizeable closet. The room feels cloying, overly warm and overly furnished to Josie, but she's not the one who has to live here. At ninety-four, Evelyn has multiple physical problems: a pacemaker, hypertension, osteoporosis, a few TIA's. Her biggest obstacle is macular degeneration. When she could no longer drive, she left the small Nebraska town where she'd lived since her husband retired from the ministry. She'd been widowed for twenty-five years, but the townspeople fondly remembered Samuel and looked out for her. She can't see well enough to read or crochet or write letters, any of the pursuits that might help fill her days. She watches a lot of TV news, which hypes both her anxiety and her tendency to pronounce judgment. She takes a regimen of pills, but her mind is sharp, except when she's overly anxious, which she often is. She can, and does, still play cards. No one understands how she does it or why she nearly always wins.

Josie hates to play cards. She also hates to lose, and with her mother and cards, losing is a given. It makes her feel stupid to lose, and who likes feeling stupid? She tries, over and over, because she's a full-grown woman and knows her reluctance is childish. Invariably, it ends badly. She wilts into displays of poor sportsmanship, which makes her feel even worse, her mother gloats over winning, the cycle as dependable as forsythia in the spring.

Josie's father, Samuel, was an imposing figure, and Josie has some sympathy for her mother having lived so long in his shadow. Evelyn accepted his way of looking at the world, disappointed that most people couldn't live up to their high standards. Though stern, demanding, and unforgiving of what he deemed errancy, Samuel was popular with his followers. Charismatic and gifted with a flair for oratory, he offered people a path of certainty. So long as nothing too far afield happened—nothing to call into question Samuel's claims that good is rewarded and evil punished—adherents could bask in a childlike acceptance of the goodness of life. It has taken Josie nearly fifty years, a college education, a master's degree in mathematics, and a lot of distance to get out from under her father's judging eye, and even now—with this latest turn of events in her life—she has to work hard not to think she's being punished at last for the sins that have haunted her.

Today, her mother wants Josie to take her shopping for a hanging plant. She and her mother do share this, a love of growing things. Though her family had moved frequently as her father established new churches, their home always held green plants. Her mother had a particular flair for growing African violets, a gift Josie has not inherited though she has tried numerous times. She remembers her mother starting plants from single leaves, the dainty flowers of pink, lavender, white, magenta. Evelyn is wearing purple today, turned out in one of the outfits Josie buys for her, knit pants and coordinated top.

"Can you help me find my amethyst earrings?" Evelyn says.

Josie opens the closet door. A plastic organizer hangs from the door, pockets with jewelry separated by color. Each pocket is labeled in large black letters. After several tries, Josie finds the amethyst earrings in the pocket labeled GREEN, but at least they are both there. She helps her mother fit them into pierced ears. When Josie was a teenager, her father forbade pierced ears, claiming some abomination or other, associating pierced ears with loose women. It pleases Josie, this small rebellion of her mother's, that after Samuel died, she consented to getting her ears pierced.

Her mother chatters about her life while Josie guides her to the car, fastens her seat belt, drives her to a local garden store, shepherds her inside. Josie doesn't pay much attention, having heard it all before, who snubbed who at the breakfast table, the handsome young man who comes to play old timey songs on the piano, the disappointing minister who leads a Sunday service. She's trying to imagine bringing up the topic of Cecile. Running it over and over in her mind. Predicting her mother's reaction. Every time, the result is disastrous.

"How about this one?" Josie says, indicating a trailing dieffenbachia. They've already dismissed aloe vera, jade, all sun-loving plants. Her mother's only window faces north.

Her mother sighs. "If you think that's the best we can do."

On the way to the checkout, they walk past a counter filled with blooming African violets. "Oh look, Mom," Josie says. She's flooded with nostalgia.

Her mother reaches out a hand, cups one burgundy flower, bends low to look at it. "Do you remember when Wilma Polinski took all my violets?" she says.

"No, I don't."

"You might have been gone to Lincoln by then."

"What happened?"

"Some of them had spotty leaves. Wilma came to see me. I said something like, My African violets don't seem to be doing well. I thought she might have some advice. She said, Get me a box. I gave her the box, and she loaded them all up and took them home."

"Why did you let her do that?"

"I don't know. I was shocked. Also, I thought she'd give them back."

"Did she?"

"Oh, no. Next time we were at her house, she said, Come look at my violets. There they all were, blooming."

"That's terrible," Josie says. She means it. "Did you ask her to give them back?"

Her mother's mouth compresses into a forbidding line as she shakes her head. "I started to, but your father laid his hand on my arm. You know, those signals husbands and wives have that no one else sees. Later, he said, People are more important than plants. So, I let it go."

42

"Oh, mom." Josie's outraged on her mother's behalf. He wouldn't have been so dismissive if someone had made off with one of his numerous Bibles.

They pay for the dieffenbachia. Josie is hauling her anger around in her mind, her mother's acquiescence, her father's moral standards. They walk to the car, get settled. They are halfway back to her mother's home when Evelyn says, "He said, there are other violets. I didn't want other violets."

Josie keeps her eyes on the road. She's thinking of violets and pierced ears, surprised at her mother's vehemence.

In a quiet, small voice, Evelyn says, "He bought one for my birthday. But it didn't survive."

"Why not?" Josie asks.

"I didn't water it," her mother says.

Josie glances at her mother, almost sends the car up onto the curb and swerves sharply. Her mother looks, unseeing, straight ahead.

Nola Jean

FRIDAY AFTERNOON. THE GUESTS ARE GATHERED OUTSIDE TOBY'S HOUSE in the front yard that George created with a hard-to-manage lawn, enclosed by a white picket fence. Friday afternoon Five O'Clocks are a tradition at Toby's Last Resort, an open invitation to gather for beer or soft drinks. On the first occasion Toby offers pie, which she does today, blueberry or apple. When there's pie, there's also coffee, prepared ahead and poured into insulated urns. In addition to the picnic table, a few lawn chairs have been set out. Some weeks, no one shows up, but today all the guests are here: Isabel, Matthew, and Nola Jean. Anita and Luis, of course. Anita is helping serve up the pie. Accompanying Matthew is a long, tall man in skinny jeans, western shirt with pearl snaps, and boots. He's wearing a string tie. He looks like someone auditioning for a part in a Western. Especially next to Gabe, who looks like the real thing—sleeves rolled up, work jeans dirty at the knees, hatband tan. Gabe hasn't changed much since he and Nola Jean were in high school. Older. A little gray. He still stands proud, that same lazy crooked grin. Right now, he's next to Isabel, looking down at her and listening in that way of his.

Nola Jean hasn't seen or talked to Toby since their conversation about her adoption. She almost didn't come to this little soiree, but she thought that might look too obvious. She doesn't want to cause Toby more grief, but she's not sure whether that means she should stay away or try to act normal. And what would normal look like? Nothing about this situation is normal.

She takes in the yard, the potted geraniums not yet flowering. The sweet peas stretching to climb the fence. An oasis, incongruous on the prairie, amid yuccas, cactus, and sage, but not that uncommon among ranchers. A taste of civilization. She knows it's likely Luis who tends this now. Anita and Toby are at the picnic table, cutting pie and laying it out on small paper plates. She decides not to disrupt them. She can't intrude on Gabe and Isabel either. Gabe will be none too happy to see her. Luis is guffawing with Matthew and the drugstore cowboy in the only spot of shade afforded by the towering cottonwood that grows outside the fence. Nola Jean ambles over to their group.

"Nola Jean," Matthew says. Warm all over, that one. "Let me introduce my guide. This is Corey Spencer."

"Howdy," the guide says. Sticks his hand out for a handshake. He's younger than Nola Jean first thought, midtwenties at most. Handsome. Dark hair and blue eyes, not a combination you see all that often. His hair falls in a deep wave over his forehead.

Anita calls to Luis. She wants him to bring out the coffee urns. He grins, rolls his eyes, and saunters off into the house.

Nola Jean shakes Corey's hand. He hangs on a little too long. Gives her an obvious once-over and says, "You're a pretty sight."

Nola Jean almost laughs. She can't get over feeling it's all rehearsed. She's surprised he didn't call her little lady. She's wearing jeans and an orange cotton smock, embroidered with flowers, ties at the neck that she's left dangling.

"So, you're the local cross expert?" she says.

Corey moves into his aw-shucks mode. "I just know the area, that's all."

"You live around here?"

"Up by Minatare," Corey says. "My folks farm up there."

Nola Jean nods. Minatare is a tiny community west on Highway 26. It's main claim to fame is a gigantic feedlot that gives the town a distinctive flavor.

"How'd you meet Matthew?"

Corey shoots a sideways look at Matthew, which seems odd. Something off script, apparently.

"I just answered his ad is all. He said he wanted somebody to drive him around the panhandle of Nebraska, looking for folk art. It gets me out of the field."

Corey doesn't look like he spends much time in a field, but Nola Jean doesn't say this. She notices that Gabe and Isabel have finished their pie. They're at the picnic table thanking Toby and Anita. Next, Gabe is holding open the fence gate for Isabel. Nola Jean's relieved that she won't have to face him. And a tiny bit deflated.

"You guys want pie, you'd better get in line," she says. "My mother's pie is a big hit."

"I forgot to tell you, Corey. Nola Jean is Toby's daughter," Matthew says.

"Like mother, like daughter," Corey says.

Nola Jean smiles but offers nothing to correct his assumption. She's learned one or two things since fourth grade.

"C'mon," Matthew says, wagging his head at Nola Jean.

"No, oh no, thanks. I think I'll wait a bit. It's early. I mean, I haven't had any dinner yet. It's early for pie."

While she stammers through her lame excuses, Matthew and Corey move toward the picnic table. Nola Jean is left standing, not sure what to do with herself. She's out of place here, even more than she used to be. George's house. The Alhambra gone. She walks around behind the house to the garden plot. Toby has already planted lettuces, radishes, each row marked with the seed packet turned upside down over a popsicle stick stuck in the ground. When it's warmer, there'll be tomatoes and beans. Beets.

She remembers another gate back here. She decides to go for a walk, swing around the pond behind Goldenrod. Maybe she'll thread her way back to the family cemetery. Check out her ancestors. Maybe in the cemetery, with the dead and buried, she'll feel at home.

Anita

LOOK AT THAT NOLA JEAN. WEARING MAKEUP. TIGHT CITY JEANS. ANITA'S relieved to see that Gabe is involved in a conversation with the poet lady. True to form, Nola Jean ignores Toby and sidles up to the group of three men. She's a man magnet, that one. Or men are a magnet for her. Either way, Anita decides to get Luis out of there. She signals to him that they need the coffee urns, even though no one, so far, has asked for coffee.

She watches Toby for signs that she's hurt by Nola Jean's snub, but Toby betrays nothing. When Luis brings the coffee, she sits down with him on the end of the picnic table to tuck into her pie. Toby sits, too, on the opposite side.

"Great pie," Luis says.

Anita reaches up to wipe a blueberry stain off Luis's chin. That man. One of these days, he's going to need a bib.

Luis leans into her hand. He looks at her and winks, and damn, if she doesn't feel herself blush. They're too old for her to be responding to his monkeyshines.

She catches Toby watching them, notes the smile lurking at the corners of her mouth. She's sorry for Toby, living old and alone.

Isabel and Gabe stop by the table to offer thanks. Everybody makes nice.

"Can you find your way back, Isabel?" Toby says.

Anita finds that comment strange. It's not like Toby to be so solicitous. Toby never shares much about her guests and their reasons for coming here. Anita knows only that Isabel is a poet, but even poets can find their way home. True, her cabin is the farthest from the house, and Isabel arrived on foot. Still . . .

"I'll walk with her," Gabe says.

Anita's ears prick up. Gabe's pickup is parked at their trailer, in the opposite direction from the cabins. He'll have to walk all the way to Primrose and back.

Aimed straight at her, Gabe says, "It's a nice evening for a stroll."

She watches Gabe hold the gate for Isabel. Watches them move off down the road. Under the table, out of sight, she reaches out for Luis, rests her uneasy hand on his thigh.

Toby

ONCE ALL THE OTHERS HAVE GONE AND THE REMAINS OF THE PIE HAVE
been carried inside, Toby sends Anita and Luis home. She's fine tidying
up by herself. Besides, she wants to visit George before she turns in
for the night.

It's dusk by the time Toby reaches the cemetery. She's comforted by the
soft coo of a mourning dove. A crescent moon dangles like a cowgirl's
earring. She loves this time of day, when quiet drapes the land, the sun
subdued by shadows. Sometimes the sun throws out spectacular color,
a last gasp or display of power before sinking below the horizon, but
today there are no clouds to bounce the rays.

She's surprised to find Nola Jean slumped on the ground in front of
Rosemary and Luther's gravestones. She would have thought it would
be Walter who'd draw her here.

Not wanting to startle Nola Jean, Toby calls her name as she moves
aside the barbed wire gate. Nola Jean moves to rise.

"Don't. You don't have to get up," Toby says.

Toby joins Nola Jean in front of Rosemary's grave. She sits on an old
stump, placed here for this purpose. She can get herself down on the
ground, but if she sits long, it's damn difficult to get up again. She found
that out the hard way once. Even the gravestones were too small for her
to get enough purchase. She had to crawl over to the fence to find a post
to haul herself up on her feet. Indignity, that's the word for getting old.
She'd had to confess to Luis, and he placed this makeshift chair here.

She and Nola Jean sit together without talking for a few moments.
Toby is surprised that it feels nice, peaceful.

"Remember how taken Lila was with Rosemary?" Nola Jean says.

Toby murmurs in assent. The summer Lila was sixteen and pregnant,
she had found an ally in Rosemary's portrait.

"What was she like?" Nola Jean asks.

"She was kind. Gentle." All the things Toby feels she couldn't be for Nola Jean.

"Seems like an odd match with Luther."

"Yes. Still . . . he loved her, in his way. I think she knew that."

"That must have been horrible for you. When she died."

Toby sighs. She doesn't like to talk about that time. Doesn't like to think about it.

"It was . . . ," she gropes for a word. "Dark." She shudders.

Nola Jean says nothing, for which Toby is grateful. What is there left to say? She couldn't get out of bed. Couldn't eat. Nightmares. Horror upon horror.

After a while, when she feels calm, Toby says, "I'm glad you told me about your search."

"Are you?" Nola Jean says.

"Yes. I'm glad I know." She can get ready. Be prepared. For what, she's not sure. Some deep unsettling. Some reckoning. She had decided, in the small, unsleeping hours of the night, that she has nothing left to lose. She already knows that she was lacking as Nola Jean's mother. Their relationship, if you call it that, is strained and distant. Polite, but not real. It may be too late for her, but it's not too late for Nola Jean. If Nola Jean can salvage some grace for her life, then so be it. But by god, if Nola Jean gets hurt by this, there'll be hell to pay for someone.

Nola Jean

NOLA JEAN IS LOST IN THOUGHT WHILE SHE WALKS BACK TO LARKSPUR. Because it's evening and the ground unpredictable, she's walking on the sandy roads. She tingles with nerves. About the upcoming meeting with her birth mother. Also, about the conversation yet to come with Toby about moving into town. She's been waiting for the right moment.

She comes upon the turnoff to Larkspur when she sees Gabe on foot. He must have walked Isabel home. And stayed a while. Well. He always did have that chivalrous streak. One of the things girls liked about him.

She hesitates. She can either wait and speak to him, or she can make the turn and head toward her cabin. Either way, it's awkward.

She waits, and when Gabe is a few feet away, she lifts a hand to wave. "Hi."

"Hi." That crooked grin. He stops. Not too close. "I heard you were back. For a while this time."

She shrugs. "Anita tell you?"

He looks down, digs the toe of his boot in the dirt. "Yeah."

She looks around, casting for something to say. "Bright star, there."

"Venus," he says.

"You know that for sure?"

"Pretty sure."

They both laugh. She'd forgotten how nice it was to hear him laugh. Bursting out of his customary silence.

"You walked the poet home."

"Uh-huh."

More time stretches between them.

"Guess you know I'm divorced," she says. Immediately embarrassed.

"Some time back, wasn't it?"

"Ten years. Sometimes it doesn't seem so long."

He says nothing.

"You?" She looks at the night sky rather than at him.

"No one. At the moment."

She nods. Then, after an awkward pause, "Heard your team did real well this year."

"Went to State."

"That's good."

"We got creamed. But it was good for the boys to find out they can be competitive."

"Okay. Well, then, I should get home. Before it gets too dark."

He nods, waits for her to turn away.

All the way down the road to Larkspur she thinks about Gabe. Not Gabe, the man, but Gabe the boy she knew in high school. His dance moves that had drawn her and a lot of other girls to him. His way of listening like he cared what you had to say, so different from the other boys who talked to impress. His lips. His hands on her flesh.

Reaching her porch, she turns and looks up at the night sky. The bright star low on the horizon. "Venus," she says out loud. "Right."

Toby

RESTLESS, TOBY ASKS LUIS TO SADDLE UP WITH HER ON SATURDAY morning. She'd prefer to ride by herself, but this is another concession she's had to make to getting old. She's fine for a ride out and back. But, damn it all, if she wants to dismount, she fears she may not be able to get back on without assistance. This morning, she wants to check on the blowout penstemon in the far northeast corner of her land. There used to be thousands of these herbal plants in the Sandhills, but thanks to modern ranch practices—less overgrazing, control of fires—the sandy depressions necessary for the penstemon's existence are few and far between. She'd learned about the penstemon's status as an endangered species one summer when a biologist from the University of Nebraska stayed in one of her cabins. Dr. Ruth Meyer came to study the blowout penstemons at the Crescent Lake National Wildlife Refuge northeast of Toby's ranch. Dr. Meyer had been shocked and thrilled when Toby told her she believed she had some specimens on the ranch. She's been in touch with Dr. Meyer ever since, taking photos that she mails to the professor throughout the season.

Besides becoming interested in the plucky little plant herself, Toby has an ulterior motive. Since meeting Dr. Meyer, Toby has harbored the hope that the university might be interested in the Bluestem Ranch someday. Or at least some part of it. What to do with her ranch on the event of her death is a subject that keeps her awake many nights. She's considered leaving the whole thing to Luis and Anita, but she doubts they'd want to continue the resort without her. Royce and Julia could use the additional land, but they wouldn't want the cabins. Besides, it doesn't seem fair to Nola Jean or Lila for her to give the entire property away. Because of the proximity to the Crescent Lake Wildlife Refuge, the university might be interested in the resort as a research center. She could sell the remaining acres to Royce and Julia, if she could work out payments that didn't stretch them too much beyond what they pay her now for the leasing arrangement.

So far this plan exists only in her mind. Tracking her own stand of blowout penstemon is one way for her to keep the ranch in the mind of the biology research department. Since she can't predict whether she's going to die soon or ten years from now, it's difficult to know how to proceed. She's put it off, knowing she should talk to Nola Jean first, and now Nola Jean shows up this summer. Toby doesn't believe in signs and portents, but she's not a fool likely to disparage an opportunity either. Nola Jean has a lot on her plate right now, but perhaps after the meeting with her birth mother is over.

Meanwhile, Luis steadies Cream, and Toby is able to mount. Luis rides Sugar, and they set out. The morning fresh and golden. Mourning doves coo, insects buzz, and Toby rests in the rhythm of the saddle. God, she loves this.

When they reach the blowout, Luis steadies the horse while she dismounts. Not gracefully, but she manages. She and Walter were never able to do much about this blowout, tucked in a corner and situated oddly so no matter what they tried, the wind carved out a depression of bare sand. She chuckles now, thinking they worked hard to eliminate the very thing that has allowed the penstemon to survive.

Luis knows what to look for. The two of them scour the surface to find sprouts. The blowout penstemon is short-lived, at most about eight years, but it has adapted an impressive arsenal for longevity. It reproduces mainly by rhizomes underground, but in addition, in late August or early September, a single plant produces as many as fifteen hundred seeds. Dr. Meyer told Toby that a single seed might lie dormant for years or even decades before wetness and abrasion cause it to open and produce a plant.

"Here, Toby," Luis says, pointing to three distinct shoots.

They keep looking, like kids on an Easter egg hunt, and in all, they find eight, two more than last year. Toby snaps photos with the small camera hanging on a cord around her neck. She and Luis will make this trip once a week throughout the summer. A few weeks from now, the stalks will be close to two feet tall, light lavender flowers clustered along the stems. Dr. Meyer had shown her how the single flowers have dark nectar lines that guide pollinators like lights on a runway. The blowout penstemon is a survivor, against impossible odds and in the worst imaginable conditions. Toby wouldn't admit it to anyone, even with a gun held to her head, but she's developed a superstitious identity with the plant. As long as it shows up each spring, she believes she, too, will survive.

Luis is good company, mostly silent. She likes that in a man. Walter had been like that. And George. Inured to outdoor life, she supposes. Because he's silent and because she knows he can keep a confidence, she thinks about telling him about Nola Jean's search for her birth mother. She imagines it on the ride back. His noncommittal responses, a nod, a murmur. She imagines how good it would feel to relieve herself of this solitary burden. That is almost enough, because of course, she doesn't speak.

Josie

LATE AFTERNOON ON SUNDAY, JOSIE LIGHTS TWO CANDLES AT THE TABLE she has set for herself and Dan. He's golfing, but he'll be home soon. She fusses with the arrangement of daffodils she cut from her garden. First, she put on a dress. Then she changed her mind. She doesn't want him to think it's a special occasion. Not like a birthday or anniversary he's forgotten. She's done all this, the flowers, the candles, a pork roast in the oven waving its aroma all over the house, because she wants him to know how much she loves him. Before. Before and after. Sickness and in health. For richer, for poorer. There's nothing in there about before and after lies.

Tan pants. Crimson blouse. She smooths her hair in the mirror, short and gray, wavy. Nothing special. Gold heart on a gold chain around her neck. His gift to her on their fortieth anniversary. She hopes he notices. Or even remembers. Small pearl earrings. He gave her those too.

She puts some music on, Chopin piano. Decides that's too much, turns it off. Walks the floors, looks out the window in the back of the house, then the front, listens for the garage door opener. When she hears it, she's not sure what to do with herself. Where to position herself. In the entryway. In the dining room. In the kitchen.

She settles on the dining room. Where the table is set for the surprise. She's decided she'll wait until after they eat to tell him. She's made his favorite meal: pork roast, mashed potatoes, fresh salad. Ice cream for dessert.

She feels silly sitting at her end of the table. She'd never do that. It's unnatural. She stands, and at that moment Dan walks in.

"Josie," he calls.

"In here," she says.

He scans the table, the flowers, the candles, her face. He takes both her trembling hands in his. "What's the matter, Love?"

At that, all her resolve evaporates. She wails. He holds her face pressed against his shoulder, soothes her as he would a frightened child. Ignoring the food, the candles, he leads her to the living room, sits her down on the couch, and lowers himself beside her.

"I think you best tell me what the hell is going on," he says.

So, she does. She tells him about Cecile. All of it. He listens. Without once interrupting. She finishes with the recent letter she received. It's upstairs in a drawer, but she'll fetch it if he wants to see it. He sits back with his hands on his knees.

"Well," he says. "Well."

"Is that all you have to say?"

"I'm . . . surprised. What did you think? Why didn't you say something before?"

"Oh, Dan. How could I? I lied to my parents. Then, when I met you, I guess I thought it was over. Behind me. I couldn't tell you and not tell them. Or that's what I thought. I just thought it was over."

"She contacted you?"

Josie nods. Lifts her hands in a hopeless gesture.

"How did she find you?"

"I don't know. Hired an investigator, I guess. That's what she said in her letter."

"Does she sound . . . I mean, what does she want?"

"She's not a nut case."

"No, I didn't mean that. I just . . . I don't know what I meant."

"I told her I'd meet her for lunch."

"My god, Josie."

"It's supposed to happen Tuesday. At the Egg and I."

"You set this all up? Without bothering to talk to me?"

She stutters. "I know. I should have. But I, well, I am talking to you."

"Forty-four years, Josie."

"I know."

Dan rubs his face with his hand. Then the back of his neck. She knows these signals. That's why she's not surprised when he stands and says, "I'm going out."

"Out where?"

He shakes her hand off his arm. "I don't know. What does it matter? Out."

She wants to throw her arms around him. Grab his hand. He stops midway to the door. Without turning, without looking at her, he says, "I can't . . . I'm not . . ." He shakes his head, makes a gesture with his arm like he's throwing off a bad scent, and then he's gone.

Josie sits, she doesn't know how long. When she does stand, she moves like a robot. On automatic pilot. She blows out the candles. She turns off the oven, but she doesn't remove the roast. She leaves the mashed potatoes and the salad on the counter. She sits at her computer and sends a message canceling the lunch with Nola Jean. What could she have been thinking?

She goes upstairs, removes her clothing. She folds every piece neatly and piles them on a chair. Her earrings and necklace tucked back in her jewelry box. She slips into a nightgown.

It's light outside, but she crawls between the covers. She's tired. She's never been this tired. She can't think. Won't think. It's broad daylight on a summer evening, and she sleeps.

Nola Jean

MONDAY MORNING, NOLA JEAN WALKS TO THE TOP OF THE HILL NEAR Larkspur to check her email for messages. She does this daily, usually first thing in the morning, but today, she spent a chunk of time packing and repacking the overnight bag she plans to take with her to Fort Collins. The drive from the ranch will take over two hours, and she wants to get there the night before her lunch with Josephine Klingman. She made a reservation at a Ramada Inn for two nights. She has no idea how she's going to feel after that lunch, maybe in no shape to drive.

She struggled with deciding what to wear tomorrow. Casual? Dressy? She wants to look her best, but she doesn't want to look like she's making too big a deal out of this. She doesn't want to send a message of expectation. She settled on jeans. Designer jeans. A turquoise cotton shirt that shows off her eyes. Long dangly silver earrings or small sapphire studs? Necklace or no necklace? Unable to choose, she popped her travel jewelry case into her overnight bag. Makeup kit. Boots or sandals? Take both.

She catches herself gnawing at her lip. If she's not careful, she'll make it bleed, and then she'll have that to deal with. Showing up with a fat lip would definitely give the wrong impression. Another thing, she doesn't know what to call the woman who is her mother. Josephine? Mrs. Klingman? If the restaurant is crowded, how will they find each other? She has no idea what Josephine Klingman looks like. She should've sent a picture with her letter. She did send her email address, in case Josephine Klingman needed to get hold of her, but instead Josephine Klingman had written back by snail mail. No phone number. No email address.

At the top of the hill, Nola Jean takes in the view while waiting for her cell phone to power up. Rolling hills. Green, this time of year. The road weaving in and out over the knolls like a ribbon threaded through eyelet lace. Cedar shrubs nestled in seams. The big blue lid of sky.

She can see her little cabin from here, the windmill, the cottonwood. Lonesome, yes, but there's beauty in the starkness. Minimalist décor, a term she's learned in the design class she's been taking. She shunned this landscape as a child, but now she's pondering how to capitalize on this feeling of serenity and space for her next class project.

She opens her emails and is stunned to see a message from JKlingman. Sent last night. A vise wraps around her chest. She makes herself click the message open. Josephine Klingman can't make the lunch. No explanation. Nothing about getting in touch later. Nothing.

Nola Jean lifts her face to the sky. She emits a howl, long and mournful. Spent and light-headed, she bends at the waist, lets her head hang to restore equilibrium. She hurts everywhere, her chest, her heart, her throat, her head, even her knees. She hurts. And what now? Nothing. Nothing. Nothing.

Josie

JOSIE SLEEPS LIKE THE DEAD. SHE FINALLY WAKES LATE IN THE MORNING. She pads downstairs in her slippers. Blankets and a pillow on the couch. So, Dan did come home. But he didn't want to climb in bed with her.

Through the patio door off the kitchen, she sees him leaning against the banister, gazing out over the easement that stretches between their house and their backyard neighbors. Mostly grass, a few tall evergreens. He likes birds. She hopes he's there to catch sight of a chickadee or a finch and not because he intends to avoid her for the rest of their lives.

She's stuck. Should she go back upstairs and wait to see if he comes to her? She smells coffee. Should she pour herself a cup and join him? After all this time, knowing each other as they do, how is it possible they've stumbled into this unfamiliar territory?

In the end, she decides the waiting is worse than the verdict, whatever it is. She forgets the coffee, opens the patio door, and steps out onto the wooden deck. The morning air is brisk. She shivers, but not from the cold.

"Dan?" she says.

He doesn't turn or speak. She moves alongside him. Rests her arm next to his on the railing. Glancing at him sideways, she can see he didn't sleep much. His face looks ravaged.

"I called it off. The meeting."

He says nothing. She waits, and when he finally turns to her, his eyes are full of pain.

"It's not what you did back then," he says.

She nods. Can that be true? Something jagged clogs her throat.

"It's that you kept it from me."

She opens her mouth to speak, but he holds up a hand like a crossing guard.

"You didn't trust me enough to tell me, and it makes me wonder. Are there other things you've been hiding from me?"

"No. Oh, Dan, no."

"How can I know that for sure?" he says.

He looks so wounded. Bewildered. She's seen him hurt like this before. When his mother died. When he was laid off unfairly. When their youngest son was picked up for illegal drug use. Normally, she'd reach out and pull him to her, comfort him. But this is different. This time, she is the source of his pain. Neither of them knows what to do.

"It . . . it happened before I met you," she says. "At first, I didn't want you to think less of me. And then, time went on. And I just . . . I honestly don't know."

Her hand trembles. They stand side by side, not touching.

"I'm so sorry," she says. She can't look at him. Can't.

"I know."

He doesn't look either. The two of them speak into the void, not sure where their words will fall. Afraid to find out.

She places her hand on his, but he pulls away. She stifles the sob that wells in her throat.

"I'm not ready," he says.

She nods.

He turns and walks into the house. She hears the front door open and close. Where will he go? What should she do? She moves inside, folds the blanket he left on the couch. She hugs it close to her chest, uncertain whether to leave it on the couch for future nights—would that be a kindness—or put it back in the closet as a signal that she wants their life to resume. She stands and turns circles, numb with grief, wishing, wishing what? That she'd never opened that letter from some stranger named Nola Jean.

Nola Jean

NOLA JEAN LOOKS AROUND THE CABIN, AT HER PACKED BAG, DECIDES she can't stand to stay in this room. Not today. She can't face unpacking either. On impulse she turns toward Isabel's cabin. She's got to talk to someone.

On the walk over, the land rises in her face, hostile to her now. Dry, dusty, desolate. A magpie flutters at the side of the path, emits a scratchy bleat. Poor magpie. Nola Jean thinks, not for the first time, that nature can be stingy. Why should a magpie, strikingly feathered black and white, be saddled with such a raucous voice? And why should the meadowlark, graced with beautiful song, be confined to a squat brown body? She admits there are practical reasons. Meadowlarks hide in the grass where they make their nests, yeah, okay, but today she doesn't care about any of that. She hears the magpie and an echo from her childhood; don't get too big for your britches. Don't expect too much. And why not? Scraping out a living in this landscape breeds an attitude of scarcity. Brown birds sing, and flamboyant birds sound like out-of-tune violins. Doling out bits and pieces, some frontier brand of justice.

Isabel is sitting on her front porch, notebook in hand. A tall glass of water on the floor. Nola Jean pauses, takes a deep breath, and walks up the path.

"Hey," she says.

"Hi," Isabel says. Nothing more.

Nola Jean can see that Isabel is working. Focused. Like she doesn't want to be bothered. Nola Jean revises the purpose for her visit.

"I'm driving into town," she says. "Maybe Scottsbluff. Do you need anything?"

"Avocados," Isabel says. She laughs, a light flutter.

"Definitely a trip to Scottsbluff, then." Nola Jean doesn't trust the small grocery in Elmyra to have avocados worth eating.

"Oh, is that a lot of trouble?"

"No. Not really. It's the big town farther west. Not that far. Besides, I need a mission."

"Are you bored?"

Nola Jean sighs. Bites her lip. "Just restless, I guess. Sure you don't need anything else?"

Isabel smiles. The lighthouse smile. "No. I'm good. Thanks."

"Okay." Nola Jean doesn't move.

"You sure you're okay?"

"Yeah. I just . . ." Nola Jean shakes her head. "Catch you later," she says, waving her hand behind her as she walks back to her cabin.

She wastes no time. Grabs the keys to her car, drives past Toby's house without stopping. She's nearly to the main road when she decides to go back. It's tricky turning the car around without sliding into the ditch, but she manages.

She knocks first and then walks in. Calls out Toby's name so she won't be surprised. She finds her mother in the kitchen, washing up breakfast dishes. She's relieved that Anita is not here. She's the last person Nola Jean wants in on her business.

"Want some coffee?" Toby says. Toby turns, then, to look at her. Nola Jean watches her expression darken, like a shutter closing. Total eclipse of the sun.

Toby dries her hands on a dish towel. "I thought you were headed to Fort Collins today."

Nola Jean swallows. "She canceled."

"Oh, Nola Jean."

Toby starts to move toward her. Nola Jean stiffens. She doesn't mean to, but she does. She doesn't want to fall apart in front of Toby. Toby grabs the back of one of the chairs.

"I'm headed to Scottsbluff," Nola Jean says. Her voice too bright. Brittle, but it's the best she can do. "If you need anything."

"Are you sure you don't want to sit down?" Toby says.

Yeah. She's sure. Then, from some animal part of her brain comes this phrase. "I think you should move into town this fall."

"What?" Toby's knuckles turn white on the back of the chair.

"You're getting too old to be out here on your own."

"Is that right?" Toby says.

"I talked to Dr. Penny about it. She thinks it's a good idea."

"You talked to Dr. Penny. About me?"

Nola Jean sets her jaw. This is familiar territory. She knows how to behave here. Her mother displeased with her. She, defiant. All right, then.

"You got some nerve," Toby says. "Talking behind my back."

Nola Jean nods. "Think whatever you want. I can't deal with this right now."

She leaves. Slams the screen door behind her. Sits in her car and bangs the heel of her hand on the steering wheel. Dammit. She hasn't spent a year in therapy for nothing. She has just enough awareness to let a shard of shame creep in for making somebody else feel as bad as she does. But then, what the hell. Toby will get over it. Nothing fazes her for long. And that confrontation—okay, part lie—got her out of the house without crying. Because if she knows one thing for sure, crying in front of Toby is not going to make her feel better.

Anita

ANITA AND TOBY HAVE PLANNED A TRIP TO TOWN. TOBY'S GOT SOME business with Malcolm Lord, the banker. Anita wants to see her daughter and grandkids.

Toby's driving, tight-lipped. Upset about something. When Anita showed up at Toby's house, she heard her banging pots and pans all the way up the walk. Toby got out of the house without her car keys and had to go back.

Anita is used to Toby's silences, but enough is enough. "What's the matter?" she says.

"Nothing."

They drive a few more miles. Normally, they might chat about what's growing in the roadside ditches, lamb's-quarters they could harvest or early wild roses. Too soon for goldenrod or sunflowers. But today, Toby is sealed like a tomb.

"Is it Nola Jean?" Anita asks.

Toby turns her head and looks at her so long she's afraid they might have an accident.

Finally, Toby turns back toward the road. "What have you got against Nola Jean?" she says.

Anita fidgets. Pulls at her pants that suddenly seem too tight in the crotch. "Nothing." She lies. What else can she do? She recognizes a mother's instinct to protect her young, even when her young is causing her misery.

"All right, then." Toby says.

When they get to Elmyra, Toby drops Anita at Delia's house. Any other day, Toby would come in and say hello. Hug the two little boys, six and four. Not today. Today Anita barely has the car door closed, and Toby drives away. Anita's surprised she doesn't peel out, she's in such a hurry.

"What's eating her?" Delia asks, meeting her mom in the yard.

"Nola Jean," Anita says. With utter certainty.

Toby

DR. PENNY SADLER IS BUSY WHEN TOBY STORMS INTO HER OFFICE. Lucy, the nurse-receptionist, informs Toby that Dr. Penny's whole morning is filled with appointments.

"I don't need an appointment. There's nothing wrong with me. I just need to talk to her for one minute."

"I can't promise."

"I'll come back," Toby says. Then, "No, I'll wait."

"Suit yourself," Lucy says and shrugs.

Toby sits down in one of three chairs in the tiny waiting room. She picks up a magazine, *People*, but she doesn't care about the overdressed celebrities on the cover. Good lord, what is this country coming to? Whatever happened to *Popular Mechanics* or *Science Digest*? Even *Ladies' Home Journal*, though she's no more inclined to fuss with her home than she is with her personal appearance.

She's waited maybe four minutes when Dr. Penny's next patient shows up. Maxine Flannery. It would have to be Maxine. Friendly enough, but also prone to talking all over town. It occurs to Toby that she's likely to know everybody coming and going from Dr. Penny's office.

"Hi, Toby," Maxine says.

"Maxine." Toby nods.

"What are you here for?" Only Maxine would ask that question straight out. No boundaries. She hefts her considerable weight onto one of the straight-backed chairs. Her thighs spill over the seat. Both shoes are runover at the heels. Everything about Maxine is uncontained.

"Nothing much," Toby says. "You?"

Like most people, Maxine is happy to launch into a litany of her own complaints. Short-winded. Headaches. High blood pressure. Her mother died of a stroke, that runs in families, you know, and she's not getting any younger, and with four kids underfoot, there's so much work to be done, her husband out in the field all day expecting a big meal at noon and another at night, she's exhausted, who wouldn't be?

Toby closes her ears and tries to nod whenever there's a lull in Maxine's recitation. Her eyes are glued to the door leading back to Dr. Penny's examination room. She knows that Dr. Penny walks with her patients back to the reception desk, hands them off to Lucy for future scheduling. When old Bob Hannity hobbles out, Toby's prepared.

She waits until Bob is directed toward Lucy. She quickly moves over to Dr. Penny. "Doc, can I have a word?" she says.

"Hey. I thought I was next," Maxine says.

Toby turns to Maxine. "This'll only take a minute, Maxine."

"I tried to tell her you were all booked up," Lucy says. "She insisted."

"It's all right," Dr. Penny says. "C'mon back, Toby. Maxine, I'll be right with you."

It's only a few steps to the examining room. When they enter, Dr. Penny motions Toby to a chair beside a desk.

"I'll stand."

Dr. Penny crosses her arms in front of her chest. "I think I can guess what this is about," she says.

"So, it's true," Toby says.

"Hold on, Toby. Before you start making accusations . . ."

"Did you have a talk with Nola Jean about me being too old to stay out on the ranch?"

"She came to me, Toby."

"I bet she did."

"She's concerned."

"I don't want her concern. Or yours."

"It's natural, with an aging parent . . ."

"You think I want to be talked about like that? Spied on, by my own daughter? Does she report to you? Toby forgot to put baking powder in the biscuits today."

The door opens and Lucy sticks her head in. "Everything all right, Doc?" she says.

Toby realizes, only then, that she must be yelling. She's shaking with rage. She can't remember when she's been this out of control.

"That's all right," she says. "I'm leaving."

She hears Dr. Penny call her name behind her, but she's so humiliated, all she wants to do is get outside. That Maxine will have it all over town how she lost it and yelled at Dr. Penny. She leans up against an outside wall to catch her breath. It's not lost on her that she's more upset about Dr. Penny than her own daughter. She might have known Nola Jean would do something like this, but Dr. Penny has been a trusted friend and ally.

She sits a while in her car, collecting herself. Here's one more thing. Gertie, her bitter sister, ten years older than Toby, ranted at everyone in the last years of her life. Toby had little patience with her. Now, she's forced to see Gertie's side of things. She had no idea what Gertie had gone through. None.

Nola Jean

THE DRIVE TO SCOTTSBLUFF SETTLES HER DOWN. THROUGH SEVERAL small towns, past Minatare, Corey's home base, the town with the feedlot. She doesn't know how anyone could stand to live near the stench, but people must get used to it. Minatare Lake, a big state recreation area is nearby, so that's something. Maybe the pros outweigh the cons. Who can say why people make the concessions they do, duty or inertia? She's no different, putting up with a no-count husband way too long or working at a job she's come to detest.

When she gets to Scottsbluff, she goes first to Safeway. Avocados, for sure. She buys four, two for Isabel, two for herself. They don't keep long. She wanders around the market, but her mind isn't on food. Or cooking.

She locates a small coffee shop and buys herself a decent cup of dark roast. She drives down Broadway, the main street littered with deserted storefronts. When she was a kid, before the mall was built on the edge of town, before Walmart moved in, downtown was a bustling place: Sears, JCPenney, specialty dress shops, a music store, fabric store, one store that sold only vacuum cleaners, jewelry, a couple movie theaters. A town big enough for streetlights. They used to come here to Christmas shop, multi-colored lights strung catty-cornered across the intersections. When she was in high school, this town was a destination for an important date. Gabe brought her here, to the Midwest Theater, famous for its sixty-foot tower covered with aluminum stars and lit by floodlights. They saw *Grease* and walked out of the movie holding hands, humming the tunes all the way home. Later, Nola Jean wondered if Gabe brought her here so they wouldn't be seen together in Elmyra.

It's close to lunchtime, but she's not hungry. She drives south, across the North Platte River to the twin town, Gering, and then west to Scottsbluff Monument. She pays the national park fee and drives a curvy road up the butte. Leaves her car in the lot and walks on a trail to the top, where there's a view of the river valley and the town stretched below. Up here, the wind blows strong. She should have brought a jacket.

From another side of the monument, she hears voices. She doesn't want to run into people. She's not up for small talk. Some folks hike from the visitor center across a wide field, then up a trail that meanders through a tunnel or two. She's done that twice, once with Toby and Walter when they took a rare day away from the ranch and once with Gabe. He kissed her in the dark of one of the tunnels.

She doesn't make her getaway fast enough and the owners of the voices come into view. Two men. She's starting down the trail when one of them calls to her.

Squinting into the sun, she recognizes them. Matthew and Corey. She waves and turns, hopes they will take the hint and not pursue, when Corey calls out, "Wait up."

Before she can decide whether to be rude and pretend she didn't hear, Corey has trotted toward her. His hand on her shoulder. He's like an overeager puppy, annoying and persistent but tough to turn away from.

She moves and shrugs his hand off her shoulder. "Hey," she says.

Matthew comes alongside Corey. "Hi, Nola Jean," Matthew says. His warm, preacher smile.

"You guys finding many crosses up here?"

"Corey's showing me around the area," Matthew says. "There's a lot of history here. It's fascinating."

"Is it?" Somehow you don't think of the place where you grew up as having history. Or being fascinating. She's spent plenty of afternoons exploring Paris, Rome, London. But Scottsbluff?

"We were just going to grab a bite of lunch. Do you want to join us?" Matthew says.

"No, I . . ."

"Oh, c'mon," Corey says. "You haven't eaten yet, have you?"

Nola Jean looks at their open, eager faces. Well, hell. Why not? If Corey wants to flirt with an older woman, why not enjoy the attention? "If you like Mexican food, there's a good place in Terrytown," she says.

"I know it," Corey says. "Meet you there."

They're ahead of her, already seated when she gets to the restaurant. Corey stands, flags her over. He and Matthew are placed across from each other in a booth. She walks past walls decorated with bright paintings, desert flowers and Day of the Dead skeletons. The worn fake red leather of the booth sinks with deep depressions where countless butts have sat. She hesitates for a moment, then slides in beside Matthew. That may have been a mistake; she can feel Corey's feet seeking hers under the table.

"What's Terrytown, anyway?" Matthew asks.

"This village between Scottsbluff and Gering. I don't know. It's always been called that," Corey says.

God, he's so young. "Named after Terry Carpenter," Nola Jean says. "Local politician. Mayor of Scottsbluff, for a while. His claim to fame was that he tried to convince western Nebraska to secede from the state."

"Really?" Matthew laughs.

"He felt the concerns of western Nebraska were underrepresented. Everything was controlled by Omaha and Lincoln. Plus, the landscape out here is more like Colorado or Wyoming."

"I take it nothing came of that," Matthew says.

Nola Jean laughs, despite her resolve not to enjoy this too much. "No. I don't know if that's because he couldn't convince people or because neither Wyoming nor Colorado wanted us."

"How do you know all this?" Corey says. "I never heard of him."

Nola Jean raises an eyebrow. Not smart, if he wants to score points with her. He's just made her feel old and anachronistic.

"He died when I was in high school. I did a paper on him. Funny, what you remember. I took Spanish, too, but I can't conjugate a single verb."

Over enchiladas, Matthew and Corey talk about their itinerary for the coming days: Wildcat Hills and Robidoux Pass, Chimney Rock, Fort Robinson.

Nola Jean listens. They won't find many crosses in any of these places, but their enthusiasm is infectious. For her, it's a trip down memory lane.

"Corey says there are fossils of dinosaurs not far from here."

"Yeah. Just north of Mitchell. West of here. Agate National Monument. Out in the middle of nowhere."

"There's that old movie theater in Mitchell," Corey says.

"The Nile? Is that still operating?"

"I think so. One of the few old ones left."

"It's art deco," Nola Jean says. "Thus, the Egyptian theme."

"Wow." Matthew says. "Hard to imagine art deco making its way out here."

"The women's bathroom used to have corsets and old hats hanging on the walls."

"Well, I wouldn't know about that," Corey says, giving her his aw-shucks grin.

He is cute, in a rakish sort of way. Nola Jean lets him trap her foot between his ankles under the table.

"You could make a big loop and swing over to Fort Robinson," she says. "If you go that way, stop in Harrison. There's a drugstore that has a café in the back. A banner across the road into town claims they make the world's largest hamburger. Baseball teams order one and cut it up like a pizza."

"You're kidding," Matthew says.

"That's the story anyway. I've never been there when anybody ordered one that size. But I know they make a good burger."

"We might spend a few days at Fort Robinson," Corey says. "You know, see Crawford. Even go into Chadron." Corey looks at Matthew and says, "That's a college town. Some good antique stores there." Back to Nola Jean. "We want to go up to Pine Ridge too. There are some great craftsmen on the reservation. Might even make it up to Hot Springs and the Black Hills. We could be gone several days."

This is a long speech. Corey looks down at his plate, his face red. Nola Jean's not sure why he's embarrassed. Talking too much?

"That sounds like a good plan," she says. "Don't forget Courthouse and Jail Rocks. Just south of Elmyra. Or Crescent Lake."

"I ain't never been to Crescent Lake," Corey says.

"What is it?" Matthew says.

"A wildlife refuge," Nola Jean says. "A few miles northeast of Toby's place. Every bird that migrates through North America comes through there."

"I've heard of sandhills cranes," Matthew says.

"Their big migration happens earlier and farther east. But you might see one or two stragglers yet this summer. I've seen trumpeter swans. Owls. Killdeer. All kinds of shorebirds."

"What's it near?" Corey asks. "What town?"

"Not near anything. You can go north out of Lisco or Oshkosh off Highway 26. You can get there from Toby's, but those roads can be tricky."

"Maybe you could show us," Corey says, looking directly into her eyes. Is that a smirk on his face?

"Maybe," she says.

"I love an excursion," Matthew says. "We could pack a picnic."

"Well, yeah, we'd need to. There aren't any restaurants around there."

At Corey's insistence, they exchange cell phone numbers. Nola Jean reminds them that they can't get coverage at Toby's unless they walk to the top of the hill.

"At that point," Nola Jean says, "you're already within shouting distance of my cabin."

They walk her out to her car. Corey opens the door for her. When she's seated inside, he leans on the door frame. "Sure you don't want to go around Bayard, see Chimney Rock with us?"

"No," she says. "I gotta deliver some avocados to Isabel. Thanks for the lunch, though. It was fun."

"See you back at the ranch, Nola Jean." Then he winks. Actually winks.

She watches the two of them walk back to their car across the parking lot. Matthew is closer to her in age, but it's Corey who seems interested. Well. She does feel better. And she could do a lot worse.

Josie

LATE AFTERNOON, DAN COMES HOME. JOSIE HAS NO IDEA WHERE HE'S been, and she doesn't ask. He says nothing, picks up a book, a thick tome dedicated to U.S. history, and heads out onto the deck. She moves around the kitchen a while, watching him, trying to decide what to do.

Eventually, she pours two glasses of red wine, opens the sliding glass doors, sets his glass down on a small table, sits opposite him. He hardly looks up from his book to acknowledge her presence. They are strangers to each other in this moment.

Josie clears her throat. She's been thinking all day, rehearsing this speech.

"There were other things," she says.

Dan closes the book. Looks at her, his face stricken. The condemned waiting for the executioner.

She winces. Her lip trembles. "Once, I bought an expensive jacket. I paid for it with cash and lied to you about what it cost."

He waits a while to respond. Then, he nods.

"Which jacket?"

"I wore it to your office party. Gold and black silk."

He looks away. Then back. "I liked the way you looked in that jacket," he says.

"You did?"

"Yeah."

She fishes a tissue out of her pocket, blows her nose.

He sips his wine. She sips hers. Neither speaks for a while.

"Remember that Emma Marie?" he says.

"The one who always wore high heels?" Her breath comes ragged.

"Once at a conference, she invited me up to her room for a drink."

"Oh." This is it, then. Josie feels the floor drop away from under her. This is the retribution part. This is what she has coming.

"I didn't go."

"You didn't?"

"No, I didn't," he says. "Why would I?"

At that, she feels a flutter of hope. A sigh.

"I felt guilty anyway," he says. "Because something made Emma Marie think I might."

"You were attracted to her," she says.

He shrugs. "I was flattered, I guess."

"You never mentioned it," she says.

"No. I didn't."

More silence. She knows him. He's looking out on the space behind her, over her shoulder. She sees his mental wheels churning. What she doesn't know is where the spinning wheel of fortune will land.

When he finally looks at her, his eyes are clear. "Anything else?" he says.

She inhales sharply. Nothing will suffice now but bald truth. "Lots," she says. "Things the boys did I never told you about. Once I dinged our car and let you think it was another driver in a parking lot."

At that, he chuckles. Not a full out laugh, but it's something. He rubs his hand along his jaw.

"Me too," he says.

"Really?"

He shrugs. "You know that gold heart necklace you like so much?"

She reaches to her throat. The one she's wearing now.

"I sent my secretary out to buy something for you. I had forgotten our anniversary. She picked it out."

She nods. Well. She doesn't like the necklace as much as he thinks she does. She only wears it to please him.

"We could go on like this all day," she says.

"Maybe we should."

"Or not," she whispers.

After a moment, after weighing the options the way he does, he says, "You're right."

Toby

TOBY'S DRIVING HOME FROM ELMYRA ALONE. SHE'D BEEN IN A FAIR state, leaving Dr. Penny's office. She'd made up that excuse about seeing Malcolm Lord, didn't want Anita . . . oh, holy hell. Anita. She had forgotten to pick up Anita. She pulled off. Turned around. She knew Anita would be surprised to see her this soon, but she was in no mood to hang around town wondering what people were saying about her. This might be one of the few times she wished she had a cell phone. She had no use for one out on the Bluestem, and the expense didn't seem worth it.

She pulled up to Delia's. Anita and Delia were outside with the two little boys. Good. She wouldn't have to go in and make polite conversation. She thought about honking her horn, but that seemed rude. They'd be alarmed, and she'd have to try to explain. No, no help for it, she'd have to get out, hug the two little guys, smile and ask Anita if she was ready to go home.

Anita had looked at her in that penetrating way she has. Though she's not a talker like that Maxine Flannery, Anita makes it her business to know what's going on with everybody. She's a good friend, when you need one, and a damn annoying nuisance when you want some privacy.

"You ready?" Toby tried to make her voice neutral.

"It's early, isn't it?"

"I got done sooner than I planned."

Anita was reluctant to leave. Who could blame her? She is adored by her grandsons. Restless, Toby shifted her weight from one foot to another.

"Hold on," Anita said. "Luis said something about making a trip in for some fence supplies. Maybe he could pick me up."

Toby had to wait while Anita attempted to call Luis. First, he didn't answer. No surprise. Most places on the Bluestem, he wouldn't get the

78

call. Then, he rang back. Turns out he'd been driving. A stickler for safety and rules, he had pulled over. Toby thinks he's more in danger of being clipped while sitting on the shoulder of the highway than if he had just picked up the damn phone, but it's not for her to say. It seemed to Toby they had a lengthy conversation, but when Anita finally hung up, laughing like there'd been some joke between them, she said he was on his way to town. He'd pick her up.

Now, Toby drives alone, grateful for the space. Her mind thrashes around. She tries to take in the sweep of the river, the calming sky. A red-tailed hawk circles above the highway. Usually, these are things that bring her peace.

When she gets home, she dumps her purse in the house, grabs a long-sleeved shirt and a hat, makes for the barn. It's been a good while since she's saddled a horse by herself. Luckily, Cream is so used to her and well trained that he trots over to her, so she doesn't have to chase him around the corral. The bridle and blanket are no problem. Hefting the saddle is another issue, but after a couple of tries, she manages to get it on. Cream indulges her by standing patiently while she mounts.

She rides out, alone. The way she prefers it. Cream's even strides, the contours of her familiar land, the grandeur of the sweeping sky, the beckoning open space, this is her life. This.

She rides to the farthest northeast corner of her land, as she knew she would when she started out. She drops Cream's reins and dismounts. Her hips are too stiff to allow her to step down on the ground with one foot still in the stirrup, but she knows if she hangs onto the pommel, she can swing her right leg over until both feet are even, then slip her left foot out and lower herself to the ground. She manages it with only a slight stumble. She knows Cream will stay put until she's ready to mount again.

She sits at the edge of the penstemon blowout. Removes her shoes and socks, digs her toes into the warm sand. She has no fear. If she can't get up and get herself home, then let her die here. That would be preferable to being hauled off to sit out her last years cooped up in town.

She spots the penstemon shoots. She speaks aloud, feeling only slightly foolish.

"How do you do it?" she says. "How do you carry on in spite of so many foes? Tell me your secrets."

She lets herself cry then. She hasn't done that in years, not even when George died. She weeps in big silent shudders. Her mother died on this land, albeit too young and violently. Her father too. Walter, Gertie, John, and even George. Why, when she is the last holdout, should she have to face dying in town? In exile?

After a while, she feels Cream nuzzle her shoulder from behind. She's comforted by it, as if a loving hand were patting her back, there, there. She reaches up and rubs the horse's nose. Cream snorts, lowers his head farther, and Toby rests her cheek against the gelding.

She recalls a conversation she overheard once. She'd stopped into the bakery in Elmyra, and two older women were seated at a nearby table. One, recently widowed, the other nursing a husband with a bad heart condition. One said to the other, This is what we do; we put our guys to bed. Toby's problem, as happens with so many women, is that there's no one left to put her to bed. With all the others, she was there—younger, stronger, able to carry on. She's lived too damn long.

She supposes, if she's honest, she knew this day would eventually come. She didn't expect it this soon. She's not ready. She has aged. Any fool can see that, and she prides herself on not shying from the truth. But what she does about it is nobody's business but her own. She has no intention of moving to town, and no one can make her. She's not of unsound mind. Not yet. But the ground has shifted, now that she knows she's being watched. People are waiting for her to stumble.

All her life, she's tried to live up to people's expectations of her strength. Now, their expectation is that she will weaken. She's out here talking to a plant because she's got to figure out how to remember who she is.

Josie

IT TAKES A COUPLE DAYS OF TIPTOEING, EACH BEING POLITE AND careful. Dan comes back to their bed, but sleeps turned away on the far edge. Eventually, the tension between them begins to thaw. Dan touches her hand when she sets down his morning coffee. They brush against each other when passing in the hall. After breakfast on the third day, Dan lays aside the paper. He picks up his cup of coffee, lifts it to his lips, and over the brim says, "So, she wrote to you?"

Josie had been on her feet, rinsing dishes for the dishwasher. She sits, right-angled to Dan. "She goes by Nola Jean," she says. "Lives in Minneapolis, but her adoptive mother lives in Nebraska. On a ranch in the Sandhills. That's where she is now, but I don't know for how long."

"Do you want to see her?" Dan's voice is gentle.

Josie's eyes fill. She nods her head. "I think so. I feel . . . I owe . . . I don't know. She deserves to know the truth, doesn't she?"

Dan looks askance at that. She can imagine what he must be thinking. He didn't deserve the truth, but this stranger does?

"I mean, now," she says. She presses the paper napkin to her eyes. The daffodils she's brought into the kitchen table are fading, the petals dropping. She fiddles with the smooth petals, until Dan reaches out and pats her arm.

"Well. Then, you should," he says.

"What about mother? The boys?" Her voice breaks.

"One thing at a time," he says. "Let's just see how it goes."

"Okay." She barely breathes.

Dan turns his attention back to the paper. She notes a big ad for hearing aids on the back page. "If you don't mind, I'd like to go with you," he says. Nonchalant, like it's no big deal.

"I'd like that." She keeps her voice even to match his tone. Her heart is pounding, a wonder he can't hear it.

He doesn't look at her, still talking to the paper. "Let's meet her in Cheyenne. Maybe at the Plains Hotel."

He's thought about this. Out of town. Good idea. Historic hotel with lots of travelers.

"When?"

"Next Tuesday? I play golf on Monday." He puts the paper down and looks at her. "I think we should meet in the afternoon, say three o'clock, in the Conestoga Restaurant. It will be pretty empty that time of day. Nobody will care if we sit a while. Easier to talk over a beer than while eating. If it gets late, we can always stay over. Same for her if she doesn't want to drive back. And the hotel is big enough . . ."

He doesn't finish, but she knows what he means. The hotel is big enough that even if they stayed over and Nola Jean did, too, they needn't run into each other. He's thought of everything. All that's left is for her to agree. And Nola Jean.

She nods but discovers she can't find her voice. He nods, too, and turns back to his paper. Taking her cues from him, she rises and finishes tidying the kitchen. An old hymn is tugging at her, something about "showers of blessing," and for the first time since receiving the letter, she feels clean.

Toby

SHE NEEDS TO TALK TO NOLA JEAN. SHE'S BEEN WAITING FOR NOLA Jean to come to her. That's the way this ought to work. After all, Nola Jean is the one who dropped this on her. Along with the news of her birth mother canceling their meeting. She knows that must have been hard, so she's cutting Nola Jean some slack. Not for going behind her back to Dr. Penny. Not for thinking she's too old to run this place. But some slack for not coming right away to apologize. Nola Jean has other things on her mind, she grants her that.

She misses the days when work took her mind off things. On a day like this, when she's sick of herself and her own thoughts, she'd have been out riding, looking for broken fence, feeding livestock, hauling hay. It's midday, not the best time to work in the garden, though there are always weeds.

She thinks about walking down to Isabel's cabin. She'd like to talk to her, but she makes it her policy not to disturb her guests. She's available if they want to come to her, but the place is not much of a respite if they're expected to entertain their bored and troubled host.

About the time she's ready to pull out a book, though it's difficult to keep her mind on the page, she hears a knock. Her door isn't closed, so when she looks up, she sees Matthew standing at the screen door.

She's on her feet, calling out to him, c'mon in, and he does. He acts nervous, rubs his hand over his beard. She's amused how men who have facial hair do that, pet themselves. Giving in to the same urge that tugs at babies with pacifiers. Self-soothing. Course we all have something, look at her, downing shots of whiskey.

"Sit down, Matthew."

"Ah, I don't want to take up your time."

"Don't be silly." She waves him to a chair. She's got more time than she knows what to do with.

"Can I get you some iced tea? Or lemonade? The iced tea is brewed, but the lemonade comes from a mix."

"Iced tea would be fine. Thank you."

He smiles. She bets he's used to this, calling on older women, setting them at ease. He's got a nice manner, she'll give him that. She can see how people would want to tell him their worries. Hell. She's tempted herself. If she had more faith in the god he prays to, she'd do it for sure.

She returns from the kitchen with two tall glasses of iced tea. He takes his, sips, says mm-mm-mm like a well-trained boy, sets it on the end table. He wipes at the condensation on the glass with his finger. She sits in the rocker across from him.

"Pretty day," he says.

"Um-hm." She nods. She's waiting to find out what brought him here. She could ask, but she wonders how long it will take for him to get around to it. She feels guilty, stalking him like a cat playing with a captive mouse, but good lord, she has to find her entertainment somewhere.

Matthew shuffles his feet. Rubs at his beard again. Toby drinks from her glass of tea and sets it down.

"Is your cabin all right?" One swipe of the cat's paw. The mouse squirms.

"Oh, yes. It's fine. Great."

He's having trouble establishing eye contact. Seems like an odd thing in a pastor. In her experience, people do that when they're hiding something or hiding from something. She's done it herself, talking to Nola Jean. Darn. The thought of Nola Jean creeps back in. Never a break from parenting. No matter how old you get, your children occupy half your headspace. It's like unrequited love. Parents go on worrying and loving best they can even though their children move away from them in all possible ways.

"I was wondering . . ." Matthew says.

"What? I'm sorry. I'm afraid my mind slipped somewhere else."

Dammit. She should never have said that. An old person's apology. And now, ammunition to use against her. She's got to stop doing that.

"You know Corey. You met him, my guide, at your evening gathering?"

"Seems like a nice young man," Toby says.

"He's from Minatare. Driving down every day. Or so. I was wondering how you'd feel if he pulled in a small trailer and parked it by my cabin? That way, he wouldn't have to make the drive. I'd be happy to pay extra. I know your cabins are for solitary use. Some days we're going to both be gone. Not that I'm suggesting it evens things out. I don't mean that. Just that . . ."

"It's fine," she says.

"Really?"

He looks overly relieved. His shoulders relax, his breathing smooths out. Toby's puzzled. Are they planning a bank heist? Making meth? She tries to imagine the two of them engaged in a life of crime and laughs out loud. Oops. That was a mistake. Matthew's looking at her now with renewed fear.

"Don't mind me," she says. "Of course, it's fine."

"I could pay . . ."

She waves a hand in dismissal. "How are you doing with the hunt for crosses?"

They talk, then. A nice, long conversation. She's found the topic that will keep Matthew engaged, fill up time for her and relax him. He tells her about Incan crosses, medieval crosses, funky crosses fashioned from barbed wire. Tiny origami crosses and quilted crosses and ornately carved wooden crosses.

"In a backyard in Minatare, there's a cross made out of old machine parts welded together. We drove by so I could see it. Corey knows the man who lives there, so we got to go inside and talk to him. He said he made it for his wife when she died. They'd been married sixty-six years. What gets me are the stories. Every cross has a story."

"I can see that," Toby says. Her mind drifts to the family cemetery, all the stories buried there. "Did you offer to buy it?"

Gently, Matthew says, "No. He'd never sell it. Besides, it's too big. My criterion is that every cross has to fit in my study at the church."

"You've been at the same church a long time, I take it."

Matthew chuckles. "Twenty-four years. Straight out of seminary."

"I thought Methodists moved their pastors around."

"Usually. But it's a small community. And my church is duly aligned, Methodist and UCC—that's United Church of Christ—and the UCC part is congregationally organized. Meaning, bishops can't tell congregations what to do."

"Sounds like that could be a recipe for conflict."

"It could. But they leave us alone. We're not big enough or important enough for anyone to get concerned about. As long as we don't do anything dramatic to call attention to ourselves, we're fine."

"I guess you won't be planning a bank heist, then?"

Matthew registers surprise. Sits back a little in his chair.

"Did you think we would?"

"No, oh no," Toby says, laughing. "Never crossed my mind." Well, that's a lie. But a small one. It's her mind, and she can cover for it any way she pleases.

Matthew shifts forward, looks at his watch. "I should go," he says. "My goodness, look at the time."

"I've enjoyed talking with you," Toby says, rising. And she has. He saved her from a long afternoon of useless rumination.

"Me too," Matthew says.

She walks him to the door. "Will we see you Friday at the Five O'Clock? You and Corey?"

"You bet," he says. "Next time, I'd like to hear more about your life."

Toby smiles at that and watches him move down the path. Next time. She likes that part. But if he thinks she's going to open up to a complete stranger about the complicated life she's led, he doesn't know much about people like her.

Josie

JOSIE'S HEARD NOTHING FROM NOLA JEAN. SHE SENT AN EMAIL YES-
terday, apologizing for her abrupt cancellation, suggesting they meet
Tuesday in Cheyenne. She sent it in the morning, as soon as she and
Dan got up from the breakfast table and parted to go about their day.
Suppose Nola Jean has already left for Minnesota? Suppose she's changed
her mind and wants nothing to do with her past? What did she think?
That Nola Jean would be anxiously waiting, ready to pounce on any
change of heart? Well, yes, she has to admit. She did think that. Nola
Jean contacted her. She's felt, up to now, that all the cards were in her
hand, that it was her decision whether to play or not. Now that she's
got her mind wrapped around the meeting, she's surprised to find that
she's on the brink of a devasting disappointment if Nola Jean opts out.

Yesterday she made chocolate chip cookies to fill the dragging time. A
recipe she's made hundreds of times, but she mismeasured something,
she still doesn't know what, and they didn't turn out right. Plus, she
scorched one entire cookie sheet full and had to throw it in the trash.
In the process, she burnt her hand and dumped the bathroom drawer
on the floor searching for gauze.

She didn't sleep. Going over what she wants to say.

Today, she's decided to scrounge through drawers and boxes to locate
some old photos. She knows she has one somewhere of Nola Jean's
father. Also, some of his letters. She's never been highly organized,
though she's a keeper. But instead of properly labeled storage bins, like
her friend Carol, Josie is more of a stuffer and a piler.

She finds it hard to breathe. A boa constrictor is coiled around her
chest.

She starts in the bedroom, rummaging through the drawers in the
bedside tables. Old cameras, an outdated passport, a sleep mask with
buckwheat seeds her daughter-in-law gave her one year for Christmas,

flashlights that don't work. Nothing. Next, she tries her desk drawers in the spare bedroom. Broken pencils, a shoebox full of greeting cards received for her birthday and Mother's Day, a three-hole punch she'd been looking for last summer and couldn't find. Old receipts. Erasers hardened beyond use. A stapler and tape and an English-to-Italian dictionary she bought for a trip to Venice ten years ago. No pictures. No letters.

She takes a break and goes to the kitchen to brew herself a cup of tea. While waiting for the water to boil, she sits at the table with her head in her hands. She's making a mess everywhere she goes. That's what she does. Makes a mess of things. She should have cards printed: Messes Made While You Wait. Thank goodness Dan is playing in a golf tournament today and won't be home until late afternoon.

She pours water over a teabag, English Breakfast, sets a timer for four minutes, and stands staring out at her backyard. She's seeing herself. Young. Scared. The tiny helpless baby lying in the hospital bassinet.

When the timer dings, she removes the teabag. Spoons in a quarter teaspoon of sugar and a splash of milk. Holding the cup in two hands, she heads to the basement storage room. Shelves and boxes. Where to start? She sits on the bottom step of the stairs to sip her tea. Get her head together. Isn't that what the young people say? Her sons, sometimes, Gotta get my head together, Mom.

She shuts her eyes, tight, against the rising images of her sons and how they will take this news. Don't think about that. She wishes she had a more disciplined mind. One she could steer. She should've taken up meditation, like her friend Carol who is a tour de force. Organized and disciplined, everything shipshape, even her thoughts.

Her chest hurts. She sets the cup on the floor, places her hand over her heart, feels it thumping.

None of the boxes are labeled. She stands on a stepladder, lifts them down from the top. First, Christmas tree ornaments. The next level, old clippings and school papers of the boys. She realizes there's an accidental method to this; the oldest boxes are on the bottom. She should wait until Dan gets home to help her. But she's already made a giant mess, and what would she do with herself all day?

By lunchtime, she's gotten all the boxes off the shelves. They're strewn all over the basement rec room floor. Her calves and arms quiver from the exertion. She prides herself on staying fit, goes to yoga twice a week, walks daily. She can still ride a bike. Gardening is a good workout. Still, up and down a stepladder, lifting boxes, not something she does every day.

She stops to make herself a peanut butter sandwich. Climbing the stairs to the kitchen is hard work. She tosses the loaf of bread onto the table. Gets the peanut butter from the cupboard, a knife from a drawer, plops down in a kitchen chair. She has trouble unscrewing the peanut butter jar. Dan puts it on too tight, damn him. She doesn't want to get up to find the silicone jar opener in the cabinet drawer. Instead, she uses the hem of her shirt. The jar opens, but she swipes a glob of peanut butter on her shirt front.

She gets it done. Makes the sandwich and eats it, her mouth dry and peanut butter stuck to her teeth and the roof of her mouth. She's too tired to get up to run a drink of water from the tap. She rests her arms on the table, her head on her arms. Dozes for half an hour. Wakes with a start, drool wet on her shirtsleeve. It takes a moment to remember what's going on, why she's like this, asleep at her kitchen table, her shirt slavered with peanut butter.

Somewhat restored, she makes her way back downstairs. She's careful to hang onto the banister. Her feet are leaden. She remembers feeling like this once when she was a kid and rode her bike twelve miles over sandy, hilly roads to get to an old quarry swimming hole. She and her sister. When they got there and shed their outer clothes to swim, the water felt viscous and thick, like gelatin. They laughed about it. How they were so tired they couldn't move their limbs smoothly through the water. They didn't have enough sense to worry about the ride home. Luckily, their mother came to pick them up, having seen the note they left on the kitchen table about where they were going. She borrowed a neighbor's pickup truck to stow their bikes in the back. She brought food and water, neither of which they'd thought to carry with them. Don't tell your dad, she said. As if they would. Anyway, now she feels like that. Only it's not water that offers resistance; it's air. The air is too thick to move through.

She makes it to the couch in the rec room. Looking around at the sea of boxes, she realizes they're taped shut. The only open ones are the first few she'd taken down, the Christmas tree ornaments and the boys' old school papers. She left the scissors in the storeroom, which is up three steps from the rec room. She thinks about crawling. It must be easier; that's why toddlers start with crawling. Don't be ridiculous, she tells herself. She uses the arm of the couch to help her stand. Okay. She's up.

Her chest seems made of wood. Her armor is too tight. She wishes she'd taken off her bra. Nobody home. Who needs it?

She trips over a box. Loses her balance and falls on the carpet. On the way down, she twists to miss the boxes. She hits hard, her head missing the boxes but thwacking on the edge of the coffee table. Unconscious, she looks like an infant, on her side, curled into herself, no blood, and that is how Dan finds her when he gets home.

Nola Jean

NOLA JEAN HAS DECIDED TO TAKE ISABEL UP ON HER OFFER. WHEN she'd dropped off the avocados, Isabel invited her to stop by for a glass of wine some evening. After a couple days of keeping to herself, ignoring Matthew and Corey and their invitation to go to Crescent Lake, avoiding Toby because she's not up for the argument about why Toby should move to town, exhausting herself as much as possible by walking the prairie, she decides she needs some socialization.

Sick of her jeans and boots, she's put on a skirt and sandals. She sticks to the sandy road to get to Isabel's, not wanting to tramp through prairie grass with bare legs and exposed toes. She hopes she's picked a good time, late enough for Isabel to be finished with dinner but still plenty of evening left. It's around eight o'clock, and the day is just starting to wind down. Nola Jean carries a flashlight for the walk home. She doesn't mind navigating these roads in the dark. Besides, last night there had been a bright moon.

When she rounds the bend, she sees Isabel sitting on the front porch. Isabel waves her arm like a signal flare and calls out her name. When she reaches the porch, Isabel stands. She's wearing all white, pants and a long top, a loose cardigan, finely woven linen. Barefoot. Large hoop earrings. She's exquisite, a model Mattel might use to craft a high-end doll or a travel company to advertise a vacation in Portugal. She waves Nola Jean to a chair and disappears inside to bring out wine and glasses.

Nola Jean sits, looks out on the rolling prairie, sees the cattails surrounding the pond not far from Isabel's porch. Tension rolls off her like dust shaken from weary feet. Once they are both seated, neither speaks for several moments. That's the marvel of Isabel. No need to fill the air with aimless chatter or words to impress.

"How is it going for you?" Isabel turns to face Nola Jean, her eyes liquid and warm.

Nola Jean sighs. "Not great." Then, before she's aware of making a conscious decision, she tells Isabel that she had tried to contact her birth mother. That the woman had agreed to see her and then backed out.

"That must be painful," Isabel says.

"Disappointing. I'm not sure what I was hoping for, really."

"Does Toby know?"

Nola Jean nods. "She took it well, actually. Better than I thought she might."

"Toby seems like a wise woman. We all hope we learn a few things with time."

Isabel looks out over the prairie when she says this. Nola Jean squirms in her chair. She's never thought of Toby as wise. Stubborn, yes. Strong. Stuck in a rancher's world. But wise?

"I found out I was adopted twice."

"How did that happen?"

"The first couple who adopted me were killed in a car accident. I was two years old. Toby and Walter adopted me, then. They didn't know."

"Didn't know?"

"They didn't know the couple who died weren't my birth parents. They picked me out at an orphanage."

"That's a lot to take in."

"Yeah, it has been."

"How did you find out?"

"I hired a private investigator. Sometimes I feel like I'm watching a movie, only I'm also starring in it."

"I know what you mean. Seems surreal. You know it's you, but it feels like it must be happening to somebody else."

They sip wine quietly. Nola Jean decides to ask. "Did something happen to you?"

"I was diagnosed with cancer. About a year ago."

"Oh, god."

"Out of the blue. Ovarian."

"That's not a good kind to have, is it?"

"No, it isn't. Not that any cancer is a good kind to have. Ovarian cancer is hard to diagnose, usually quite advanced when it's found. Vague symptoms. Could be anything—bloating, changes in bowel habits. I had no risk factors. Ate right, exercised."

"That doesn't seem fair."

"Well, what's fair about being born with risk factors? At first, I asked why me? But then, reading the statistics and who gets struck, I realized why not me? We just don't like to know how random life is. And how vulnerable we all are. Here's an irony. My doctors kept saying one point in my favor was my overall good health . . . apart from having cancer. I think they thought it would help me withstand the treatment, which is brutal."

Isabel pauses to sip her wine. Then, she says, "I had a hysterectomy. Eighteen weeks of aggressive chemo."

Nola Jean doesn't know what to say. Isabel is thin. Her hair super short. Still, she seems so alive. Vibrant, even.

"Are you okay now?"

"I don't know. You never really know. I'm cancer free, at the moment. But it could come back. Ovarian cancer often does."

"That sounds awful. Like living with a ticking time bomb."

Isabel shrugs. Raises her hands, as if to say, what can you do?

"You seem so, I don't know, so centered?"

"Do I?"

"I noticed it right away. When I'm around you, I feel it. A kind of peace."

"Well. Don't be fooled. I've railed. I've been scared. I've been despondent. I'm still all the above at times. But there are compensations."

"Like what?"

"For one thing, you find out how kind and loving people can be. I had a lot of support."

"Good."

"You learn to pay attention. I thought I knew how to do that. I am a poet, after all. But cancer crystallizes things."

"When I'm sick, I just want to sleep."

"I only felt sick when I was in treatment. Then, I craved ordinary things. Like going to a movie and not having to think about whether the seats would have a headrest. Food that tasted good. Being able to buckle my pants."

"Maybe I know a little of what you mean. When my husband and I divorced, it was the daily things I missed. Things I'd taken for granted. His hand pushing my hair behind my ear. His coffee mug staining the end table. We were miserable together, for a lot of big reasons, but still I missed him humming in the bathroom, even though it drove me crazy when he did that while I was trying to sleep."

"Exactly." Isabel laughs, and Nola Jean laughs too. How can they be laughing over a conversation about divorce and cancer? Then again, how can they not?

"I've spent a lot of my life meeting adversity by gritting my teeth until it's over," Isabel says. "But this is not going to get over. I'm never going back to the way I used to live. I've lost my capacity to deny mortality. But right in the middle of the worst days, I decided that this, too, is life. You know what I mean? Suffering and illness and fear are all part of what it is to be alive. I want to dwell in my life, no matter what comes, instead of looking for escape."

"My concerns seem so small."

Isabel turns to her, eyes flashing. "Don't say that. Don't ever think that. That's . . . you know, a lot of people shunned me. Oh, a lot were wonderful, but some couldn't get too close because they didn't know what to say or because I reminded them that we're all going to die or they felt that whatever was keeping them up at night was trivial. It's all our work. All of it."

Nola Jean stares at her for a moment. Then she chinks her wine glass against Isabel's. "Okay. It's a deal," she says. "My lost mother and your cancer. We both play our cards."

"Deal," Isabel says, flashing her signature smile.

They sit a while in silence. A few bugs show up, flitting through the air aglow.

"Look at that," Nola Jean says.

"Lightning bugs."

"Some of my friends call them fireflies."

"I like that. Fireflies. Much more poetic."

"Some of the kids used to catch them and scrape them against their foreheads to make themselves glow in the dark. I never did, though. I loved pretending I was one of them, spinning and darting, turning my face up to the nighttime sky."

"I can see you doing that."

It's been a while since Nola Jean's had a friend who could see her dancing with fireflies. She lays her head back, closes her eyes, sees herself lifting her arms, spinning and spinning and free.

Josie

WHEN DAN GETS HOME AND FINDS JOSIE ON THE BASEMENT FLOOR, not sure whether she's asleep, dead, or passed out, he has trouble waking her. She hears his voice as if it's coming to her under water. She sees images of long twisted horns, like trombones only vast and complicated, and Dan's voice is lost inside all the turns and twists. Her eyes fly open and then shut. She tries to speak to reassure him, but she can't get air into her windpipe. She feels exactly like she did once when she pitched a ball to a kid who smacked the ball right into her stomach and knocked the wind out of her. The teacher stood over her, yelling her name, the kid who hit the ball screamed, She's dead!, and Josie, who couldn't speak, was terrified they'd bury her alive. Dan lifts her to her feet, supports her by draping her arm over his shoulder. He has one arm around her waist and the other hanging on tight to her hand. He shouldn't be doing that. He's too old to bear her weight like that, but she's weak. He half walks, half carries her to the stairs. Then out to the car. Loads her in awkwardly, bending and straightening her limbs like you might a child who's resisting a car seat, reaches over her and fastens the seat belt, drives to the hospital emergency room.

A wheelchair, a lot of fuss, blood pressure high. A lump on her head but no blood. A residual headache, to be expected. The doctor on call is young, female, small-boned with a mountain of curly brown hair. Josie is fully awake now. Calm. Embarrassed. "I'm fine," she says. I'm fine, I'm fine, I'm fine.

Doctor Head-of-Hair asks a lot of questions. Was her chest tight? Yes. Did she have trouble breathing? Yes. Has she been under stress lately? Oh, yes. What did she do today?

Josie takes a deep breath before answering. Looks at Dan, knows he's not going to be happy when he hears what she did, tells the doctor she'd been taking boxes down from shelves. I know it was foolish, she says, directed at the doctor but meant for Dan.

The doctor wants to run some tests, make sure she hasn't suffered a heart attack. She wants to keep her overnight for observation. In case she has a concussion. But her best guess: a panic attack. The doctor explains how acute anxiety mimics a heart attack, causes an adrenaline rush that pushes blood around the body and simultaneously hyperventilation constricts the blood vessels. All this results in a spike in blood pressure that is not dangerous unless there are underlying heart health issues. The fact that Josie fell and hit her head hard enough to knock herself out but not so hard that it seems to have caused lasting damage is a stroke of luck. Josie finds that last statement confusing, but she guesses the doctor means she's lucky not to have damaged herself more from hitting her head, not that she's lucky to have hit her head in the first place. Maybe she's not thinking straight. She nods and tries to smile and waits patiently until the doctor leaves the curtained cubicle.

She turns to Dan. "I'm so sorry."

Dan rushes to her side, grabs her hand. "Shh," he says. "I never should have left you alone."

"I feel like a fool. All this fuss. Because I got a little upset."

"C'mon, now."

"I'm going to forget all about her. Clearly, she wants nothing to do with me now."

"You mean Nola Jean?"

"Who else?"

"Shh. Let's not think about her right now."

Josie closes her mouth but not her thoughts. How can she not think about her? She's bungled this so badly. Every part of it. From the original deed to now.

"Dan, I can't stay here tonight. I can't."

"The doctor wants to keep you under observation."

"I need to go home. Ask the nurse. Ask her what signs you should watch for."

She knows she's condemning Dan to a sleepless night. If she can go to sleep, big if, he'll be propped awake watching her.

"I think it's better if you stay. The doctor said . . ."

"I don't care what she said. It's not a prison. They can't make me stay, can they?"

She tries not to let her voice rise. She doesn't want to be written off as a hysterical woman. But this part of Dan drives her crazy. He's a rule-follower. Like her father and her mother. Rules take precedence over compassion, and this time, this once, she's not going to stand for it. She knows she's right. She knows if she sits in this hospital bed tonight, alone, no comforts of her own home, she'll only be more anxious. Her chest is tightening now, just contemplating it.

In the end, they work out a compromise. The doctor runs her EKG, all normal. Josie's speech is not slurred, she's not disoriented, she has a slight headache. The doctor sends them home with a list of signs to watch for in case of concussion. She offers Josie a prescription for anxiety medication, but Josie doesn't want to go down that road. She does accept a temporary sleep aid.

While Dan is downstairs in the kitchen scrambling eggs for their supper, she checks her emails. Nothing. She was a nervous wreck before, at the thought of meeting Nola Jean. Now, she's a wreck at the thought of not meeting her. She decides to try once more. She writes a longer email. She confesses that she got cold feet the first time. She admits she was unprepared for Nola Jean's entry into her life, but now, she's anxious to meet her. She thinks better of it and deletes the word anxious. Instead, she types, I will be disappointed if we don't meet. She assures Nola Jean that she respects her answer, but she hopes Nola Jean will grant her this second chance. As an afterthought, she adds, My mother—your grandmother—is still living and would love to meet you. (She doesn't write, if I can bring myself to tell her about you.) Then she signs off. Please let me know soon. Josephine.

She's finished before Dan brings her supper upstairs. He serves it to her in bed, on a tray, as if it's a special occasion. Scrambled eggs with sliced strawberries on the side. He sits in a chair close to the bed with his dinner on a TV tray.

"I think you're right," Dan says. "This has gone on long enough. Our life has been perfectly fine without Nola Jean, and it's good to go back to being ourselves."

Josie stops to peer at him, her fork poised midair. She smiles. He has no idea. None. But then, how could he? If Nola Jean never responds, she'll grieve alone. If Nola Jean does respond? Well, she'll cross that bridge when and if.

Nola Jean

SHE'S ON HER WAY TO TOBY'S HOUSE, MIDMORNING, BECAUSE SHE wants to talk to her before they face each other at tonight's Five O'Clock. She regrets dropping that comment about Toby moving into town. She had planned to take it slow. Introduce the thought over a piece of pie. Let Toby feel it was something to consider together. Maybe, even, Toby would think it was her idea, though Nola Jean knows that's unlikely. She's learned over the years how to deal with difficult passengers, how to gentle the scared ones and maneuver the obstinate ones, but she's never figured out how to handle Toby. Still, knowing Toby, she likely didn't give her comment much thought. Toby probably dismissed it the way she dismisses everything she doesn't want to do. So then, Nola Jean will feel foolish bringing it up. Dancing, that's what this is. Like two awkward teenage wallflowers, she and Toby, neither knowing which move to make.

The day is blossoming into beauty, a gentle breeze doing the hula through the prairie grass. The sky wields an open invitation, cloudless except for a few tendrils low on the horizon. Weather forecasts don't mean a lot out here, but they could use some rain. She had hoped to see a rolling thunderstorm, watch it drag its ragged skirts over the land. Plus, she longs to see the yuccas in bloom, clusters of white bells like peace flags dotting the landscape. She read somewhere that they're edible, at least some species, though maybe not raw. Something about making your throat itch.

There's nothing keeping her here now, except she's in no hurry to get home. Her design classes won't start up again until fall. She hasn't decided whether she'll go back to the airlines or take Liz Dahlberg up on her offer. Liz wants to open a small home design specialty shop, and she wants Nola Jean to partner with her. They met through their school program. They share an aesthetic, an appreciation for simplicity of line, space, and saturation of color. They'd offer some home furnishings along with design services. Liz inherited a chunk of money three years ago when her father died, so she's not asking for capital. She wants Nola Jean for her ideas and creativity, which is flattering but terrifying. What if she can't deliver? Liz says Nola Jean knows foreign markets, which is true. In her travels, she's shopped in Paris, Rome, London, Prague, Berlin, Barcelona. She doesn't know Asian or South American markets, but it would be fun to explore them. Not right away, of course. But eventually, she'd get to travel to make purchases for the store without having to wait on crabby sleep-deprived passengers. No wearing of uniforms. Also, no secure paycheck. No company-provided health insurance. The store would be a long shot, at best, but when will she ever have this opportunity again?

Her therapist says she has difficulty making decisions. To which Nola Jean, tied in knots, replied, You think, and wondered why she was paying a lot of money to have someone tell her the obvious.

She hasn't checked her email for days. She stops at the top of the hill and pulls out her cell phone. While waiting for it to find a signal, she turns in a full circle. Rolling green as far as she can see. A fence or two, scattered cottonwoods and brush, sage and yuccas, clumps of cactus blooming pink. Compared to Minneapolis with its lakes and lush parks and mature trees, this is a desert. She recoiled from the isolation as a child, but when she and her husband bought a house in Minneapolis, she chose one with big windows across from a park so they'd have an open view. The first thing she did was hire a tree service to chop down the overgrown yews plastered up against the living room and dining room windows. Neighbors gathered in their front yard, shook their heads in disapproval, but she could not understand why they would tolerate no light inside the house and not being able to see outside. Like everything else in her life, she's conflicted about this landscape. Still, like it or not, she's deeply imprinted with it.

She opens her emails, scrolls through a few ads from clothing companies and theaters, and then sees an email from Josephine Klingman. Actually, two emails, one a cryptic apology with a suggestion they try again. The other, a plea, including—good lord—a living grandmother.

Nola Jean is torn between wanting to leap into the air to click her heels together and wanting to throw her phone as far away as possible. Clearly, Josephine Klingman wants to make certain no one sees them together. Transported to fifth grade, Nola Jean remembers snotty girls dropping notes on her desk, saying she had cooties because she was from the country. By then, Nola Jean was being driven to a consolidated school closer to town. There were town kids and country kids, the line between solid and unmovable. Like those town kids, Josephine is afraid of being tainted by association. Plus, who's to say Josephine won't cancel again? Nola Jean has no idea what kind of person she is. Perhaps she's unstable. Or worse, malicious, and this is her idea of a fun little game.

Forgetting about Toby and her original mission, she stands for a long time, looking but not seeing, lost in indecision, and wishing to hell she'd never started this search.

Anita

ANITA IS WORRIED. SOMETHING IS EATING AT TOBY. OVER THE YEARS, they've fallen into an easy companionship. Though Toby's never been chatty, they work side by side in the garden, can beans late in the season, get the cottages up and running, or close them down when it's time. Sometimes, she helps Toby clean or do special projects like painting a room. While Luis and Gabe are out working on the land, she and Toby have been known to enjoy a glass of lemonade on the front porch. Lemonade laced with something stronger if it's late in the day. She helps Toby prepare for the Friday Five O'Clocks. Always pie the first week. Then they might bake cookies or brownies or make a pasta salad. Sometimes, when they are both bone weary or it's too damn hot to think about cooking, they put out salsa and chips, which requires a trip to town because Toby never stocks such things. Then they treat themselves to a cone or a pecan sundae at the drive-in. Toby would never admit she likes anything but homemade ice cream, but on a hot day, she'll settle for store bought.

Anita checks in every morning to see what needs to be done. The last few days, Toby has dismissed her. Sent her home. Without so much as an explanation. She just says, I don't need you today, Anita. As if she's nothing more than a servant. She's used to that kind of talk from some people. There are a lot of Mexicans in this part of Nebraska. Most of them, like her parents and Luis's parents, were children of migrant workers who labored in the beet fields or in the sugar beet factory in Scottsbluff. The housing then was horrible, tar-paper shacks or uninsulated hovels. The lucky ones, like Luis's grandparents, came west for the summer but then went back to Omaha for winters where they had small houses near the feedlots or railroad yards. Her own grandfather built an adobe house in Scottsbluff out of dirt, hay from the livestock railroad yards, and rocks from the sugar beet factory. He tore down the company house and used it to make a roof. Her mother worked in the fields from the time she was ten years old. She endured four miscarriages between Anita's birth and Gabe's and believed her health was ruined by the grueling field work. Her mother told her many stories of people calling them ugly names, saying they were dirty or that Mexican Americans brought crime to their neighborhoods. Poverty kept them isolated, but they survived by forming strong community bonds. Religion was a big part of that, along with monthly dances and sharing food. When Anita was four, her family moved to a small house in Elmyra because her father got a job at the local farm implement company. Luis's family was already living in Elmyra. His father got a job at the Sioux Army Depot, stacking ammunition in miles of bunkers that would be shipped out to soldiers fighting in the Korean War.

Anita is proud of her heritage. She knows her grandparents and her parents were strong, good people. Until he died in a farm machinery accident at age fifty-eight, her father's primary goal was to equip her and Gabe for a better life than the one afforded to him. He was a firm believer in education and hard work. He prayed the rosary and practiced kindness to his neighbors. He also taught them to stick to their own kind. They could attend school, show off their moves at the community dance hall, participate in band or chorus or FHA for Anita and sports for Gabe, but he said no one would take kindly to their dating a gringo. Besides, why would they want to? Who, besides their own, would ever understand?

Now, a Black man is president of the United States. A long time coming, that's what she has to say about that. She's supposed to feel there's progress because she and her family have done what others assume is normal. She had her own business, a fabric store on the Main Street of Elmyra. Gabe is a respected teacher and coach at the high school. Luis retired with a pension. Their son went to college and works as a hospital administrator; Delia went to nursing school and will go back to work once her youngest is in kindergarten. They earned their way, like everybody else. And yet. Ugly things get said about people with brown skin on the television. There's lots of agitation over immigration. She's grateful that she and Luis were born in the United States and so were their children and grandchildren, but somebody in each of their pasts was an illegal immigrant, venturing north out of desperation and hope for a better future. They worked hard, paid their taxes, obeyed the rules. They've had a renegade or two in the family, somebody who ran afoul of the law, but what family doesn't?

Still, she believes it's better to stick to your own kind. Their close friends are mostly through their church. She doesn't trust most Anglos, doesn't get too close. But Toby has been different. She has felt safe with Toby. Even though she's technically their boss, Toby has never made her feel that she's less. Until now. Something is eating at Toby, and she won't talk about it.

Luis says that's just Toby's way. She's private. But Anita is not so sure. Also, if Toby was one of Anita's friends, she would sit her down and ask, what's going on? She wouldn't stand by while her friend stewed in her own juice without at least trying to help. Something is stopping her from asking Toby, some inhibition that she's not been aware of before. She doesn't know whether it comes down to Toby being the boss or Toby being white. Either way, she feels put in her place, and she doesn't like it.

That's why, on this Friday morning, when she shows up to help prepare for that evening's Five O'clock, and Toby says, "Go on home, Anita. I haven't even thought about what we'll serve," she erupts.

Toby is seated in her living room, on the old threadbare futon with wooden arms. Anita sits opposite her in a rocking chair. Anita takes a deep breath, leans forward, props her arms on her knees. "All right," she says. "What is going on? You haven't been yourself for three days."

Toby's hand flutters through the air, lands on her throat. She looks off to the side. Anita is truly alarmed. Has Toby had a stroke?

"What do you think, Anita? Am I getting too old to run this place?"

Anita is taken aback. Sure, she and Luis have wondered how long Toby can go on with this. Hell, they've wondered how long they can manage to keep up with it, and they're younger than Toby. But she hasn't seen any obvious change or decline. Has Toby had a diagnosis she's keeping to herself? Is she noticing symptoms?

She decides to play it safe. "Where is this coming from?"

Toby doesn't answer. In fact, she presses her lips together like someone who won't tell a secret. Then it comes to Anita. She sits back in her chair. Nola Jean. It has to be. All this has come up because that ungrateful girl is here. Of course, Toby doesn't want to betray her own daughter. That was obvious in the car the other day. Anita knows she has to be careful, or she'll push Toby into defending her. She tries to take the sneer out of her voice and says, "Nola Jean?"

Toby stands up. She moves to the window, her back to Anita. Then, with a big sigh, she says, "She talked to Dr. Penny."

"That's what had you so upset in town the other day?"

Toby nods. "Nola Jean wants me to move into town for the winters."

"Hmm." Honestly, that doesn't sound so bad to Anita. Still, knowing Toby, she can see how this would wound her pride. Toby can't see herself anywhere but on this land.

"And Dr. Penny agreed?" Anita asks.

Toby turns and looks at her. Then she shrugs and pivots back to the window. "I didn't stick around long enough to find out."

Anita stands. She has no idea what to say. It's not like Toby to give a damn what other people think. She raises her hands, then drops them.

"Is that why Nola Jean is here?"

"Maybe. I guess . . . I don't know. She's got some other stuff going on."

Anita moves toward the window. She stands beside Toby looking out over George's front yard, the picket fence, beyond it to the flow of prairie grass.

"The two of them." Toby's voice is flint, making sparks with each word. "Talking about me behind my back. Like I'm some kind of specimen."

"Seems like you need to talk to Nola Jean."

Toby snorts. Tosses her head. If she were a threatened mare, she couldn't have done it any better.

"For what it's worth," Anita says, her voice gentle and quiet. "I don't see you any different."

Toby turns to her then, her eyes rimmed in red. She hasn't been sleeping, clearly. Toby takes a deep breath. It quivers on the intake, but when she speaks, her voice is strong.

"Let's make rhubarb muffins for tonight. I got all that rhubarb in the garden."

Nola Jean

NOLA JEAN AND ISABEL ARE HEADED TO A COTTONWOOD GROVE THAT runs along the bottom of a draw extending north from the Primrose pond. There's a path threading through the trees that has been there as long as Nola Jean can remember. Some ancestor, her grandfather or his father before him, placed wooden benches in a few choice spots on the land where a person could sit and contemplate. Nola Jean used to come here as a child, perch on the weathered bench and dream. The bench is still there, rebuilt with new legs. Luis's handiwork, probably. Or Gabe's. When they sit, they are ringed by seven deeply furrowed trunks stretching toward the illimitable sky.

"These are amazing," Isabel says.

"When I was a kid, I called them the seven sisters. I could place my whole hand sideways in the grooves of the bark. Look." Nola Jean stands, wedges her hand inside one of the nearest trees. "I still can. Of course, they've grown right along with me." She sits again. "They were my pretend family. Or sometimes my court. You know girls, their heads full of princess stuff."

The trees arch over them, high and higher, 100 to 150 feet tall. The afternoon sun dapples through the leaves, glints off the waxy surfaces, bathes the central space where they sit in golden ambient light. In the stillness, they hear the scurry of a squirrel, a flutter of a wing. An occasional birdsong. The air smells damp and clean.

"My god, it's a cathedral." Isabel's voice is hushed, reverent. She holds out her hand and turns it, watching the play of light on her flesh.

"Have you been to Barcelona?"

"No. Have you?"

Nola Jean nods. "Gaudi's famous cathedral, La Sagrada Familia, has giant pillars that branch as they reach for the ceiling hundreds of feet above. He was inspired by trees. When I saw it, I thought immediately of this place."

For a while, they don't speak. They rest in the solace of beauty and grandeur.

"When I was in chemo," Isabel says, "I used to sit outside on my patio. I looked at blooming geraniums and squirrels dashing about, and I would think, we are the same, you and I, sinew and bones and cells, and all of us will die in order to give rise to new life. I found it comforting."

"It's odd, isn't it? When I come here, I feel both smaller and expanded. I don't know how to talk about it."

"Transcendence."

Nola Jean smiles. "Maybe."

"No, I mean it. That's what that is. Lifted out of our small selves and into connection with the whole universe. We are literally moved. Displaced. Nature does it for me. A fine poem. Music, sometimes."

"Sex?"

"If it's good."

More silence. "Speaking of sex," Isabel says.

"Were we?"

"Gabe has come to see me."

"Oh. Oh, I see."

Nola Jean feels her face growing hot. She's surprised, though she shouldn't be. She watched them together at the first Five O'Clock, which was—what—only one week ago.

Isabel shrugs. "Just to talk. So far. He's very attractive, isn't he?"

"Yes, he is," Nola Jean says.

Isabel turns to her. That direct gaze. "Would you mind?"

Nola Jean leans back. Her response holds too much heat, but she can't help it. "No. Of course not. Why should I?"

"He told me you and he used to have a thing."

"We were kids. It was a lifetime ago."

"You're sure?"

"Yeah, I'm sure. Watch out for Anita, though."

"Why do you say that?"

"She's protective of her little brother."

"I'm pretty harmless."

Isabel turns away then. Nola Jean is not sure Isabel is harmless, where Gabe's concerned, but he's a grown man. She doesn't mind. Does she? And if she did, what good would it do?

On the way back to Isabel's cabin, when they are walking side by side rather than single file on the narrow path through the trees, Nola Jean finally says what she's come here to say. "My birth mother contacted me again."

Isabel stops in her tracks, turns to Nola Jean. "She did?"

"Yeah." Nola Jean stoops, pulls the tip off a blade of grass, sticks it in her mouth to chew on.

"What did she say?"

Nola Jean resumes walking, and Isabel falls in step with her. "She wants to meet. On Tuesday. In Cheyenne this time."

"That's good, isn't it? That's what you wanted."

"I don't know. I feel batted around. Maybe she's just playing games with me."

"Did you answer her?"

"Not yet." They are at Isabel's cabin. "What do you think I should do?"

Isabel smiles. "You know I can't answer that."

"If it were you?"

Isabel looks off in the distance, focusing on something beyond the horizon. "If it were me, I'd have to find out. Take the chance. But that's me."

"Yeah. That's what I thought."

"So. Will you?"

"I don't know."

Nola Jean watches Isabel turn into her cabin. Isabel stops and blows her a kiss from the porch. She's wearing black cropped pants and an ivory linen sleeveless top. She's lovely and ethereal and Nola Jean feels a tinge of fear for her. She remembers a line from a Robert Frost poem, "Nothing gold can stay," and wonders if Isabel is too good for this world. She shakes her head to ward off such superstitious thoughts—her mind too much on loss these days—turns to walk home. She's halfway back to Larkspur before she remembers that she had intended to go and talk to Toby. Well, that can wait. First, she has to decide what to do about Josephine Klingman, and she's not ready to do that. A chicken hawk soars overhead, its shadow dipping on and off the road. Nola Jean watches, her heart climbing with the bird in flight.

Josie

SHE HEARS NOTHING FROM NOLA JEAN ALL OF FRIDAY. SHE DOES WHAT most of us do when confronted with the untenable, she stays busy. She goes to see her mother. Evelyn is in rare form, complaining about everything and everybody. The food is bland. The help is inattentive. Her bed is too hard or too soft. Her back hurts or maybe her arm, Josie has stopped listening. She waits for a lull in her mother's voice and murmurs what she hopes are reassuring sounds while adjusting her bedspread, wiping her countertop, folding the clothes brought back from the laundry.

In her mind, Josie rehearses what she will say to her mother. Remember that baby that I said died? Well, it didn't. It was a girl, and she was born. She's alive and well and fifty years old. Any way she plays it, she comes back to her mother's dismay. You lied, she will say. You lied to me all these years. And what can Josie say to that, except yes, I did. And why did she lie? She scarcely knows herself. At the time, it seemed the only possible course. Her parents were so angry and righteous. She was afraid. Possibly. Or wanted to punish them? Or was simply out of her mind. Check all of the above.

"Josie. Josie, are you listening to me?"

"What? Oh sure, Mom. Do you need something?"

"What's gotten into you today? You act like you're somewhere else."

Josie forces herself to sit in the chair opposite her mom. Knots her hands in her lap. "I'm sorry. I have a few things on my mind."

"Like what?"

"Oh, you know." Josie laughs, a nervous tinkle that sounds false even to her ears. She reaches up and brushes her hand across her hair. "The garden. Mindy's birthday coming up. Lists of things to do."

"You worry too much. Always have."

This is a recurring theme from her mother. Pronouncements of things wrong with her disguised as reassurance. She worries too much. She's too sensitive. She takes things too seriously. She should turn things over to the Lord. Josie hears all of it as a recipe that would enable her to be more available to meet Evelyn's needs. If she had no concerns of her own, she could focus entirely on her mother.

"You're probably right," she says. She clamps her mouth shut, her jaw sore from tension. Then she stands. Bends and gives her mother a kiss on the cheek.

"You just got here," Evelyn says.

"I'll be back. You have that doctor's appointment on Monday."

"I thought it was Tuesday."

For a moment, Josie is swept with panic. Did she get these dates wrong? She rifles through her purse, a large leather bag with too many compartments. She zips and unzips, sorts through receipts, keys, a fingernail file, two combs, a bag of gummy worms she bought for her grandson, tissues, paper clips, chewing gum, ticket stubs. Some of this detritus lands on the floor, some on the chair, she knows she looks hysterical and is making a giant mess, but she can't help it. Finally, she lands on her phone. Checks the calendar.

"It's Monday, Mom. Ten o'clock in the morning."

She stoops to pick up all the junk, shoves it back in her bag.

"You ought to clean that thing out," Evelyn says.

"You're right," Josie says.

"You always were messy, that way. Never taking the time to organize."

Josie stops in her tracks. She looks down a rifle barrel at her mother. A loaded rifle. If her mother says one more negative thing, she'll pull the trigger.

"I gotta go, Mom. We have a busy weekend, but I'll call you."

She escapes her mother's room, leans back against the door to breathe and gather herself.

"You okay?" a nursing attendant asks.

"Yeah. Fine," Josie says. Though clearly, she isn't fine. She is definitely not fine. She's not even sure, at this point, what fine would look like.

Anita

LUIS DOESN'T FEEL WELL. HE CALLED OFF WORKING EARLY THIS AFTER-
noon, has been sitting in the recliner with his feet up. He left Gabe
finishing a stretch of fence by himself. Anita flutters around him,
brings him a glass of ice water, pushes the hair back from his forehead,
straightens the cover on the arm of the chair. She's sure he doesn't have
a fever, but she feels his brow every five minutes to make sure. He's pale.
Ashen, a gray cast underneath his golden skin.

"Would you sit down, woman? You're making me crazy."

She sits opposite him on the couch, perched on the edge.

"You're like a tiger about to pounce."

She doesn't laugh. It's so unlike him. He's never sick, and he never
complains.

"What's wrong with you?" she says.

"Nothing that a little rest won't cure. I got overheated, that's all."

"It's not that hot."

"I'm not as young as I used to be."

She doesn't believe him. Not one word. What can she do?

"I think I should call Dr. Penny," she says.

"And say what? That I got tired working today and knocked off a
couple hours early? I'll tell you what you should do. You should go help
Toby with her Five O'Clock."

"You aren't coming?"

"Not this time. I'll just stay here with my feet up while you do all
the work."

He smiles, warming her insides the way he does.

"I don't feel right leaving you here."

"Gabe'll swing by to clean up when he's done. He can check on me."

She stands. Wipes her hands down the sides of her jeans. She's wearing
a flowered shirt, one of Luis's favorites, and a necklace with a gold cross.

"If you're sure," she says.

"Go on," his voice gentle.

She leans over him and kisses him on the forehead, checking once more for fever. He reaches one hand up and squeezes her arm.

From the doorway she looks back. His eyes are closed, his breathing even. Lord, how she loves the man! She'll kill him if he's lying to her.

Toby

THEY ARE ALL GATHERED FOR THE FRIDAY FIVE O'CLOCK. EXCEPT LUIS.
Anita says he's not feeling well. Gabe arrived a little late, wet-haired, having stepped straight out of the shower. Toby can't remember a summer when Gabe showed up for these gatherings, but then Nola Jean wasn't here. Or Isabel. It doesn't take a wizard to see that there's a spark between Gabe and Isabel. Toby catches Anita watching them, eyes narrowed, lips clamped. Corey has zeroed in on Nola Jean, standing too close, leaning. Nola Jean is wearing a black above-knee skirt, sleeveless lilac shirt. Corey has traded in his cowboy gear for a T-shirt and jeans; he looks like a teenager, lean and boyish. Toby watches all this with bemusement, the way she might occasionally tune in to an afternoon soap opera. Once, she was the subject of conjecture, the epicenter of love and attraction and jealousies. All that seems like another lifetime, and now, whether she's older and wiser or just older and dried up, she can hardly recall what all the fuss was about.

Matthew seems outside the circle, for the moment. He wanders over to Toby and Anita, who are standing by the picnic table with the drinks and muffins. He's in baggy shorts and a blue polo shirt.

"I wore this for you," Anita says, lifting the gold cross from her neck.

Matthew smiles. "Nice. Not a crucifix, I see."

Anita chuckles. "No, though I have those too. This one was a gift."

"Oh? Who from?"

"A childhood friend. We used to play hopscotch and jump rope together. She died a few years back."

While Matthew and Anita settle into a nice chat, Toby steps aside. She's hoping for an opportunity to catch Nola Jean's attention, but she's not sure how to pry her away from Corey. She's thinking about asking Nola Jean to give her some help in the kitchen when Nola Jean excuses herself from Corey and moves toward her. Corey casts around for a moment, notes that Isabel's and Gabe's heads are curved together like a croquet hoop, then ambles over to join Matthew and Anita. Matthew instinctively steps back to widen the circle for Corey.

Toby stands as tall as she can while her daughter moves closer.

"This seems to be going well," Nola Jean says. Real casual like. Well, if that's the way she wants to play this.

"Yes. I think so," Toby says.

When the pause becomes too awkward, Toby says, "So, what have you been up to? I haven't seen you for a few days."

"I know," Nola Jean says. "I was pretty thrown by Josephine's backing out of seeing me."

"Of course, you were," Toby says.

"But I heard from her again."

"You did?"

"She wants to set another meeting. Tuesday. In Cheyenne. At the Plains Hotel."

"I see."

"Where she won't run into anyone she knows."

"I guess I can understand that."

Toby's on two tracks now. One part, the mother instinct, listening and aware of Nola Jean's pain. The other part hurt that her anguish doesn't seem to be on Nola Jean's radar. She's distracted by the internal war, wondering at what point in life a parent's needs come before a child's, if ever, or if it's only when the parent wanders so far into old age that they become the child. She doesn't want to give up her status as an adult, and yet, a piece of her is stamping a foot and clamoring for attention. It takes energy she's not sure she can sustain to navigate through these shoals. At some point she realizes Nola Jean is talking and she has no idea what she's said. Not wanting—especially now—to look doddering, she decides to fake it and hope she can catch up to the conversation.

". . . don't know if I can trust her," Nola Jean says.

My feeling, exactly, Toby thinks. I don't know if I can trust you. But, she says, "You're afraid she'll cancel again?"

"Or I'll drive all the way over there, and she'll not show up."

"Which way do you have the most to lose?"

Nola Jean takes a moment to look at her. Toby sees a note of appraisal, then Nola Jean nods.

"You're right," she says. "Thanks."

"Do you think we could talk? Maybe tomorrow?"

"I promised Corey I'd take him and Matthew to Crescent Lake tomorrow. Can it wait?"

Wait? That's all she's been doing, and she's running out of patience. It's on the tip of Toby's tongue to tell Nola Jean that she talked to Dr. Penny when Isabel calls the whole group to attention.

"Hey, everybody. I found out that Nola Jean has a hidden talent."

Nola Jean groans. The others chime in, urging Isabel to tell.

"Nola Jean confessed to me this afternoon that she can play 'Amazing Grace' on a cottonwood leaf."

"No way," Corey says.

Laughing, the group moves to the side of George's lawn where the cottonwood branches spread across the fence. Anita comes to stand beside Toby, and the two of them watch, like spectators at a rodeo afraid the cowboy will get bucked off. Nola Jean plucks a leaf from the tree, folds it in half, pinches it at the top and bottom, blows into the opening and uses her fingers on the leaf to change the pitch.

Matthew speaks first. "That might be 'Amazing Grace,' if you've got a good imagination."

Nola Jean laughs too. "I never said I was a virtuoso."

"How'd you learn to do that?" Gabe says.

"Walter, my father, showed me."

Toby's surprised to hear that. She never knew Walter to blow on a cottonwood leaf. After all these years, to think she could learn something new about him.

"Show me," Isabel says.

With that, they all pluck a few leaves. Nola Jean demonstrates how to fold the leaf—careful not to crease it—and where to place their fingers. At first, no one can get anything resembling a pitch out of the leaves, but eventually first one and then another gets the hang of it. Along the way, all of them fall into laughing, punch-drunk and giddy.

"Let's do the 'Blue Danube,'" Matthew says. Then he proceeds to sing, "Dah-dah-dah-dah-dah," and the others all chime in with two high toots, followed by two low toots.

They try 'We Will, We Will Rock You,' and 'When the Saints Go Marching In.' They keep it up a long time, howling and hooting, releasing the tension that all adults and maybe this group in particular carry, stomping their feet to the rhythms when the tunes are unrecognizable.

Anita shakes her head. "They've gone mad," she says, but she can't help smiling.

Toby watches in amazement. The sheer joy of it astounds her. She watches them, clothed in summer colors, bending in half with glee, stomping and dancing like a living floral ballet right there on her front lawn, and she is swept with sorrow. She cannot fathom how she has not known that Nola Jean is capable of spreading this kind of light.

Nola Jean

THE WHOLE GROUP WALKS TOGETHER BACK TO THEIR CABINS. IT'S DUSK by now, and they're still laughing and talking about their impromptu cottonwood band. They reach the turnoff to Nola Jean's cabin. While they're lingering, saying good night, Matthew extends an invitation to Isabel and Gabe to join them for the Crescent Lake tour. It's not lost on Nola Jean that everyone has accepted that Gabe and Isabel are a pair.

"Guess we could," Gabe says, in his slow drawl. "Luis says no work tomorrow. He's not feeling great."

"Do you usually work on Saturday?" Matthew asks.

"Depends on what needs doing," Gabe says. Gabe looks at Isabel as if to say what do you think.

"Why not?" she says.

"Great." Matthew literally rubs his hands together. Nola Jean sees that he likes this role, bringing people together. A little community. "What time shall we get started, Nola Jean?"

"Earlier is better, if we want to see birds. But I suppose Corey has to drive down from Minatare."

"Oh, no. He's got a camper at my place now." Matthew looks sideways at Corey.

"Yeah, we thought it'd save me, you know . . . ," Corey stammers.

"Save him driving," Matthew adds.

"Just convenient," Corey says.

"Toby said it'd be okay," Matthew says.

They're falling over each other trying to explain. Seems odd to Nola Jean, but then who is she to talk about odd? In fact, they're all a little out of the mainstream, or they wouldn't be at Toby's Last Resort. Even Gabe. He's not seeking solace here, but his life has not exactly followed a predictable path. He entered the navy straight out of high school, counting on the GI bill to help finance college when he finished his tour of duty. The talk around town was that while stationed in Hawaii, he fell in love and got engaged to a woman from Idaho. She finished her stint six months ahead of him and was supposed to meet him in San Diego. When she didn't show up or answer his phone calls, he drove to Idaho and found that she was married to someone else. And pregnant. The story was that she cried and said she just didn't know how to tell him. Without another word, Gabe got in his car, drove back to Nebraska, and enrolled at Chadron State College where he majored in history. After graduating, he hopped around Nebraska and Iowa schools teaching and coaching until seven or eight years ago when he was invited to come back to Elmyra to coach the boys' basketball team. As far as Nola Jean knows, he's never married, though he's obviously attractive to women.

Yanking her mind back to the present, Nola Jean says, "How about if we start out about eight o'clock? We can be civilized about this. Bring water, a hat, sunscreen, and a lunch. We'll need two cars."

"I can drive. I know the way," Gabe says.

"We could take my car," Isabel says. "I'm not sure I want to be jostled around in your truck."

Nola Jean and Gabe look at each other and laugh.

"I don't think so," Gabe says. "The roads are sandy. That area can be wet. Jostled is better than stuck."

"You can go with us, Nola Jean," Corey says.

"Why don't you and Matthew come to my cabin in the morning? We'll take my car. It'll do fine, better than Matthew's Escort. And I've seen that jalopy you drive, Corey. Gabe, shall we meet up in front of Toby's? We might as well try to stay together on the drive over."

It's settled, then. Nola Jean tells them to go ahead. She wants to check her emails while she's standing on this high point. Matthew and Corey move down the road toward the turnoff to Goldenrod. Gabe and Isabel start down the path to Primrose, and Nola Jean watches just long enough to see Gabe take Isabel's hand. She's guessing Gabe won't be driving back to Elmyra tonight.

She takes her cell phone from her pocket, waits for it to boot up. She looks again at Josephine Klingman's plea to meet, pushes reply, and says only, Okay. She thinks about writing more, but what else is there to say at this point? Instead, she presses send and lets out the breath she's been holding.

On the road to Larkspur, she spots a shooting star low on the horizon, just visible in the fading light. Soon more stars will appear as the night deepens. It's always seemed like a grand secret that the stars hide in broad daylight. Out here on the prairie, away from city lights, the darkest skies provide a backdrop for a spectacular display, the Milky Way wiped across like a chalky eraser's swath on a blackboard. But to see the sparkling stars, you must be willing to brave the night.

Josie

SHE GETS THROUGH THE REST OF THE DAY. SHE SNIPES AT DAN OVER lunch. She tries to work on a quilt in the afternoon but makes so many mistakes that she has to rip out every seam. She forgets to thaw meat for dinner, so she serves pancakes. Dan doesn't complain, but he's oblivious too. She can't talk to him. He'll tell her to let it go. He thinks she has let it go.

By the time she gets Nola Jean's cryptic email response, late Friday evening, she's so exhausted she can barely register any feeling. For sure, she's too tired to broach the subject with Dan. She goes to bed thinking she has three days to explain to Dan and wondering how she's gotten herself into another predicament where the person she loves and trusts most in the world has no idea what the hell she is doing.

Nola Jean

NOLA JEAN'S TOUR PARTICIPANTS, EXCEPT FOR GABE, ARE SURPRISED to find that Crescent Lake is not a lake but a conglomeration of lakes and wetlands that cover a wide expanse. The small tourist office is closed on Saturdays, but there's a boardwalk with signage and accompanying brochures in a lidded box. Matthew, who likes facts and statistics, announces that the area is designated a national wildlife refuge and covers forty-six thousand acres.

"Good lord," Matthew says. "Forty-six thousand acres! That's huge. Who manages it?"

"It's owned by the federal government, so I suppose the Fish and Wildlife Agency," Nola Jean says.

"Or the National Park Service," Gabe offers.

Isabel has wandered apart, kneeling to study plants, take photos. Sensing that she wants some private space, Gabe sticks with the rest of the group. Matthew is still quoting from the brochure.

"You know how many species of birds have been spotted here?"

"A lot?" Nola Jean ventures.

"Two hundred seventy-nine! Not individual birds. Different species. That's incredible."

"We'll see a lot of birds today if we keep our eyes open. And don't make too much noise," Gabe says.

"Hey! It says here this place was founded in 1931."

Gabe and Nola Jean exchange a look. Matthew sounds like a tent evangelist, but his enthusiasm is infectious. It's impossible not to smile. Corey's head rotates side to side like a periscope, hands in back pockets, bored.

"Thirty-five species of mammals now," Matthew shouts. "Including, long ago in the age of bison, the plains grizzly bear, plains wolf, and black-footed ferret."

"There's been a team of scientists studying turtles here for years," Gabe says.

"You know a lot about this place," Nola Jean says, teasing him.

"I bring students here sometimes."

"I thought you taught history."

"This is natural history. Besides, gets us out of the classroom."

"Your students must love you."

"I bet you don't know this," Gabe says, sluffing off her attempt at a compliment. "There was a snapping turtle here that once laid ninety-seven eggs in a single nest."

"I bet you tell that to all the girls." Nola Jean shoves her elbow into Gabe's side. He feigns pain, grins. It feels good to be close to him.

"You think that's impressive? One species of turtle, I think it's called a yellow mud turtle, nests completely underground."

"That doesn't sound like much fun," Nola Jean says.

Corey, waking up, suddenly throws his arm around Nola Jean's shoulders. "I bet it could be fun with you."

Nola Jean sees Gabe smirk. She bends and slips out from under Corey's arm, but it's too late. Gabe has already moved away, headed toward Isabel. Isabel is pointing out in the middle of a lake where a blue heron stands majestic and still.

The whole morning goes on like that. Surrounded by water and grass, insect buzz and birdsong, the only human sounds of their own making, their feet clumping on the boardwalk and voices echoing. Isabel is transfixed with the beauty and stillness of the place, Gabe at her side narrating. Matthew keeps his head in the brochure, reciting names from long lists of birds and mammals and plants. Corey sticks to Nola Jean like a gnat on yellow. They see a myriad of ducks, teals and mallards, more wading birds. In a distant tree, a bald eagle. Shore birds galore, including the ubiquitous killdeer. An owl in a tree alongside the road when they drive to another area. Trumpeter swans. They find a dry spot to pull out their picnic lunches. Nola Jean thought to bring along a blanket, which she spreads on the grass.

"It says here," Matthew says, "that this area is a 'sea of grass in a sea of grass.'"

Silenced, for once, he turns and pivots to take in grass in every direction. Blue grama, buffalo grass, sedges, and wildflowers, a woven tapestry as rich as anything that once hung in a medieval castle.

"There's a reservoir underneath here," Gabe says.

Corey lies on his back, munching a peanut butter sandwich. His long, lean body is stretched out beside Nola Jean. He moves slightly to nudge his hip next to hers. Nola Jean reaches forward to pluck a twig off the blanket, an excuse to shift her weight away from him. Corey swivels his hip to make contact again. Nola Jean sighs and tries to remember that he's a harmless puppy.

Meanwhile, Gabe and Matthew are deep into a discussion of the Ogallala Aquifer, the underground ocean that stretches all the way to Texas, feeding this Sandhills area with moisture to keep all this going. Isabel has brought along a small notebook, and she's jotting in it while nibbling on her lunch of carrot sticks and celery. She looks up and catches Nola Jean's eye.

"It's beautiful here," Isabel says.

Nola Jean looks around, seeing the familiar through Isabel's eyes. "It is," she agrees, "in its own way."

Isabel chuckles. "That's all any beauty has, isn't it? Its own way? How else could it be?"

"I've lived in Minnesota a long time," Nola Jean says. "There, it's all trees and lakes. Not lakes like these. Forested."

"That's beautiful too," Isabel says. "It's not a competition. Is it?"

"I think you two ladies are beautiful," Corey says. He sits up, one knee bent, props his elbow on the knee. He's the invention of swagger. "That's where beauty is, if you ask me."

Nola Jean and Isabel try not to laugh. They're way too old for this. Still, the sky is clear, the air cool and laced with birdsong. They pass a pleasant hour.

"I hate to see this end," Isabel says.

"I'm ready to go." Corey lurches to his feet, wipes his hands at the back of his jeans to knock off any lingering grass or bugs.

"Is there anything else down this way we should see?" Matthew asks.

Corey groans, but Matthew pays no attention.

Gabe looks at Nola Jean. He's chewing on a blade of grass. "We could go to Ash Hollow."

"Lovely name," Isabel says.

"What's there?" Matthew asks.

"Just an old sod house," Corey says.

"A small museum. It's near the most significant army–Native American battlefield in Nebraska," Gabe says.

"Really?" Matthew says.

"I didn't know that," Nola Jean says.

"What about the battleground?" Matthew asks.

Corey lets out a giant sigh, plops down on the blanket, lies back, and shields his eyes with his arm.

"It's located a few miles away from Ash Hollow. Called the Battle of Blue Water. Or sometimes, the Harney Massacre. Later, it was known as the First Sioux War."

"What happened?" Matthew, again.

"Some time in the 1850s, a band of Lakota warriors raided Fort Laramie and killed some soldiers, maybe thirty. In retaliation, Colonel William Harney led an army of six hundred into an Indian camp of three to four hundred people, killed eighty-six, wounded seventy, and marched barefoot women and children 140 miles to Fort Laramie."

"You have those numbers in your head?" Matthew asks.

"What can I say? I'm a history teacher."

"What about the army? Any losses?"

"Among Harney's troops, a handful died, four, I think. A few more were wounded. One missing, presumed dead."

"I hate this part of American history," Isabel says.

"There are other parts to hate," Matthew adds quietly.

"Why didn't we learn about this?" Nola Jean says.

Gabe shrugs, as if to say, you know why. "There was a topographer along named Warren. His job was to make maps of the area as Harney moved west. He didn't take part in the battle but stayed to the rear, tried to nurse the wounded. He also wrote about the battle in his journal, and he collected a lot of artifacts."

"Wouldn't that be looting?" Isabel asks.

"Maybe. There was a lot of that. But Warren gave his collection to the Smithsonian. Sixty-eight items, including a beaded ammunition pouch, a child's doll, moccasins. There are plans to display some of those items at Ash Hollow in 2017. That's the 150th anniversary of statehood for Nebraska. There's to be a big shindig featuring the shared histories of Native Americans, settlers, cowboys, fur traders, people going west, anybody who came through here. Soldiers, too, I guess."

"Can we go to the battlefield?" Matthew asks.

"It's on private land now. But we can go to Ash Hollow if you want. It was a famous part of the Oregon Trail. There's a hiking path to the top of the hill."

"How far is it?" Isabel asks.

"We're about thirty miles from the highway. Then, it's not too far east from there, just outside a little town called Lewellen," Nola Jean says.

"If we go now, we could spend a little time there and then have supper in Oshkosh," Gabe says.

Matthew is immediately enthusiastic, Isabel agrees, Corey complains, but in the end, they decide to pack up and go. On the drive, Matthew sits in front with Nola Jean, Corey in the backseat where he closes his eyes and sleeps. Matthew is uncharacteristically quiet, and Nola Jean is grateful for the silence.

Toby

TOBY SPENDS SATURDAY MORNING AT HER KITCHEN TABLE WITH A
notepad and successive cups of coffee. She jots, scratches out, stands,
and paces to look out the front window. When she's stuck, she sits on
the futon and imagines George sitting opposite her in the rocking
chair. Her hips feel stiff today, a reminder that it's time. That, and Nola
Jean's impatience to move her off her own land. She runs her hand
over her wiry hair, dismisses the slight tremor as too much coffee and
nerves. Sits again at the kitchen table, turns to a fresh sheet of paper,
writes #1, and goes after her list. It's nearly noon before she's satisfied.
She conjures George again, reads through her plans aloud, watches
George's face to see if he thinks she's nuts. Some will. Let them. If she
doesn't want other people making decisions for her, she better damn
well make them for herself.

Nola Jean

ONCE THEY HIT HIGHWAY 26, THE GOING IS EASY. OUTSIDE LEWELLEN, they pass a small hillside cemetery before pulling into the parking lot at the visitors center for Ash Hollow. Matthew bounds from the car and heads inside before Corey laces his shoes. Isabel and Gabe are studying a sign posting hiking trails, where Nola Jean joins them.

"The best hike is the one to the top of Windlass Hill," Gabe says.

"I do remember that," Nola Jean says. "That's where people venturing west came down off the tableland into the river valley."

"What's there?" Isabel says.

Gabe and Nola Jean look at each other and laugh.

"Not much," Gabe says. "Except a spectacular view."

"Big ruts," Nola Jean says.

"From the wagons?" Isabel asks.

"The drop was about three hundred feet. They'd lock the wheels of the wagons, hook ropes on them and let them slide down the hill. I read an account by one settler that said it took three hours to get one wagon all the way down." Gabe says this while gazing into Isabel's eyes.

By this time, Corey has sauntered over to see what they're doing. Matthew emerges from the museum to find out if there's a plan. He arrives just in time to hear Gabe's last explanation.

"We gotta go up there," Matthew says.

"Not me," Corey says. "I'll wait for you in the picnic area down the hill."

"I think I'll stay too," Isabel says.

Gabe catches her elbow. "You okay?"

Isabel flashes him her million-dollar smile. "Yeah. A little tired. You go ahead. I'll be happy making notes."

Corey spreads his arms wide. "C'mon, ladies. You're with me."

Nola Jean bites her lip. The last thing she wants to do is spend an hour fending off Corey's advances. Meanwhile, Matthew starts up the trail.

Isabel sees Nola Jean's hesitation. "Go on," she says.

Nola Jean tips her head slightly toward Corey, rolls her eyes.

Gabe, noting this silent exchange, puts his arm around Isabel. A warning to Corey to leave Isabel alone. Corey turns to Nola Jean.

"I guess it's you and me, Nola Jean."

"I'm hiking too," she says.

At that, Corey, too obtuse to be wounded, turns on his heel and heads toward the picnic area.

"I'll be fine," Isabel says. "I can handle Corey. If he gets in my face, I'll start reciting poetry."

Relieved, Nola Jean joins Gabe. Matthew's yards ahead of them, and Nola Jean and Gabe fall into an easy pace together. She's thinking of all the times they walked like this when they were young and wonders if Gabe has similar thoughts.

"I remember pageants out here," she says. "People dressed in old-timey clothes, barbershop quartets, chuckwagon dinners."

Gabe chuckles. "Yeah. They still do those. Every year."

They walk farther in silence. Then Gabe says, "I seem to recall you doing that. You had a long pink skirt with a ruffle on the bottom. And those weird sleeves that poof at the top."

Nola Jean laughs. "Leg-of-mutton."

"What?"

"That's what those sleeves are called. Puffy at the shoulder and tight from the elbow to wrist. Shaped like a leg of mutton."

"Big hat too."

Nola Jean stops. Gabe stops, and she turns to him. "You tied the bow under my chin."

Gabe raises an eyebrow, that crooked grin. "Yeah. I remember."

Nola Jean feels her face warm. What neither of them says is that after tying the bow, Gabe kissed her.

They walk a few more steps when Gabe says, "I was heartbroken, you know. When you broke up with me."

"Oh no you don't," Nola Jean says. She laughs, but there's an edge to it.

"I was." Gabe's voice soft, a catch in his breath.

Nola Jean stops. "But . . . you broke up with me."

Gabe turns to her. Nola Jean sees that he is truly puzzled.

"You did," she says. "You stopped calling me. You just . . . disappeared."

"That's what you think?" Gabe says.

"That's what happened."

"Only after you told Anita you didn't want to see me anymore."

"What?"

"You told Anita you weren't comfortable dating a boy with brown skin."

Nola Jean hears the sneer in his voice, the hurt. After all this time.

"Gabe, listen to me. I never. Anita told me that you were only dating me to prove that you could date a white girl."

"She said that?"

"She said you didn't care about me. You just picked me because I was a cheerleader and people noticed me. So, then when you didn't call . . ."

"You believed her?"

"Well, yeah. I guess I did."

"How could you think that of me?"

"I don't know, she . . . I . . . oh, c'mon, you believed her too."

Gabe lifts his hands, a gesture of defeat. He looks past her, over her shoulder. She senses the emotion roiling through him, matching her own. Quietly, she says, "I was heartbroken too."

Gabe looks down, shakes his head from side to side. "I could kill her," he says.

They stand a while in silence. Nola Jean's a ball of writhing emotions. Without either of them speaking, by some mutual consent, they fall into walking again, step by measured step.

When they both stop, as if on a rehearsed cue, Nola Jean says, "She wasn't entirely wrong, you know."

"About us?"

"We always went out of town. When we were together."

His breathing slows. "Well, yeah. That's because . . ."

"I know why it was."

Matthew has reached the top of the hill and is waving at them, urging them forward.

"We better get moving," he says.

She nods. They stride out this time.

"I liked your voice," she says, keeping her tone light. "And you could dance. And you were gentle."

"You," he says and pauses. "You were smart, funny, and kind. Also, beautiful."

"We were kids."

"I know. You would've gone off to college."

He lets that thought hang. She knows what he means. As a couple, they were destined to wreck on the muddy banks of life. Still . . .

"You know what I resent most?" Nola Jean says. "All these years since, I've avoided you."

"Anita warns me when you come to town."

"Does she think I'm that dangerous?"

"She's probably afraid we'll find out the truth."

"Well," she says. They've reached Matthew now. He's standing with his hands on his hips, exclaiming over the panoramic view. "All that, a long time ago." She waves her hand in a gesture of futility.

"Still," Gabe says. "It's nice to know."

Josie

ALL DAY SATURDAY, JOSIE WAITS FOR A MOMENT TO TELL DAN THAT SHE contacted Nola Jean. Dan puts his hand on her shoulder when he gets up from the breakfast table for their second cup of coffee. She can't tell him then. They spend the morning on normal household chores and errands. He vacuums, she dustmops and dusts, an easy camaraderie they've honed over the years. She can't bring herself to interrupt their patterns.

It's Dan's idea to order a pizza for dinner and watch a movie on television. They bicker over what to watch, but it's good-natured, familiar, and she happily gives in when he suggests a classic John Wayne movie. She could care less about John Wayne, but she snuggles close to Dan, settling herself and her nerves against the familiar contours of his body. By the end of the movie, his hands are moving over her, and she tucks her face into the soft folds of his neck, inhaling his scent, and when they make love, right there on the sofa with the TV muted but flashing, she feels young and loved and safe, and naturally, she can't possibly mention, then, that she is scheduled for this potentially disastrous meeting on Tuesday.

Nola Jean

AFTER ASH HOLLOW, THE GROUP HEADS INTO OSHKOSH FOR A HAM-
burger and fries. Isabel sits between Gabe and Nola Jean on one side
of a booth, Matthew and Corey on the other. Matthew keeps them all
laughing with his exuberant discourse on all he's seen and heard today,
peppered in between with questions: What Indian tribes lived here?
What kinds of grass grow on the prairie? Does Oshkosh have anything
to do with the overalls company? Corey endures all this with a litany of
sighs and signals of boredom, but nothing dampens Matthew.

By the time they head back, the sun is being lowered in the western
sky like a yoyo on an invisible string. They drive straight into a blazing
sunset. When Nola Jean heads through the gate to the Bluestem and
down the drive, she doesn't stop at Toby's house. The lights are all on,
though Toby's car is not in the usual parking space. She takes Matthew
and Corey to Goldenrod, drops them off. It's a tight turn around now
that Corey's trailer is parked there, but she manages it. She's headed back
up the main road toward the spur to her cabin when she comes upon
Gabe's pickup parked on the hill where the roads diverge to Larkspur
and Primrose. She pulls up alongside to say good night.

One look at Gabe's face, and she sees something is wrong. He's got
his cell phone to his ear, motions to her to wait a moment. Leaning
across him, Isabel mouths, "It's Luis."

Gabe snaps his phone off. "Damn," he says. "I had my phone with
me. I just didn't think to check it. All day. It was turned off."

"What is it? What's happened?"

"Luis is in the hospital."

"In Elmyra?"

"He didn't feel well yesterday." Gabe smacks the steering wheel with
his fist.

"That must be where Toby is," Nola Jean says. "I noticed her car was gone."

"I gotta get there," Gabe says.

"I'll go with you," Nola Jean says. Then, remembering Isabel, she says, "Unless . . ."

"No," Isabel says. "I'm tired. You go. You know the family."

Gabe drops Isabel at her cabin. Nola Jean drives to her cabin and leaves her car. Gabe picks her up and they drive, without speaking, to the hospital in Elmyra. They walk in together and find Toby and Anita in a small waiting room. Delia is there, too, looking young and scared.

Anita's eyes widen when she sees them together. Then she collapses into Gabe's arms. Nola Jean moves toward Toby who is sitting, still and pallid. Pulls a chair close.

"It's his heart," Toby says. Her hand flutters helplessly before she corrals it in her lap.

Nola Jean reaches, but Toby has turned away. Nola Jean lets her hand rest for only an instant on her mother's shoulder. She has no idea how to comfort her.

Anita

THEY'RE LUCKY. THIS TIME. DR. PENNY TELLS THEM LUIS HAS SUFFERED a minor heart attack. She wants to keep him another day or two to run tests. See if she can isolate the cause before they settle on treatment.

"He may need to go to Fort Collins," Dr. Penny says. "Depending on what we find. They have heart specialists there."

Anita sags against Gabe as she listens to Dr. Penny.

"Is Luis a smoker?" Dr. Penny asks.

"He used to be," Anita says. "When he was younger. But he quit ten, fifteen years ago."

"Heart disease in the family?"

"His father." Anita grips Gabe's hand when she says this. She knows this is not good.

"Okay. You can see him. Briefly. He's sedated, so he may not respond much. Then I think you should all go home and get some rest."

"Can I stay here?" Anita gestures at the waiting room.

Gently, Dr. Penny says, "Get some rest, Anita. Nothing bad is going to happen to him tonight. He's where he needs to be."

Anita thinks about staying in town with Delia, but in the end, she decides she wants to go home, collect a few things for Luis and herself in case she decides to stay in town later. Delia tells the nursing staff to call her immediately if there's any change, hugs her mother tearfully, and heads home to her young family. Nola Jean offers to ride with Toby so Gabe can drive Anita home in his truck. On the road, Anita cannot get Luis's gray-tinged face out of her mind. She didn't recognize the signs. She'd found him slumped in the recliner, unresponsive. What would she do without him? How could she live her life? And what now? He can't continue to work so hard.

Gabe doesn't talk to her all the way to the ranch. She's grateful for his silence, busy gnawing at her worry.

When they reach her trailer, Gabe lays a hand on her arm. "Will you be all right?" he says. "I can stay with you. Sleep on your couch."

Anita thinks she will not be doing much sleeping. She'd feel confined to the back bedroom if Gabe is on the couch. "I'll be okay," she says. "I'll meet you early at the hospital. Unless . . ."

"Unless?"

She turns her face away from him. "Unless you're not going home tonight. Then you can pick me up in the morning."

She senses Gabe wrestling with how to answer her. She waits, and when he does not speak, she turns to him and says, "Nola Jean." She cannot keep the bitterness out of her voice.

"This is not the time."

"She told you, didn't she?" Anita knows she's poking a stick in his eye. Maybe her own eye. She doesn't know why she's doing it, but she can't stop.

"I don't care about that now."

"You can't trust that girl. She told you what I said to her."

Gabe flashes. "And I told her what you said to me."

Oddly, she's gratified to see his anger. She wants it. She needs a repository for the tornado that is swirling inside her. Then, so quickly, the heat fades, and she is swept with sorrow.

"I knew this day would come," she manages to say, her voice barely above a whisper.

"You lied."

She looks away. Sighs. "Maybe I did. I was trying to protect you."

Gabe answers softly. "No one asked you to."

"Oh? That was my job, since I was fifteen."

"Maybe it's time you retired from it."

Anita rubs her hands over her face. She opens and closes her mouth twice, afraid of what she might say. She became his mother, dammit. She can't just turn off her concern for him, like a spigot. She looks him in the eye, musters all the love she holds for him. "You gave up easily. So did she. Maybe you ought to ask yourselves why."

He looks at her, then shakes his head. "I'll pick you up in the morning," he says.

"Fine."

She opens her door to step out.

"'Nita," Gabe says. "I'm sorry about Luis."

"I know."

She watches him drive away. He does not head back down the lane toward the cabins. Instead, he turns toward Toby's and the main road. Maybe he intends to pick Nola Jean up from Toby's house, assuming they're back. Or maybe he's going to drive into Elmyra and back out in the morning. Either way, she can't care about that. Not now. Her heart is only half here, the other half in the hospital with Luis. With half a heart, she can only carry so much.

Toby

NOLA JEAN DRIVES, AND TOBY SITS RESTLESSLY IN THE PASSENGER seat. When Anita called and said she couldn't wake Luis, Toby jumped in her car and drove to their trailer. They decided they could get Luis to the hospital faster than if they called 911 to send an ambulance. Somehow, the two of them roused Luis enough to support him between them. They wrestled him into the backseat of Toby's car. Anita squeezed in with him, held his head in her lap, and Toby broke the speed limit and all measures of good sense driving off the Bluestem and into Elmyra. She knows the highway patrol sets up radar for speeders on this stretch, a source of revenue for the county, and she hoped they would stop her so she could have an escort. No luck.

Now she's worried about Luis. And Anita. And what it will mean for the ranch. And the future. Good god. Of all the things she thought might happen, losing Luis was not one of them.

Nola Jean drives confidently and silently. She's a good girl. That's what goes through Toby's head. Girl. At age fifty. Lord.

Nola Jean pulls up to her house.

"No need to come in," Toby says. She knows Nola Jean has had a full day.

"You'll be all right?"

"Sure."

"In the morning . . ."

"Let's see what tomorrow brings. Just take my car to your cabin."

"I can walk."

"It's dark."

"I don't think there's much . . ."

"Just bring it back in the morning. I'll want to go into Elmyra, at some point. Maybe not first thing. Give Anita some space."

"I could go with you."

Toby nods her head. She's flooded with emotions she can't sort. Bowled over by Nola Jean's kindness, partly. Surprised that she does want her near. Afraid for Luis. And Anita. And she's exhausted. She has not forgotten Nola Jean's betrayal. She's not sure she wants to be in the same room with Nola Jean and Dr. Penny. How can they pretend they haven't ganged up against her? And this will only give them more ammunition. She knows it's selfish to be thinking about herself and the ranch when Luis's life and future hang in the balance, but damn it all, she never claimed to be a saint.

"Let's just see," she says.

She closes the car door without looking at Nola Jean's face. She doesn't want to register any hurt there. Nola Jean waits until Toby's opened her door. Toby steps inside, and she does not look back.

Nola Jean

NOLA JEAN RESTS HER HEAD ON THE STEERING WHEEL. SLIGHTED.
Rebuked and scorned, a phrase rising up from the depths of her cerebral
cortex, some Bible reference Gertie used to cling to or maybe Bob Dylan
lyrics. She has friends who complain about their needy mothers. Her
complaint? A mother who won't let her near.

She has half a mind to leave Toby's car and walk to her cabin. Would
she be doing that out of spite? The reptilian brain taking over? She
knows it's ridiculous to be sitting here uncertain whether to do what
her mother has asked or defy her, drive the car a few hundred yards
to her cabin or walk. She knows it's not even about that, and above
all, she knows none of this should matter right now. She knows, too,
that in the morning, she'll go through all this again. Should she drive
up to Toby's and offer to take her to town? Should she drop the car in
the morning and walk back to her cabin? She has no idea what Toby
needs. Or what she wants. And most of all, she hates that she's sitting
here dithering over this, at her age, wanting the approval of a mother
who is not likely to give it.

She backs the car around to drive it to Larkspur. As she does, she
sees the taillights of Gabe's pickup truck headed toward the main road.
Their day together already feels like another lifetime.

She parks Toby's car behind her CRV. She goes inside her cabin, turns
on a light, stands in the middle of the room. She dumps Toby's keys
on the desk. Retrieves a bottle of white wine from the refrigerator and
stands with it against her cheek, unable to decide if she wants it. She's
agitated. It's late, but she's not ready to retire. She grabs a flashlight,
her cardigan sweater off the hook, and heads outdoors. Walking has
always been her way of dealing with stress. Soon she's at the top of
the rise where the road triangulates, splitting off between the narrow
lanes to her cabin and Isabel's and the larger road that continues on to

Goldenrod. From here, she can see that Isabel's lights are off. The day proved to be taxing for her. It's not surprising that she's gone to bed.

Nola Jean keeps walking on the main road. At the turnoff to Goldenrod, she hesitates. Matthew and Corey would probably like to know what's going on. She doesn't want to be alone. Matthew is a minister. Right now, she could use a comforting presence.

She starts down the long lane to Matthew's cabin. She turns off her flashlight, thinking if there are no lights on in Matthew's cabin, she'll go on past and take the path around the pond that lies beyond Goldenrod. She doesn't care whether Corey is awake or not. She's in no mood to put up with his advances.

Around a slight bend in the road, she hears voices. Then, laughter. Good, they're awake. Nearing the cabin, she sees that the front door is wide open, the screen door keeping out the bugs but letting in the evening breeze. Lights blaze, and she can see Matthew through the window standing near the desk. When she has one foot on the porch, Corey enters her line of vision, carrying two wine glasses. Matthew takes one, Corey leans down, and they kiss.

Standing on the porch, unable to censor herself, Nola Jean says, "What the hell?" At the exact moment that they turn and see her, she pivots and heads away down the lane. She's moving at a fast clip, but she hears Matthew call to her, "Nola Jean. Wait. Wait."

She stops but doesn't turn. The day piles up on her, all of it too much. She turns around, marches back, stands with her hands on her hips below their porch steps.

"You . . . you . . ." she splutters, so furious she can't even think what to call them.

Matthew tries his cajoling voice. "Why don't you come in?" He holds the screen door open for her.

She doesn't think about it. She marches in, straight up to Corey, pokes her finger in his chest, and shouts in his face. "What the hell do you think you're doing? You think it's funny to hit on women? Is that your game?"

"Wait. Nola Jean. It's not like that," Matthew says.

She spits her words at the two of them. "I suppose the two of you have a lot of fun, mocking the older woman, so stupid she thinks you're interested in her." She's dangerously close to tears.

"I didn't . . . I don't . . . I think you're real pretty," Corey stammers.

"Oh, for god's sake," Nola Jean says.

"I didn't mean . . ."

"Didn't mean what? Of course, you didn't mean. Any of it. You think that makes it okay?"

"He's trying to protect me," Matthew says.

"From what? Me?" First, Anita. Now Corey. What do they think she is? A man-eater?

"I'm not out," Matthew says.

"You think I care who you or what you . . ." She waves her arms in a wide circle, glaring at Corey. "You. You made a fool of me."

"I'm sorry." Corey looks stricken. And young. So young.

"I can't be a Methodist minister and be gay." Matthew's voice is quiet. Dredged with sorrow.

Nola Jean looks from one to the other. Their haunted faces. Weakly, she says, "You came on to me."

Corey lifts his hands in a shrug. "I thought it would deflect attention. We're spending a lot of time together."

Nola Jean sags. She's spent. A day-old balloon losing air. She collapses into a half-squat, rests her hands on her knees, and then she starts to laugh. She laughs so hard that she gets the hiccups.

Matthew takes her by the arm. Gently, he says, "Why don't you sit down, Nola Jean?"

She sits on the love seat.

"How about a glass of wine?" Corey says.

"The quicker, the better," she says. She mops at her face with her hands. Matthew hands her a tissue, and she blows her nose. She feels roughly ten years old.

When they are seated together enjoying their wine, Nola Jean and Matthew on the loveseat, Corey in the rocker, Nola Jean says, "So, the two of you. Are you . . . ?" She's not sure how to go on, what to ask.

"Did we know each other before?" Matthew suggests.

"Did you?"

"We met last year," Matthew says. "At a bar in Omaha."

"A gay bar," Corey adds.

Matthew smiles at him. "I was in Omaha for a conference. On small churches."

"So, you cooked up this gig so you could be together?" Nola Jean asks.

"I was due for a sabbatical."

"The whole cross-collecting thing, that's just a cover?"

"Oh, no. That's for real. I do collect crosses."

Nola Jean turns to Corey. "Are you even from Minatare?"

"Yeah," Corey says.

"Do your parents . . ." Nola Jean lets the sentence fade away.

"No. Not really. They just think I'm different. A disappointment. I'm going to get out of there soon as I have enough money saved."

Nola Jean nods. Sips her wine. "I thought churches were more open now."

Matthew nods. "Some are. Not my denomination."

"Why don't you leave?"

Matthew sighs. Spreads his hands in a helpless gesture. "I've asked myself that question a million times. I have twenty-four years at this church. I love the people. I believe . . . I feel God has called me to this specific ministry."

"Wow," Nola Jean says.

"Yeah, wow," Matthew echoes.

"So, you have to . . ." she is unable to finish.

"Lie and pretend?" Matthew says.

"I guess."

"We're used to it," Corey says.

"We have a right to privacy," Matthew says.

"I don't know how you manage, I really don't," Nola Jean says. Twenty-four years is a long time.

"Do you reveal everything about yourself?" Matthew asks. "Even to those you love?"

Nola Jean thinks about Toby. Gabe and Anita. "No. No, I guess I don't," she says. "I doubt anyone does. Hell, half the time, I'm a mystery to myself."

"What now?" Matthew asks.

"You mean, will I tell the others?"

Matthew nods.

"Don't you think they could handle it?"

"Hard to say."

"Why would it matter?"

"They could out me to my church."

Nola Jean nods. It's hard to fathom, having to live your life so carefully. But then, is their fear of disapproval so different from her own?

"I won't say anything. That will be up to you," she says. Then, to Corey, "But stop coming on to me. And Isabel."

"Okay," he mumbles.

"It's humiliating. Also, you're not that good at it." Seeing him deflate, she adds, "Though you are cute."

Corey blushes. Matthew and Nola Jean look at each other and laugh. With that, they clink their glasses in a toast.

When they've settled, Matthew asks, "But why did you come here tonight? Something on your mind?"

Nola Jean sighs. "I came to tell you that Luis had a heart attack."

"Oh, no," Matthew says.

"When?" Corey asks.

"Today. While we were all gone. Toby and Anita managed to get him to the hospital in Elmyra. Gabe and I drove into town. The doctor says it was a mild heart attack, but they're keeping him overnight. Maybe a few days. Running some tests."

"He must be getting up there. How old is he?" Corey asks.

Matthew and Nola Jean share a glance. Only the young would see Luis as an old man.

"I don't know," Nola Jean says. "Late sixties, maybe."

"Tough for Anita," Corey says.

"And your mother," Matthew adds.

"Yeah. Toby needs Luis and Anita to keep this place going."

"If we can do anything . . ." Matthew offers.

"Right now, we don't know enough. I better get going."

"How about I walk you to the end of our drive?" Matthew stands.

"I'll clean up," Corey says, waving them out the door.

Nola Jean and Matthew walk silently. The night air smells of grass and Matthew's soap or cologne, spicey and hints of orange. She waits for Matthew to say what's on his mind. When he doesn't, she says, "Kind of young for you, isn't he?"

"Does that bother you?" Matthew asks.

"I don't know. Maybe." Nola Jean stops walking. She turns to Matthew because it's not her style to swipe sideways. "If he were a young woman, I mean, we read these stories of clergy abuse . . ."

Matthew runs his hands through his hair. A coyote howls in the distance, then another and another.

"Look," he says. "Corey's not in my congregation. He didn't come to me for counseling. He walked into a gay bar, looking for experience. A long-term, committed relationship is not exactly open to me now. When he tires of me, he'll move on."

"You've done this before," she says.

He nods. "Some of these young men, like Corey, are laced with self-loathing. I help them feel better about themselves, and for a little while, I'm less lonely."

"Seems like a hard bargain."

"We all make bargains," he says.

She nods, and they walk to the end of their lane in silence. "I can take it from here," Nola Jean says. Matthew murmurs g'night and turns. When he's a few steps away, Nola Jean calls to him. "Matthew."

He half turns to her.

"You're right," she says. "About that bargain part."

He smiles and waves. She watches him move away into the darkness and then starts back to her cabin. Her legs feel weighted, filled with plaster like a sculptor's mold. She lifts her heavy feet, trudges to the high point where she stops to breathe and survey the land in the starlight. Sad and overcome with loss, she lifts her head to the sky and adds her voice to the coyotes' chorus. She rests her hand on her chest to stifle the rising sobs. This can't be over Corey, can it? Or even Gabe? Luis is going to be all right. What's the matter with her?

She pictures Corey and Matthew, doomed to fail, and yet, for now, they shelter each other. Gabe and Isabel have something, a connection. Anita and Luis share the comfort of a long marriage, though who knows what lies in store for them. Toby is alone. She's alone. A wide gulf between them. She sighs and searches the nighttime sky until she finds Orion. Then the Big Dipper. She traces the front stars of the Big Dipper to the tail of the Little Dipper, the North Star, the one that is supposed to guide you home. "Show me," she says out loud, thinking she has no home, not anywhere. Not with anybody.

Josie

JOSIE RISES GROGGY SUNDAY MORNING, THINKING IT'S GOING TO BE a long two days. She didn't sleep well. She woke in the night from a bad dream, something about corridors and a baby crying that she couldn't get to. She lies in bed awake, revisiting their Saturday. She felt whole and safe, except for the miniature judge sitting on her shoulder. Now that judge has invaded her dreams. She's got to tell Dan today.

She's standing at the sink, filling the coffee pot with water, when Dan slides his arms around her from behind. He kisses her on the neck. She reaches one arm up and behind his head, leans into him. Oh, lord.

She waits until he's seated with his coffee and the newspaper. "Dan," she says.

"Mm-hmm." He doesn't stop reading.

"Dan." Sharper than she wanted.

He lowers the paper. "What is it?"

"I need to tell you something."

His eyes widen. She can read alarm, and she quickly adds.

"Nothing terrible. Not like that. Just . . . well, the other night, when I got home from the hospital, when I was so exhausted—which is why I didn't mention it then—I decided to try once more with Nola Jean. I didn't hear anything from her all of Friday. So, I thought she'd say no. Or say nothing at all. Which is why I didn't see any reason to bring it up."

"I thought we agreed not to contact her again," he says. His tone is terse. Cryptic.

She nods. This is an old pattern between them. He needs closure. In his mind, once something is stated, it becomes a given. She's prone to revisit decisions. Reopen discussions he's left behind.

"I know. But I just . . . well, I changed my mind. I guess." She adds this last weakly.

"I take it she agreed," he says.

He sounds like a courtroom lawyer. An unfriendly lawyer questioning a hostile witness. She bristles.

"She did." Her jaw sets. Clamps.

"When did you find out that she agreed?"

Oh, now really. That is too much. She shakes her head. Half rises out of her seat. Tosses her cloth napkin on the table.

She forces herself to take a deep breath and settle in her chair. Face the music, that's the thing.

"Late Friday night," she says.

"So, you knew all day yesterday?"

She nods. One quick assent. Next, he'll accuse her of making love to him to soften him up. Oh, god. Did she?

"So, last night?" he says.

Look at him. The dear man. So lost.

"Oh, Dan," she says. "I don't know what I'm doing. We had such a nice day yesterday. Everything . . . everything was sweet and us, you know what I mean? I couldn't bring myself to spoil it. Please . . ."

Please what? She doesn't know. She waits to see what his response will be.

Dan sighs. An admission of defeat. "Tuesday, then?" he says.

"Yes. At the Plains Hotel. Your idea."

She stands. Pours him another cup of coffee. Waits until he's had a sip.

"Dan, I've been thinking."

"There's more?"

She sits, leans toward him across the table. "I think I'd like to see her alone. I don't want her to feel ganged up on. Or overwhelmed."

He studies her. She hopes he doesn't know what she's thinking, which is that she won't feel free to talk about the past if he is with her.

"O-o-o-kay," he says, drawing it out to let her know he's not really okay. "Do you want to drive over by yourself too?"

"It could take a while," she says. A non-answer, and she knows it.

He waits without speaking.

"I mean, you'd have to wait somewhere," she goes on. "A coffee shop or something. And I don't want to feel hurried. Because you're waiting, I mean."

"I see," he says.

She holds her breath. She knows what she's up against here. The male ego, that fragile thing, though it's not typical of Dan to succumb to it or put it on full display. He stops to consider, a good sign.

She gets up from the table and busies herself with putting away the breakfast leftovers to give him space and time to think this over. When she's finished, she sits again. And waits.

"Okay," he says.

"Really?"

She sees a light start to dance in his eyes. It's all right, then. He understands.

She lays her hand on his arm. "You don't mind, do you?"

"You'll be all right?"

"I'll call you right after. If I think I'm not fit to drive, you can drive over and meet me. It's not that far."

"We'd have two cars," he says.

She waves, dismissing this as a trivial concern.

She decides on another cup of coffee. They sit in silence a while. Then, she says, "Would you help me with those boxes? I think I've found the one I was looking for."

Dan chuckles, without even looking up from the crossword he's working. "Sure, Dear. Whatever makes you happy."

She knows he's teasing her. She rests in it. God bless him. And their happy home. She hopes she's not about to light a bomb under it.

Toby

SUNDAY DRAGS. TOBY DECIDES NOT TO GO INTO TOWN. SHE HEARS Gabe's truck go past early in the morning. He must have driven out to get Anita, though it's a long drive round-trip. Still, he's the one to comfort her now. Anita and Luis have a rattletrap pickup they use to haul their small trailer, but Anita is not comfortable driving it. She's too short to see over the steering wheel. They don't design pickup trucks for short women, just one item on a long mental list Toby keeps for the ways the world is rigged against members of her sex.

Early still, she hears Nola Jean pull her sedan up to the house. Toby hears the car door. Waits to see if Nola Jean will knock. She doesn't. Toby, still in bed though she's been awake for hours, slips the curtain aside. Sees Nola Jean walk away.

She rolls on her side, pivots to get her feet on the floor. She doesn't want to examine why she's miffed when she had already decided not to go to town. Best not to think about Nola Jean. Or her motives.

She pads on bare feet out to the kitchen. Starts a pot of coffee. She sits at the kitchen table with her head propped in her hands until the coffee is done. She rises, pours a cup, the acrid odor singeing her nostrils. She doesn't know why anybody drinks this stuff.

She sits again to make another list. It doesn't have a title, but if it did, it would be something like: How to Get Along without Luis. She writes down only one item: ask Gabe if he can manage the horses and the fencing. She chews on the end of the pencil, a bad habit since childhood. Then she writes down a second item: see if Royce and Julia can take Cream and Sugar for the rest of the summer. They already board the horses in the winter. It's not fair to expect Gabe to trek out here every day. She can certainly lift a forkful of hay, and she hates to lose the freedom to ride, but hell, she has trouble saddling anyway.

This summer is already up and running. Not much to do until the cabins have to be winterized, but she can find somebody to help with that. What about next year? Or the year after?

She decides to fry an egg. That takes up some time. Getting out the pan. Butter and egg from the fridge. Toast. She likes her eggs sunny-side up with the shades drawn, so that requires a lid.

While the pan splatters a nice coating on the egg, she looks out the west window. The garden. She can manage that too. It'll be good for her to have work to do. Weeding is no big deal. If she finds the thought of freezing or canning too much when the harvest comes, she'll just take produce into town and dump it off at the old folks' home; they're always glad for something fresh.

She eats her breakfast, gets dressed, spends more time ruminating when the phone rings. She answers; it's Anita. She says Luis is doing fine. The doctor wants to keep him another day. Anita will stay overnight with Delia, in town. Toby murmurs what she hopes are comforting words.

When she hangs up, it dawns on her that if Luis can't work, needs recovery time and to be close to his doctor, Luis and Anita may want to pull their trailer into town. Be close to Delia. Anita's not thinking past this day, but Toby knows it's too soon to gamble on anything. The hand hasn't been fully dealt.

Admonishing herself not to borrow trouble, she grabs a garden hat and heads out behind the house. She grabs a long-handled hoe from the garden shed and starts down a row of beans. She's already alone on the ranch in the wintertime, and she copes just fine. She gets lonely, but she's accustomed to that. Plus, most times the roads are clear enough she can drive into town if she needs to. Once in a while, she might join a bingo game at the senior center. She can handle the summer, too, though she would miss their company. Especially Anita. She's nosy. Likes to know everybody's business. But she's a good worker. Toby leans on the handle of the hoe. She has to admit Anita is the best friend she's got. Maybe the best friend she's ever had if it comes to that. Still, she's not about to give Nola Jean or Dr. Penny the satisfaction of knowing that she's uneasy about all this. If this is to be her future, she'd better get on with adjusting.

She sticks the hoe in the soil. She miscalculates and slices a bean plant right out of the ground. Damn fool. If she could kneel, she'd be able to see better, but she might have trouble getting back up. She moves on, stepping carefully between the rows.

She stops. Puts her hands in the small of her back and arches backward. Overhead, a plane trails a jet stream across the sky. She wonders for a minute what it would be like to be on that plane. Fly away from all this. Migrating birds do it. Leave behind one home to go in quest of another.

She drops the hoe, leaves it lying on the ground. If it rains and the blade rusts, so be it. She's in no mood to attend to this today. She notes there are some potato bugs gnawing on some of the early shoots.

She goes back inside and draws herself a tall glass of cold water, stands at the sink, and drinks it down. Out the window, she can almost see the pale riders coming for her. They're in the distance, but she can hear the clomp of horses' hooves inside her head.

Anita

GABE SITS WITH ANITA AND LUIS WHILE DR. PENNY GOES OVER THE tests. Some of it is good news. No major blockages. No surgery needed. Some of it is not so good news. Luis has something called degenerative heart disease. His heart is showing wear. It's possible he was born with a congenital defect that is only now showing up. Or his early years of heavy smoking damaged the muscle. Because this heart attack was minor, Dr. Penny feels he can be treated with medication. But this is a warning sign. He will need to moderate his diet, his activities, and have regular checkups. They'll start him on a new medication today, so Dr. Penny wants him to stay one more night to make sure he doesn't have a bad reaction.

None of this sounds so bad to Anita, but Luis looks like a man who's been handed a death sentence.

When Dr. Penny leaves the room, Gabe announces he's going to step out for coffee. Anita knows he's not that big of coffee fan, but he's giving her time alone with Luis. Gabe has been her rock. Nothing more has been said between them about Nola Jean or any of that foolishness. All of that seems silly now. Anita can't fathom why any of it mattered to her.

Luis is sitting in his hospital gown on the bed. She moves from the chair to sit beside him. Takes his hand. She leans into him. In spite of the hospital, he smells like himself, and she turns her face into the bend of his neck. She doesn't want him to see her cry.

"Luis," she begins, but he holds up one hand like a stop sign.

She waits. The silence stretches. In a whisper, she ventures, "Delia sends her love. She wanted to be here, but the boys . . ."

Luis nods.

"Gordon too." Their son-in-law, who works in the local bank. Who Luis has always found soft and bookish.

Anita takes a breath. "Delia thinks we should stay with her a few days. See how you do."

"No. We're not doing that."

"She thinks . . ."

"She thinks she can watch over me like a mother hen. Just because she's a nurse doesn't mean she knows what's best for me. Besides, it's noisy there."

He's right about that. With two small boys, Delia's house is full of commotion.

"I want to go home, Anita. Our home. I want to put my feet up and listen for the meadowlarks."

"Okay. Gabe will drive us. In the morning."

Luis stands. He tests his balance, his strength. They walk out of the room together for a short stroll down the hall. At a window, Luis turns his face toward the sky, shuts his eyes, and lets the sun warm him. His fingers tighten on Anita's.

She does not tell him what she and Delia have decided. There's time for that. Thank God and all the saints in heaven, there is still time.

Toby

MIDAFTERNOON, NOLA JEAN STOPS BY. SHE KNOCKS ON THE DOOR. THAT seems odd to Toby, but at the same time, she's grateful Nola Jean doesn't barge in. She doesn't want to be caught with cookie dough on her face or literally with her pants down in the bathroom. She guesses it would be different if she still lived in the house where Nola Jean was raised. This must feel like George's house to Nola Jean. Hell. Most of the time, that's how it feels to Toby, like she's a long-term guest here. She balks at putting a nail in the wall. Maybe why she hasn't hung any family pictures.

Nola Jean asks if she wants to go for a walk. She does. She grabs a hat, and the two of them set off toward the old Alhambra site where Luis and Anita's trailer is parked, eventually pass it and walk along a little-used path that threads to the pond behind Goldenrod. They keep pace silently for a while. The sun's warmth feels friendly. Their eyes watch the ground so as not to be surprised by a rattlesnake or step on a cactus.

"Anita called," Toby says. "Luis is coming home tomorrow."

"I heard," Nola Jean says.

When Toby looks at her, she says, "Gabe called."

"You and Gabe mending fences?"

Nola Jean pauses. Toby wonders if she's overstepped some boundary. Then, Nola Jean says, "You knew about that?"

"Guessed more than knew. Seems like you've gone out of your way to avoid running into him in the past."

They walk a few steps in silence. Toby senses that Nola Jean is wrestling with what to say. How much.

"We went out a few times. Our senior year. When I was staying in town."

Toby grunts. "You never said."

They both know there are lots of things Nola Jean did not tell her parents.

"Would you have minded?" Nola Jean asks.

Toby hadn't expected that. Would they have minded?

"Probably," she admits. "Back then. Not now though."

Toby could swear Nola Jean blushes before she answers.

"That was a long time ago. We were kids."

Toby chuckles. She's thinking about her own life. How the past leans on the present.

"What split you up?"

"Turns out it was a misunderstanding."

As the path narrows, Toby steps in front of Nola Jean.

"Anita have anything to do with that?"

"Why do you ask?"

"She's like a cat near water when you come."

Nola Jean laughs. She offers no further explanation, and though Toby is curious, she doesn't press. She respects Nola Jean's decision to keep counsel on the whole topic.

They make their way around the pond. Memories crowd Toby's mind, a lifetime of walking this path with different partners, men she has loved. She and Gertie used to come here as girls to cut cattails. They'd carry them home, and their mother would put them in a vase with water until their spikes burst open. Then the girls would take them outside and spin in circles, spreading the tan fluff on the wind.

When they get back to the house, she asks Nola Jean if she'd like to have a lemonade on the porch. Nola Jean sits, and Toby fills two tall glasses with ice, pours lemonade over the glistening cubes. She'd mixed up the lemonade that morning from dry powder, but it's been chilling in the refrigerator and after a walk in the afternoon sun, it tastes good. Toby sits beside her daughter and thinks how nice it is to have a peaceful time together, to sit and enjoy each other's company.

"Are you driving over to Cheyenne tomorrow?" Toby asks.

"No. I thought I'd go Tuesday morning. Who knows? She could cancel again. I might stay over Tuesday if . . . well, I just might."

Nola Jean is quiet, then. Toby doesn't know what to ask or say, so she sits quiet too.

"Mother," Nola Jean says.

Instinctively, Toby clenches. She hears the hesitation in Nola Jean's voice.

"I thought you might like to go into Elmyra with me tomorrow."

"Oh?" Toby's suspicious. Something about Nola Jean's tone.

"We could see Luis."

"Course he might be dismissed by then. I'd like to be here when they arrive."

"You think they'll come back out here?"

"They might. Why not? It's their home."

"I'd think they'd want to stay with Delia for a few days."

"Is that what Gabe said?"

"No. Nobody said. I just thought they'd want to be close to the doctor. In case. You know."

Actually, Toby does know. This was her own thought, precisely, but she's put off by Nola Jean assuming it.

"I guess we don't know what they'll do until they do it."

"Okay." Nola Jean leans back in her chair. Waits. For what Toby thinks of as a respectable period. Then, she begins again.

"I made an appointment," Nola Jean says.

"For what?"

"With Deb Perkins."

"With Deb . . . you mean, the realtor?"

"I understand there are some new senior apartments going up not far from the hospital. She said they have models ready for viewing. They're going fast. People are signing up. Some of your friends."

Toby lets Nola Jean ramble on, sentence after sentence. She's stuck back on the shock that Nola Jean has called a realtor. Without even asking her first.

Toby stands. She knocks her lemonade off the small table, the glass falls to the porch floor and rolls to the edge. She doesn't care. "That's why you came here honeying me up this afternoon?"

"It's just to look. You don't have to decide anything now."

"You're damn right I don't."

Nola Jean is on her feet now too.

"You must see that Luis isn't going to be able to work this place for you."

"I don't think any of us knows what Luis can or can't do. Or what he wants or doesn't want to do. People have heart attacks. They recover. They don't just . . ." she waves her arm aimlessly, trying to land on the word she wants. Finally, she sputters, "Stop. They don't just stop."

"What can it hurt to look?"

"Hurt? The whole town will be talking about it. Toby's too old. No, worse. Toby's daughter thinks she's too old." She narrows her eyes. "Is this about your inheritance. Is that it?"

"No, of course not." Nola Jean steps back, as if Toby has tossed ice water in her face.

"Because if it is, don't you think it's ironic that you're worried about getting your inheritance out of me at the same time you're looking for your real mother?"

Toby shoves past Nola Jean and enters her house. She slams the screen door behind her. Stands with her back to the doorway, fists clenched. She cannot believe she said that to Nola Jean. What part of her gave rise to such nasty words? Damn it all to hell.

Nola Jean

NOLA JEAN'S APPOINTMENT IS SET FOR TEN O'CLOCK MONDAY MORNING. She picks Isabel up at nine o'clock, and they head into town. When Nola Jean left Toby's house the day before, she walked straight to Isabel's. Isabel invited her in, and for an hour they drank wine and worried together about Luis. Isabel had heard nothing from Gabe. Nola Jean did not tell Isabel that Gabe had called. No sense complicating things. She and Gabe share a history, and sometimes it's too much work to fill in a newcomer on your past. Nola Jean didn't tell Isabel about her conversation with Toby either. She didn't want to come across like a snotty teenager whose parents don't understand her, even though that is exactly how she feels. Fourteen and in trouble for wanting to go to a Friday night dance.

Instead, she invited Isabel to go with her into town. They could swing by the hospital. Nola Jean mentioned that she had an appointment to scout out some senior apartments and would welcome another eye on the place. Isabel raised an eyebrow at that but said nothing. We can have lunch, Nola Jean said. There's a good Mexican place. Or if you don't like Mexican . . . and Isabel had interrupted to say Mexican's fine.

On the way into town, Isabel hums softly, a tune Nola Jean either doesn't know or doesn't recognize. Isabel seems unaware, and because Nola Jean finds her sounds comforting—like a mother crooning to a baby—she doesn't want to interrupt her. The sky spreads open and cloudless, the ditches teeming with wild roses here and there.

They swing by the hospital first. Out front, Gabe is leaning on the fender of his pickup, chewing on a toothpick or matchstick. Nola Jean pulls up alongside. Isabel rolls her window down, and Gabe strolls over. He props his hand on the open window frame, ducks down to say hi to Nola Jean, then glues his eyes into Isabel's.

"How are you?" she says.

"Tired."

He looks tired. His hair is disheveled, like he only ran a hand through it when he got out of bed. Missed at least one day's shave. He's wearing a T-shirt and jeans. Isabel reaches one hand up to cradle his face. Nola Jean looks away, embarrassed to be watching this display of intimacy. She's trying to decide how she can get herself out of this picture, whether she should park the car and let them have a real conversation, walk herself around the block.

"How's Luis?" she hears Isabel ask.

She turns back to hear Gabe's answer. "Better. He's getting released right now. Anita is with him."

"Do you two want . . ." Nola Jean begins. "I could park. Walk to my appointment."

"Appointment?" Gabe says.

She leans across Isabel to look up at him. "I'm looking at those new senior apartments."

"You plan on retiring here?" Gabe, that crooked grin.

"Very funny," she says.

Isabel pats Gabe's hand that's gripping the door frame. "I told Nola Jean I'd go with her. I can stay here, if you want."

"No. You two go on. I promised Anita I'd drive them home or wherever they want to go. They shouldn't be much longer."

Gabe steps back, gives them a low wave. Nola Jean drives off, wondering if this is Gabe not wanting Anita to know he's falling for Isabel. Or, if he feels this is not the time to pile things on for Anita. Those two have a complicated relationship, but then, who doesn't? Midlife, and she's only starting to understand that all relationships are complicated. The question is whether you want to fight for them or not. Whether the dividends outweigh the deficits.

Deb Perkins shows up ten minutes late. She's in her midforties, starchy snow-dusted hair, sturdy build, jeans and a red plaid blouse. She's perky and upbeat while she shows them through the model apartment. The rooms are furnished with cheap furniture, nothing to give them personality. The point is to be able to see the size of the rooms with furniture taking up space. A living room opens into a small kitchen. An alcove for a table and chairs. A bathroom. Deb is careful to point out that most units will have showers with seats and handrails. If someone wants a tub and can handle getting in and out, that can be arranged. Nola Jean wonders how a prospective occupant goes about proving they can get in and out of a tub, but she doesn't ask. One bedroom with a sliding door closet. Some units have two bedrooms, Deb explains. Hallways wide enough to accommodate a wheelchair. Carpet everywhere but the kitchen and the bathroom, which seems like a wheelchair hazard, but then, Toby is far from needing a wheelchair. Still, you never know.

"Do any of the units have wood floors?" Nola Jean asks.

"That could be negotiated," Deb says, which Nola Jean takes to mean at an additional cost.

They linger in the living room. Deb chatters on about the common rooms and dining hall. Residents—she calls them residents—can choose to purchase a meal plan rather than cook for themselves. Yes, it will require walking outside, but all the snow removal will be taken care of. Each apartment has a stacking washer and dryer in the back hallway off the bedroom. Isabel looks attentively at Deb the whole time she's reciting this. Nola Jean peers out the window, which faces west and the hospital parking lot.

When Deb stops to take a breath, Nola Jean says, "Will any of these units face east?"

"You mean the living room windows?" Deb asks.

Nola Jean nods.

"Sure. The living rooms face east, west, and south, depending on which unit you select."

Nola Jean closes her eyes. West is the hospital parking lot. South, residential streets and houses. East is wide open space, part of a field that still belongs to a farm on the edge of town. She starts to breathe a little easier when Deb says, "The community hall and dining room will be on the east. Just a few steps from any resident's door." So much for an open view.

When they leave and are back in the car, Isabel says, "Well, what'd you think?"

"Can you picture Toby there?" Nola Jean says.

"No. No, not really," Isabel says.

Isabel has known Toby for five minutes, and she has more insight than Nola Jean has mustered after fifty years. Scratch that, forty-eight years. Then again, Isabel has no responsibility for an aging mother in a shrinking western town.

"What happens to these old people?" Nola Jean says.

Toby

TOBY SITS IN MALCOLM LORD'S OFFICE. THE BANKER IS A SMALL MAN behind a big desk. Toby has little use for this pudgy sawed-off version of his father. Curtis was a good man, knew how to help local ranchers and farmers stave off the lean years. Malcolm had nearly foreclosed on her ten years ago and would have if George hadn't come through with his surprise investment. He'd threatened to sell her ranch to a corporate conglomerate, anathema to her, and it would have ruined Royce and Julia. They need her six thousand leased acres to sustain their progressive style of ranching. She finds it amusing that refusing chemicals and moving the herd so they don't overgraze a pasture is considered progressive since it's a return to the way ranching was done in the thirties and forties, but there you have it. The modern world claims they've invented something their grandparents did out of necessity.

Malcolm wears a pin-striped shirt and a tie. Pictures of his teenaged sons sit atop a credenza behind him. His ex-wife remarried, lives now in Scottsbluff with the two boys, but to his credit, Malcolm has worked at keeping a relationship with them. Begrudgingly, Toby admires him for that. Malcolm has never remarried, though he sees the local Spanish teacher. He's been dating her for years, and while the rumor mill is persistently active regarding the two of them, they seem content not to change their status. They keep separate homes, are seen together often, his car frequently parked overnight in her driveway. They don't appear to give a damn. So, that's two things Toby is forced to admire.

"What can I do for you, Toby?" Malcolm asks. He leans back in his chair.

Toby shifts her weight. Reaches up and tugs one earlobe. Now that she's here, she's not sure what he can do for her. She hadn't planned to make this trip to town today, but after Nola Jean's bombshell, she decided she better get started working out her own future.

"I'm looking at long-range plans for the Bluestem," she says.

That gets his attention. He sits upright and leans forward, props his forearms on the desk. A dog who's been proffered a bone.

"You thinking of selling?"

"Not all of it."

"You want to split up the Bluestem?"

He looks genuinely shocked. She knows it would have more value to a conglomerate whole. But then, she has no interest in selling it to a corporate operation like Western Cattle. She waits. Considers her options. She knows Malcolm's first concern is profit. And his last concern is profit. She despises that about him, though she concedes that his job is to keep the bank afloat. He wrangled with her about putting money into Toby's Last Resort, but in the end, he granted the short-term loans she needed to pull it off. That was mostly an issue of cash flow, and he knew she was good for it, but still. She looks at the photos of his two boys. Grinning and wholesome. Maybe he has a heart after all.

"I have a plan for the resort." She doesn't tell him that her plan is only a half-baked idea. "I'm concerned about the acres I lease to Royce and Julia."

"You don't want to continue the leasing arrangement?"

He looks puzzled. She sighs. Guesses she will have to spell it out for him.

"I'm not talking about now, Malcolm. If I die." That's a fudge, of course. With the uncertainty around Luis, she might have to implement her plan sooner than she intends, but Malcolm doesn't need to know everything about her business.

"Oh." He has the good manners to blush. "That could be a long way off."

"Or not," she says.

"Toby, are you okay?" Could that be a look of actual concern?

"Only one thing wrong with me that can't be cured. I'm old."

Malcolm chuckles and leans back. "So, what is it you want to know?"

She takes a deep breath. She's going from here to see her attorney. To reconfigure her will. But first, she needs to know if what she has in mind is feasible. "If I were to sell those acres to Royce and Julia, could they swing it?"

Malcolm shakes his head side to side. "Now, Toby, you know I can't divulge that kind of information."

"I'm not asking you for state secrets. I'm asking if you would help them to make the purchase if they needed it."

"Would I give them a loan?" Malcolm asks.

Lord, the man is dense. Toby nods.

Malcolm laughs, his good ole boy laugh. Leans forward. Talks to her like she's a third grader. Says he can't possibly predict. No one knows what the market will be when the—uh—event (referring to her death) occurs. Or what circumstances Royce and Julia will be in by then. Ends by saying it's unreasonable for her to extract any promise from him based on such sketchy and uncertain information.

Unreasonable. How Toby hates that word. She wants to stand, stomp her foot, and storm out.

Instead, she smiles. Forces her voice to a level of calm. "Let's pretend this happens in, say, five years. You know Royce and Julia's financial situation as well as anyone." She doesn't say, but he ought to know, that finances are not the sort of thing anyone around here discusses with their friends. Or family, for that matter. For instance, she knows nothing about Nola Jean's finances, whether she has any retirement. She's certain the divorce set her back. She wouldn't be having this conversation if she wasn't worried about Nola Jean's future. And Lila's too. "Would you do your best to support a purchase of my land?"

He drums his fingers on the desk. Purses his lips. Smacks his open hand on the desk and says, "Sure. Why not?"

His response seems glib to her. Too easy. Full of holes like a sieve and not at all what she'd hoped for. But it will have to do.

Nola Jean

IT'S TOO EARLY FOR LUNCH WHEN SHE AND ISABEL FINISH WITH THE appointment. Nola Jean decides to take Isabel on a town tour. She drives through the state recreation area on the west edge of town, a cluster of man-made lakes that were once part of a sandpit. Cottonwoods shimmer on the shorelines. Milkweed will later sport clusters of butterflies. Campers are parked here and there, a couple motorboats towing skiers around the largest lake. The road weaves in a figure eight, circling two lakes, moving through a picnic area and playground.

"This is lovely," Isabel says.

"A lucky boon for the town."

"Did you spend a lot of time here?"

Nola Jean sighs. "It's pretty far from the ranch. I think town kids did. There's a sand beach for swimming, though no lifeguard. I came out here sometimes when I was in high school. One day, three other girls and I skipped our afternoon classes. Came out here. Dared each other to strip nude on one of the more secluded beaches. We played in the water, laughed, and had a great time."

"Did you get in trouble for skipping class?"

"Sure," Nola Jean says. "But it was worth it."

Isabel laughs with her.

"A few parties with bonfires, that sort of thing. Necking in parked cars. There were a few tragedies. Somebody dived in shallow water and broke his neck. He wasn't from here but scared all of us."

Isabel says little. She doesn't hop on to talk about her own teen exploits. Nola Jean doesn't ask, either, preferring to stick with her own reflections of the past.

From the sand pits, they head south of town to Courthouse and Jail Rocks, two sandstone monuments that jut up out of the prairie like lighthouses. They served that function for settlers trekking west on the Oregon and Mormon Trails. They turn off the main road and wind their way to the parking area at the foot of Courthouse Rock. Courthouse looms like a rectangular layer cake, stretching east to west. The smaller Jail Rock is shaped like an upside-down funnel, the base a wide skirt topped by a narrow tower. A maze of dry gulches leads from the foot of the hills to Pumpkin Creek that runs on the south side. Posted signs warn of rattlesnakes and climbing hazards.

Nola Jean stops the car, and they get out. The air sings with insect buzz. A lone meadowlark warbles from a fencepost. Yucca and sage and wild grasses sweep the land until they give way to cultivated crops. The parking lot is high enough to afford a wide view over the fields to the north and east.

"It's beautiful," Isabel says. "Quiet."

"I used to love it here," Nola Jean says.

"Do people actually climb these?"

"Oh, sure. Well, we did. I don't know about now. They're sandstone, so slowly eroding. I was only on top of Jail once. See that big vertical crack? It seemed less safe. There's a fantastic view from the top of Courthouse."

"With Gabe?"

"Sure," Nola Jean says, not risking a look at Isabel.

Isabel smiles. "I like picturing the two of you here."

Nola Jean lets that settle, surprised, though by now she shouldn't be. "There's a marker on the other side. A boy fell off. Died. He wasn't from here."

"Seems to be a theme. Don't risk the local pleasures if you're an outsider."

"I'm an outsider now," Nola Jean says.

After a long pause, Isabel says, "Everyone is an outsider. Now and then. Here or there."

Nola Jean bristles. Feels dismissed. "I suppose," she says.

Isabel picks up on her tone. "I didn't say it doesn't hurt. To be left out or forced out."

"I can't imagine that happening to you."

Isabel flashes. "Can't you? Try thinking you're going to die for six months. How about being refused tenure because everyone else thinks you're going to die."

"I'm sorry. I didn't think."

"No. You didn't."

"Do you . . . do you want to talk about it?"

"No. I really don't."

Nola Jean is shocked to see Isabel capable of anger. She feels awful that she's the cause of it, but underneath, she's also relieved. She identifies with anger and flash more than with Isabel's serenity.

They stand in silence for a while. Nola Jean decides to try to breach the gap. "My therapist says I place myself outside. Self-protection. Get ahead of the rejection."

Isabel shrugs. "I choose to be outside sometimes. On purpose, I mean."

"Why?"

"Perspective. Not wanting to be identified with the crowd."

"Maybe it's okay if you choose it."

Isabel sighs, a great heave that shakes her body. Nola Jean knows they're both thinking that choice is available a lot less than most people want to believe.

They walk along a worn path to draw closer to Jail. Isabel is smaller and walks slower, so Nola Jean matches her stride. Then, she says, "I decided to go tomorrow. To meet my birth mother."

"I wondered," Isabel says.

"I wanted to tell you Saturday but didn't get the chance. Things got chaotic because of Luis. Yesterday, well, I had just come from Toby's. Anyway, I'm going."

Isabel stops. That intense look of hers. "That's good. I think. Do you?"

Nola Jean shrugs.

"Do you want me to go with you?" Isabel asks.

Nola Jean smiles. "That's tempting."

"I would. You know that."

Nola Jean takes a deep breath. "I do know."

"But?"

"I need to do this. Alone, I think."

Isabel nods. "I understand."

Nola Jean believes she does. Such a relief, to trust somebody. They keep walking.

When they reach the bottom of Jail Rock, Isabel cranes her neck to scan the summit. "That's a lot higher than it seems from the parking lot," she says.

"When I was in high school, there was an eagle's nest on top of Jail. A young eaglet fell out of the nest and was alive but trapped on these lower rocks. No one knew what to do. The game warden said leave it alone, either the mother would rescue it, or it would die, but if we attempted to intervene, it would be abandoned. We'd drive out here during lunch to check on it, and it was sad, the mother—we supposed it was the mother—circled high overhead, unable to reach her baby."

"What happened?" Isabel asks.

"I don't know. One day, the baby was gone. Mother too. We never knew."

Toby

TOBY'S NEXT STOP IS HER ATTORNEY, WILSON BARNES. SHE CALLED him at home that morning and asked him to meet her at his office on Main Street. He no longer keeps regular hours. Toby's known Wilson most of her life. He was a younger classmate when she was in high school. Took over his father's law practice, so the Boldens have been entwined with the Barneses for a long time. Wilson's wife died a few years ago. He has one daughter, also an attorney, but she has a practice in Lincoln.

He's waiting for her. A stocky man crowned with a mane of white hair, glasses. He's wearing a white shirt and tie, but unlike Malcolm Lord, he looks distinguished, like an elder statesman. Toby sighs with relief, thinking how good it will be to speak to someone of her generation. Like her, he must be wondering what's going to happen to him in his later years. She'd never ask, but she'd like to know if he has a plan.

Wilson points to two easy chairs arranged around a small table. Offers her water, which she declines. The room smells stale; he probably hasn't been down here in some time. He hasn't taken on any new clients in years. She notes that he sits with some difficulty.

"Hips," Wilson says with a wry smile.

"You a candidate for a replacement?"

"Already did that once. I may have to do the other one."

"I hear that's not much fun."

"The docs have got it down pretty good. The recovery takes a while."

"Must be hard to manage on your own."

"They send you to a rehab outfit."

"I s'pose. That's what they do now."

Wilson pauses. Rubs his hand over his jaw. She recalls that he used to wear a beard.

"Now, Toby, I don't think you called me down here to talk about my hips. What's on your mind?"

From her bag, Toby pulls out the notepad with her list. They dive into a long conversation. At one point, Wilson says hold on, he needs a pen and a pad of paper. He retrieves both from a desk drawer and sits, this time behind the desk so he can use it as a writing surface.

When Toby has wound down, he glances over his notes.

"This is fairly complicated. But it can be done. You sure this is what you want?"

Toby pinches her brow. "Do you see problems?"

"I thought your main goal would be to preserve the Bluestem."

Toby looks down at her knotted hands. It's taken her a long time to get to this point. It's hard to say out loud. "I don't see how that is possible," she says.

"You could find a buyer. You could stipulate, in your will, that it's not to go to any off-site enterprise. Might take a while, but individual buyers are still out there."

"I know Luther wouldn't approve. Maybe not his father before him. But right now, I'm more concerned for the people I care about than I am about land. I want Royce and Julia to have a chance. I want Nola Jean and Lila to have some future financial stability and their fair share. I think my plans—if they work out—do preserve a portion of the Bluestem, at least the spirit of the place." She doesn't say what they both know, that Nola Jean would get a whole lot more if the ranch was sold whole.

"There are a lot of contingencies that might not work," he says.

She nods. "I know that. But I want my wishes written down. In case, by some miracle, those contingencies fall in place."

"You talked to Nola Jean about this?"

Toby doesn't answer. She sees Wilson take in her non-answer, the set of her jaw.

"Don't you think you should?"

Toby stands. This session is over. What she talks over with Nola Jean is none of his damn business.

Nola Jean

NOLA JEAN'S SURPRISED TO SEE TOBY'S CAR PARKED ON MAIN STREET when she and Isabel head to El Burrito. Maybe she came in to check on Anita and Luis. But then, why would her car be on Main Street?

"You seem miles away," Isabel says.

"Oh, sorry. I just noticed Toby's car back there."

"Really? She could've come in with us."

Nola Jean says nothing.

"She know you're looking at senior living?"

"Oh, yeah," Nola Jean says.

She feels Isabel peering at her, but she says nothing. One of the great things about Isabel, she knows when to back off.

The restaurant buzzes with people. Situated on a corner, a long, narrow space. Scattered tables in front, red plastic upholstered booths along the wall. The counter for take-out and settling the bill lies opposite a side door. Restroom in the back.

Nola Jean and Isabel grab a booth. "What's good?" Isabel pages through the menu.

"Anything," Nola Jean says. "They even have Mexican Coke. No high fructose corn syrup."

A teenage girl comes to take their order. She's Latina, long black ponytail, glasses. They each order a luncheon platter, beans, rice, and enchilada.

Not long after they order, another party of three slides out of a booth that sits deeper into the café. Three women, one of them Dr. Penny. The other two head to the counter to pay, and Dr. Penny moves toward the front door. "I gotta get back to the office," she says to the other two who wave her away with calls of We got this, next time, you pay.

Dr. Penny is nearly past them when she notices Nola Jean and stops to say hello. Nola Jean introduces Isabel.

"How's Luis doing?" Nola Jean asks.

"On his way home today. He's lucky. This was a warning shot."

"Tough on Anita," Isabel says.

Looking at Nola Jean, Dr. Penny says, "Toby too."

"Yeah. She relies on him," Nola Jean says.

"She tell you that she came to see me?"

"No. She didn't. When did that happen? Is she okay?"

"Not about her health. About the conversation you and I had. Apparently, you told her."

"Oh. Oh, I see. No, she never said a word." Nola Jean backtracks in her mind. Tries to recall exactly what she had thrown at Toby from that place of hurt. She'd convinced herself that Toby let those words roll right off her back.

"She's under the impression that we are ganging up on her."

Nola Jean knows her cheeks are burning. "I'm sorry. I never should have . . . I did mention that we'd talked."

"She was pretty upset."

"I can imagine."

Dr. Penny pauses and sighs. Her mouth moves from side to side, as if she's considering what else to say. Finally, she says, "Toby's been my patient for a long time. I need her trust if I'm to be of any use to her."

"I know. I'm sorry. Really. I'll talk to her."

"If there's to be any further discussion, I think the three of us should sit down together."

Nola Jean nods. Feels chastised. Everything she tries to do around her mother backfires.

Dr. Penny smiles. Briefly lays a hand on Nola Jean's shoulder. "Nice to meet you," she says to Isabel.

After a few moments of silence, Isabel says, "That was kind of rough."

"I deserved it," Nola Jean says. She's lost her appetite. Tosses her napkin on the table.

"You and Toby . . ."

Nola Jean shrugs. "It's complicated," she says.

Isabel takes a couple bites. Surrenders her fork and napkin. Her food is half eaten, but these are generous portions. "Know what my mother said when she learned I had cancer?"

"What?"

"She said, 'I can't understand why this is happening to me.'"

"Really? To her?"

"Yeah."

"Was she . . . I mean . . ."

"Complicated," Isabel says.

They look at each other and start to laugh. Other people in the restaurant stare at them. They clink their water glasses together in a toast to life's impossible complexities and drink to the life available to them. In that moment, Nola Jean knows they will be friends forever or so long as they both inhabit this earth. She'll drive to Iowa City or whatever it takes to never let this wise woman slip away from her.

Josie

JOSIE PICKS UP HER MOTHER A HALF HOUR BEFORE HER DOCTOR'S appointment on Monday. It's a routine appointment, but her mother fusses on the drive over. They'll be late. Josie should've come earlier. Evelyn is wearing pale blue pants, a floral bloused top with ribbing at the bottom, long-sleeved because she gets cold in air-conditioned spaces. She doesn't like the collar. It's not pressed properly. Doesn't lay down the way it should. She repeats this complaint multiple times during the ten-minute drive.

"Didn't you have anything better to wear?" Evelyn says.

Josie glances down at her jean skirt, pink T-shirt. She wore the same thing yesterday and threw it on without a second thought. She recognizes what's going on here. Her mother is anxious, morphing her anxiety into criticism. Still. They're going to the doctor's office and then to lunch at the local Egg and I, not to the Taj Mahal. Besides, what's wrong with what she has on? She clamps her lips and does not answer. A sure way to goad her mother into further barbs.

Right on schedule, Evelyn says, "You really should color your hair. Men don't like gray-haired women."

Josie has never colored her hair. Evelyn still pays the beautician that comes into the assisted living facility to color hers. As a concession to her age, she's stopped dying it mahogany brown and goes instead for ash blonde, resulting in a soft peach color. She looks nice. Always. Josie tells her regularly how nice she looks. Evelyn rarely returns the compliment. Only one of the many ways Josie doesn't measure up.

"Dan's hair is gray," she says, hoping to throw her mother off the scent.

"With men, it's different. Men are lucky if they have hair."

"Here we are." Josie threads the car into a parking space close to the front door of the doctor's office.

As she helps her mother out of the car, Evelyn says, "I hope we're not late. I hate to be late."

The appointment goes smoothly. Evelyn's blood pressure is too high, but the doctor chalks that up to being in the doctor's office, decides not to adjust her medication. Her weight, stable. Long conversation about stools, consistency, color, regularity, whether there is accompanying pain, after which the doctor suggests a daily bowl of muesli. At that, Evelyn raises her eyebrows and looks at Josie who knows her mother will never succumb to a daily dose of muesli, Miralax, or any other digestive aid that would require her to eat or drink something yucky. What, then, would she have to complain about?

When they are seated at the Egg and I, they go through the usual routine over what to order. The portions are too big. Would Josie split something with her? Josie points out that she can order a half sandwich with a cup of soup or small salad. What if she wants an omelet or skillet breakfast? Those are huge. Do you want that? Well, no, but what if she did, she couldn't possibly eat it all. Mom, decide what you want; then we'll figure out whether to split it or order separately. Okay. Nothing sounds good. She just doesn't have much appetite. What about the chicken salad sandwich? You had that last time. What did you have last time? I don't know, probably one of the sandwiches. What difference does it make? I might like to try something different, and I want to know if it's any good. (The waitress arrives.) No, I'm sorry. We're not quite ready to order. Could you give us a minute? I guess I'll have the chicken salad and a cup of tomato basil soup. Okay. What are you having? A salad. Maybe I should have a salad, but aren't those big? Mom! Where is that waitress? I don't think much of the service here. She's giving us a minute. Well, I'm ready now. I don't like to be kept waiting.

Josie sighs. She orders a chicken salad and cup of soup for her mother. The same dish her mother eats every time they come here. She orders a Greek salad for herself. When the waitress walks away, Evelyn says, "Maybe I should have had that Greek salad."

"You don't like olives, Mom."

"Oh, does a Greek salad have olives? Couldn't they just leave the olives off?"

They chat a few moments about the grandchildren, the weather, the past weekend. Josie takes a big breath and decides to dive in. She leans (as much as is possible) across the table because she doesn't want the whole world to hear her confession.

"Mom, there's something I need to tell you."

Evelyn is distracted by a couple young women who come and take the table adjacent to their booth. Both are dressed in short shorts and sleeveless T-shirts. Why not? It's warm outside. The dark-haired one wears glasses, sandals. The other, whose hair is dyed an unnatural shade of candy apple red, wears a nose ring, an eyebrow ring, and one arm is tattooed from wrist to shoulder with what appears to be a wrapped peacock's tail.

Evelyn clicks her tongue against her teeth, that age-old signal of disapproval. "Look at that," she says.

"Mom." Josie nods her head at the girls, trying to warn her mother to keep her voice down, but Evelyn has no intention of censoring herself.

"Why would a young girl want to spoil her looks like that?"

At that, both girls turn and glare at them. Josie tries to smile and wishes she could crawl under the table.

Evelyn meets their gaze and speaks directly to the girl with the sleeve tattoo. "Your mother know you did that? Or your grandmother?"

The girl lifts her lip in what could only be called a sneer. "My Granny rides a Harley," she says. She picks up her menu with her middle finger on the outside edge in a gesture that Josie hopes her mother cannot interpret. Then both girls (they can't be more than eighteen) start giggling behind their menus.

Evelyn turns her attention back to Josie. "Well, I never," she sputters.

At that moment their food arrives. Evelyn immediately says it's too much; she'll never be able to eat all that. But she does. And throughout the meal and all the way back to her assisted living establishment and while Josie is telling her goodbye and during Josie's drive back to her house, Josie is thanking her lucky stars, her guardian angels, and any other talisman she can think to conjure up. What possessed her to try to tell her mother about Nola Jean? Without first assessing the situation. What if Nola Jean has purple hair or tattoos? Furthermore, why should she subject Nola Jean to her mother's withering disapproval? For a moment there, against her better judgment and a lifetime of accumulated data, she slipped into needing a mother. Oh, she knows Evelyn loves her. But she forgot, for one nearly disastrous moment, that Evelyn's love is predicated on Josie supplying what Evelyn needs, not the other way around. If she could, she'd send those two teenage girls, teetering on the brink of a complicated adulthood, a bouquet of flowers.

Toby

TOBY WAITS UNTIL MONDAY EVENING TO WALK OVER TO CHECK ON ANITA
and Luis. She finds them sitting outside, under the arms of a 140-year-old
cottonwood, planted by Toby's grandfather, the original homesteader of
this place. The leaves tinkle in the breeze like wind chimes. Dragonflies
and bees buzz around the potted plants. The remnants of the Alhambra's
foundation are still visible, haunting in the slanted afternoon sun. In spite
of Toby's protests, Anita rustles up another folding lawn chair tucked under
their trailer. They situate themselves in a semicircle, Anita in the middle.

"How're you doing?" Toby asks Luis.

"Not too bad," he says.

Toby's wondering if this is the right time to talk about how they'll
move forward. Maybe not. Give the man a few days' rest. She's content
to sit with these old friends and say nothing, soak up the beauty of the
waning light.

She's not there long when Matthew's car pulls up. He and Corey
emerge. Corey hangs back, not sure what to do or say. Matthew strides
straight over.

Anita stands to fetch more chairs, but Matthew waves her back down.

"No, no," he says. "Don't bother. We just stopped by to see if there's
anything we can do."

"You heard, then?" Luis says.

"Nola Jean told us."

A look passes between Anita and Toby. Toby can read Anita's mind,
knows she's thinking she would. And Toby telegraphs back, It's no
secret, is it?

Matthew, unsure what has transpired, says, "She was concerned."

"I bet she was," Anita says.

Toby bristles. "We all were," she says. Damn, she hates being put in
the position of defending Nola Jean when she herself is furious with her.

"I'm sorry . . . did we?" Matthew raises his hands to indicate his confusion.

"Never mind," Luis says. "People out here. We like our privacy. But you're fine. You're here now. Nita, can't we find these two gentlemen a couple chairs? And maybe some iced tea? I think I'd like a little coming home party."

After that, there's nothing for it but Anita to move into the role of hostess. She directs Matthew to the stack of chairs. While he and Corey retrieve chairs for themselves and widen the circle, Anita goes inside to make a pitcher of iced tea.

Toby moves with Anita to their kitchen. "Glasses in there," Anita says. She points to a cupboard.

As Toby counts out five glasses, places them on the counter, she realizes she's only been in this trailer twice. Once when she went to hire Anita and Luis and then two days ago.

"There's ice in the freezer compartment," Anita says.

Toby knows Anita's irritated. She's curt, slamming through the motions of making iced tea from an instant mix.

"Fool man. He ought to be resting," she says.

Suddenly, loud laughter erupts outside. Both Anita and Toby look through the screen door. Matthew is leaning forward, elbows on knees, talking directly to Luis. Corey hangs back in his chair, looking like the teenager he almost is.

"Maybe it's good for him," Toby says.

"Hmmph," Anita concedes. "Maybe."

Anita rustles up a tray, and they carry the five full glasses outside. Once they're handed around, Anita asks, "What was so funny?"

Luis says, "Oh, Matthew, here, was telling me how he once found a cross made out of goose poop."

"Is that so?" Anita says, not finding this humorous.

Luis starts chuckling again.

"The guy had been fired from a high-level job," Matthew says. "Needed something to occupy his time while he looked for another position. He was very entrepreneurial."

"Is that what you call it?" Anita's tone implies that she thinks the guy was simply wacky.

"He used a wood base," Matthew says. "But he spread the goose poop in textures. Kind of like a Japanese sand garden."

Anita and Toby look at him. Neither says a word. Nor do they laugh.

"It . . . uh . . . it has no odor when it's dry," Matthew says, and this sets Luis off again.

"Did you purchase a goose poop cross?" Toby asks. Completely deadpan.

Matthew looks down at the ground. Then, back up, as if to face his accuser in a trial. "Yeah, sure, I did."

And Luis laughs still more. Even Corey joins in this time. Anita and Toby look at each other, shrug as if to say what the hell, but Toby is secretly thrilled to see Luis laughing. She guesses Anita is, too, though she has yet to relax her grip on Luis's arm.

Once things have settled down, Matthew turns to Toby. "Corey and I thought we'd take off for a few days. Head up to Fort Robinson. But if you need help here . . ."

"No, you go on," Toby says.

"It's beautiful up there," Luis offers.

"Like here," Matthew says, as he stands to take his leave.

Toby stands along with the two men, not wanting to tire Luis too much.

"Yes, this place is a balm, that's for sure," Luis says, as Matthew reaches to shake his hand.

Relieved to hear Luis say this, Toby notes that Anita's lips are pressed so firmly together that they appear blue. She waits until Matthew and Corey have departed. Anita walks with her a few paces.

"He's doing good," Toby says.

"He's got to rest."

"Of course."

Anita stops and looks back toward Luis. "Those two boys. Do you think . . ."

Toby arches her eyebrows. "Yes," she says.

Anita shakes her head. "The world is a changing place."

"Some of that's for good," Toby says.

Anita stands silent for a few moments. Something on her mind, besides the behavior of two men who are strangers to them both. Her toe scuffles in the dirt. Finally, she looks up at Toby.

"I'm not sure Luis can rest here. Let go."

Toby nods. "Whatever you need."

"I may hold you to that." Anita squeezes Toby's arm and turns to join Luis.

Toby moves down the path over the rise to her house. Now what could Anita have meant by that? She stops to look at the emerging stars. Star light, star bright, she thinks. And if wishes were horses, couldn't we all ride?

Anita

ONCE TOBY RETIRES, ANITA SITS WITH LUIS. SHE BASKS IN THE SILENCE, the comfort of being the two of them. She flutters around Luis, goes inside for a blanket she tucks around his knees and a pillow she fluffs behind his back, offers him an apple (heart-healthy). Luis nods or murmurs, finally he opens his hand, and she places hers in it.

"I'm sorry, Nita," he says.

"What are you talking about?" She puts her other hand over their clasped hands. Leans over to kiss him on the cheek. "Listen, old man, you didn't plan this."

She's alarmed to see his eyes fill with tears. In all the years they've been together, she's only seen Luis cry once, when his mother died.

"You're going to be fine." She smiles, tries to radiate positive energy straight into his heart through her gaze into his eyes. "We're fine."

She clears her throat. "You're going to have to take it easy for a while." Luis nods. "I know. Most of the fencing is done. Gabe can finish it on his own." Luis rubs his forefinger against his upper lip. "What about the horses?"

Anita raises her hands. Exasperated. What about the horses? Maybe Nola Jean can help. Or Matthew and that Corey. How should she know? And why should they care? That's not their problem and above all not her primary concern.

"There's the garden too," Luis says.

Anita wrings her hands. She pats her face. She's nervous. Good god, she knows this man, what has gotten into her? He must be thinking they'll leave, too, if he's worried about the garden. She's the one who helps Toby with all the harvesting once the garden is planted. So, they are thinking along the same lines. She sighs, relieved to discover this. Of course. She should have known.

"Toby can manage without us," she says.

"Us?"

"Once we move into town."

Luis is quiet for a long time. Too long. Anita studies him, the look of longing as his eyes rove over the east pasture, linger on the potted geraniums. She knows that look. Pure love, and only now does she realize that to Luis, this spot is home in a way it never has been to her. For her, home is where Luis is. Where her kids and grandchildren are. This is a job with nice benefits. She does love Toby (in a certain way or so she supposes), but Toby is not family. Toby is not home. And places don't qualify for that honor. She swallows hard against the lump in her throat. She's marshaling her argument for leaving when Luis says, "If I'm not able to work, do you think Toby will let us stay here?"

Toby

EARLY TUESDAY MORNING, TOBY IS SURPRISED TO FIND GABE ON HER doorstep. She's dressed, luckily. Been through breakfast. She invites Gabe in. Sits him at the kitchen table. Pours two cups of coffee. Offers him yesterday's blueberry cobbler, which he declines.

"I'm guessing you got something on your mind."

Gabe chuckles. "Luis," he says.

Toby takes a sip of coffee. Looks at him over the brim of her cup. He's nice to look at, she gives him that. There's something about his stillness, his attentiveness that makes you trust him. If she'd had a son, this is the kind of man she would have wanted him to be. Listen to her! Old fool.

"I thought perhaps I could fill in for Luis. For the rest of the summer."

"You'd do that?"

"Sure. I like working out here. I know the place. Know the horses."

"I thought I could send Cream and Sugar to Royce and Julia."

He nods. "You could. But don't you like to ride?"

She considers. "You got any other reasons for hanging around here?"

He looks away. Drums his fingers on the tabletop. "You're as bad as Anita." His tone is bitter.

Caught off guard, Toby says, "I was thinking of Isabel."

"Oh." He laughs. Embarrassed, perhaps. Caught. "Maybe. But I don't want to crowd her."

"Long way to drive every day."

"I noticed Corey pulled in a trailer. I thought I could pitch a tent on the homestead place alongside Anita and Luis. I'd have access to water. A shower and a bathroom. I'd be close, if . . . well, if they needed me."

"A tent? You don't think you're a little old for that?"

"They make cots. And air mattresses. It's not that far to town if I need to sleep in a bed for a night or two."

"I don't know how much longer Nola Jean plans to stay. You could have Larkspur once she's gone."

"It's a deal, then?"

"I can't pay you a whole lot."

Gabe shakes his head. "No. I'm doing this for Luis. Just pay me what you usually do for helping him."

"I want to pay Anita and Luis as I have. They depend on it, and now, with medical bills."

"Of course. As it should be."

He stands, then. His business done. Toby walks him to the door, watches him walk away. She's thinking she could get used to this, having Gabe around. It's a blue sky morning. This is the day Nola Jean will meet her mother. Things change, and that's life. Well, then. Best get on with it.

Nola Jean

NOLA JEAN TIMES HER ARRIVAL AT THE CONESTOGA RESTAURANT IN the Plains Hotel a half hour early. She crosses the sizeable lobby, past the doors to the Wigwam Bar, which is closed this time of day. A large stained-glass skylight drops hints of rose and blue on the mosaic tiled floor. Marble columns. The central chandelier, a teepee with metal buffalos circling it. A grand piano. Several sitting areas, here and there. A grandfather clock, stopped at two o'clock for want of someone to wind it. A shoeshine bench. Upholstered chairs with wooden arms, leather inserts, the upholstery in good shape, red with Native patterns. Gorgeous old rugs. Saddles. Floor crocks. Lanterns. The overall effect is stately and tasteful, except that several giant urns and pottery vases are filled not just with ubiquitous silk flowers but with actual plastic ferns. If Nola Jean weren't so nervous, she'd take her time to explore the décor and architectural design elements of this grand old place.

The Conestoga Restaurant is tucked off the main lobby behind a set of stairs. Nola Jean enters under a canvas canopy draped over curved ribs like a covered wagon. A painted tile mural depicts cowboys on horseback roping steers. The place is empty except for a bartender wiping stemmed glasses behind an elegant curved bar made of mahogany and carved leather. Sit anywhere, he says. Nola Jean notes the long-legged high-backed stools at the bar, but she needs more privacy. Twelve wooden booths are laid out in rows of three. Green leather seats, high backs upholstered in a brick-and-brown print, lanterns attached on the side. Atop the booths, more western accoutrements—battered teakettles, an ancient coffee grinder, woven baskets. A seating area for reserved groups sits behind a partition, though no one is here today. On the wall, a framed newspaper entry boasts of the famous fourth-floor ghost, Rosie, who shot her husband when she caught him on their wedding night leaving the Wigwam Bar with a prostitute. Smaller tables and chairs fill the front area close to the bar and a second street entrance. Nola Jean takes her time, finally chooses a booth farthest from the bar where she has an angle on both entrances, the one from the main lobby and the one from the street.

A young waitress comes by; Nola Jean orders an Arnie Palmer. She tells the waitress she's expecting someone, an older woman. The bartender has disappeared, and the waitress retreats through double doors to what must be a kitchen to retrieve her drink. Then, she waits.

The wait has already been interminable. Nola Jean woke early, before five o'clock. Watched the sun rise from her porch. Went for a walk. Showered, dressed, changed clothes three times. She settled on skinny jeans, sandals, a cornflower blue collared shirt with long sleeves that she rolled twice. Long, dangly silver earrings. Ate breakfast in her cabin. Tried to read. Following the advice of her therapist, she made notes to remind herself what questions to ask: Who was her father? What were the circumstances of her birth? Any hereditary health issues she should be made aware of? Does she have half siblings? She has no idea if any of these questions are appropriate to ask the woman who gave her away fifty years ago.

She read and reread the letter and emails she's received from Josephine. She mentally walked through what Toby told her about her adoption into the Bolden family.

There are some things she did not do. She did not talk to Toby again, after the way their last conversation ended. She can't deal with that right now. Nor has she said anything to Lila about seeking out her birth mother. After all, Lila may find herself in that spot someday, though her process with the adoptive parents of her baby girl has been far more open. Nola Jean plans to travel to Germany to see Lila in September, and it will be far better to tell her in person, after the fact.

She does, of course, wonder about her granddaughter. She never questioned Lila's decision. Lila was way too young to take on a child. And truth is, Nola Jean was in no position to step up at that point, her own life in shambles. Knowing how Lila agonized over her decision, how torn she was afterward, and how long the healing process had taken propelled Nola Jean into thinking about her own birth mother. Up until then, she'd supposed her birth mother was callow, maybe even callous. That she had handed her baby off to an orphanage and never looked back.

Her granddaughter would now be ten years old. Nola Jean knows Lila will always love her, that she has learned to live with the ache in her heart. She knows this because her own heart aches for the granddaughter she will never know. Is it possible that her birth mother aches for her?

The woman who joins her at the booth also arrives early. She comes in from the street entrance and scans the place quickly. Cropped wavy gray hair. Tall. Glasses. Wearing a navy blue skirt, blue-and-white flowered blouse, small earrings. A white sweater draped over one arm. A small shoulder bag. She's carrying a large manila envelope. She moves swiftly to the booth where Nola Jean is seated.

"Nola Jean?" she says.

Nola Jean swivels her feet outside the booth and stands. She can't find her voice. She nods, and the woman smiles.

They both laugh a bit, the way people do when a situation is awkward. They don't touch.

"Well," Josie says. "Let's sit."

They do, and immediately the waitress appears at Josie's elbow.

"Oh, I uh . . . what are you having?"

"An Arnie Palmer."

"That sounds good. Me too."

When the waitress moves away, Josie opens the manila folder and slides out a pile of photos. She chooses one of a young woman who can't be more than a teenager, light hair, sparkling blue eyes. She slides it across the table to Nola Jean.

Nola Jean looks from the photo to Josie's face. A resemblance, but not the same.

"This is Cecile. My younger sister. Your mother," Josie says.

"Oh." All the air rushes out of Nola Jean's stomach. Gut-punched.

"You didn't know?"

190

"No, I thought . . ."

"Oh, dear god," Josie says. She reaches out a hand, places it on Nola Jean's arm. It's an awkward stretch across the big table. She removes it immediately, as if she's touched scorching coals. "I assumed . . . when you contacted me, I thought your detective would have found out."

Nola Jean searches her mental rolodex. In her introductory letter, she said only that her hired detective found Josephine's address. She had written that she was searching for her birth mother.

"But . . . your name was on the birth certificate. It said Josephine Taylor."

Josie shakes her head. "I never knew that. Though I can see how a mix-up could have happened. There was . . . well, it was chaotic. And confusing. I'm so sorry."

"Is she . . ."

Josie nods. "She died a long time ago."

"I see. Well, I . . . I think I need a minute. Is there . . . ?"

Josie points toward the main lobby. "Across the lobby, past the desk. Turn left. Take all the time you need."

Nola Jean points herself toward the lobby. She walks past what used to be a gift shop, not noticing the lime-colored stained glass above the display windows. Walks down a hallway, red and blue Southwest-patterned carpet. Into a bathroom with the same mosaic tiled floor, white with rosettes of blood red and black. Stares at her face in the mirror above the sink.

She had prepared. She had pictured her mother fat, homely, destitute, beautiful, talented, everything but dead. Never dead.

She splashes cold water on her face. Doesn't care if her mascara runs. She grips the edge of the counter until her fingernails turn white. Her knees threaten to buckle. She's twelve, waiting for her turn at the barrel race. She's not good at it, the horses frighten her, but she's practiced, practiced, and Toby puts her hand on her back, calms her, says Breathe. Breathe. It's Toby's hand she imagines now. Toby's voice. And she breathes and she stills. She straightens her spine. Pulls her shoulders back. Act like a Bolden, she says out loud to the stricken woman in the mirror.

Anita

MIDAFTERNOON, WHILE LUIS CATNAPS, ANITA WALKS TO TOBY'S. SHE finds Toby behind the house, pulling weeds in the garden. Toby has dragged over one of the lawn chairs, sits precariously tipped forward, one hand steadying herself on the ground while the other yanks at thistles and ragweed. Good god.

"Here, now." Anita places both hands on Toby's shoulders, pulls back until the chair rights itself on four legs. "What are you trying to do? Break a hip?"

Toby looks up from under the brim of her gardening hat. Anita can see she's juggling the attitude she wants to take. Toby's mouth tightens, then gives way to a sly grin as she reaches a decision. "How about a cup of coffee?"

Anita nods. Probably for the best that Toby ignored her concern. That would only start them down a path of bickering, and soon, one or the other would say something she'd regret. She responds to Toby's offer by lifting one hand off Toby's shoulder and patting it down again. Hell, yes. That's what she means, and Toby knows it.

Once they're seated at the kitchen table, these two old friends, Toby says, "How's he doing?"

"Asleep. He had a rough night."

"Is he in pain?"

"I don't think so. Not his body."

Toby grunts. At their age, they know all about other kinds of pain. "And you?"

Anita only shakes her head.

"Well. It'll take some getting used to," Toby says.

Anita's eyes brim with tears, but she doesn't trust herself to speak. When you mold your life with someone else, you always know that something can happen to one of you that will alter your life. You know it when you say I do and promise through sickness and in health, but somehow, when you're young, you think you have all the time in the world. Then, when you're older, if you've escaped, you don't believe it will happen. She'd crawl through a desert or run through fire to be beside Luis. She'd live in squalor. Compared to losing him, which is unthinkable, these trials are nothing. Still, that doesn't mean there are no losses for her. They don't know yet how this will play out in the long run. But in the short run? Less travel. Less freedom. Luis has always been her rock. She relies on him to be the strong one. There's this too. She's never kept things from him, but now she feels she must keep her fears and grief to herself. She doesn't want him to think that she sees him as anything less than he was. Which brings her to why she wanted to see Toby this afternoon.

"How about some blueberry cobbler?" Toby asks. "I made it yesterday."

"No, thanks."

"Sure? You'd be doing me a favor."

"I could take some home with me."

"Great." Toby starts to get up.

"Wait. Luis isn't supposed to have carbs and stuff. Fruits and vegetables. Less meat."

Toby, half between sitting and standing, says, "Blueberries?"

Anita laughs. Amid all the fear and anguish, it feels good. "Oh, hell. Give me some. A little bit."

Toby's busy for a few moments arranging the cobbler in two bowls. Her idea of a little bit is a brimming bowl, but Anita does not protest.

After a few bites, she says, "Toby. I need you to do something for me."

Toby, poised with her spoon in the air, says, "Okay?"

"I want you to tell Luis that we can't stay out here."

She doesn't look up from her bowl. She can feel Toby's intensity, the look she is giving her. She waits for Toby to find words.

"And why would I do that?"

"Because Delia and I think we should move into town. Be closer to her. And to the hospital."

"No, I mean what reason could I give?"

Anita stands, takes her bowl to the sink, rinses it. With her back to Toby, she says, "He won't be able to do the work."

"You can't think that would matter to me."

"No, but it will matter to him."

"You think he won't be able to stand idle."

Anita turns, leans back against the counter. "What do you think?"

Toby's eyes are bright. "I may have a solution."

Anita doesn't want Toby's solution. She wants Toby to accept her solution. Why can't she, for once, go along with someone else's idea?

"Gabe came to see me early this morning," Toby says.

"Gabe?"

"He wants to bring a tent out here. Take on Luis's duties for the rest of the summer."

"A tent?"

"He can have Larkspur after Nola Jean leaves."

"You and Gabe cooked this up, all on your own?"

Anita has turned, grabbed a dishrag, scrubs at the counter. She doesn't see crumbs or dirt. She needs something to do with her hands.

"We didn't cook anything. Gabe's trying to help."

Anita flings the wet rag in the sink, turns. Because she's standing and Toby's sitting, she looms over her, an unusual advantage. "You should have talked to me first."

"I would have. There wasn't time . . ."

"Gabe should have talked to me. Before he started spouting off behind my back."

Toby stands. "Well, did you ask Luis what he thinks?"

"No. No, I didn't."

"Well, then . . ."

"That's not the same. Luis is . . . he's hurt. And he's not in a position, right now, to decide what's best."

"And you are?"

"I'm sure as hell a damn sight more able than Gabe."

Toby braces herself against the table. Her face drops, the color drains out like water from a bath after someone's pulled the plug. She slowly lowers herself to her chair. "Oh, dear god," she says.

Alarmed, Anita waits until Toby's color returns. Not sure what to do with herself, she shifts her weight from one foot to the other.

Finally, Toby says. "I'm not sure I can lie to him." She glares at Anita. "That's what it would be. A lie."

Anita has lost all patience. Or sympathy. She's a mother bear. "Not the first time you've told a lie. Is it?"

With that, she walks out. She leaves Toby sitting at her kitchen table. Let her stew for a while. She walks back to their trailer, but she's in a shitty mood and doesn't want to take that inside to Luis. She decides to use the hose to water the potted plants. The geraniums need deadheaded, so she drops the hose to pluck the dead flowers off. While dropping faded blossoms on the ground, she thinks about seeing Nola Jean drive by early in the day. She'd been looking out the window above the sink, saw Nola Jean's car, and thought, Where the hell can she be going now? She's a flighty bird, that one. Can't sit still for a minute. So, Gabe and Nola Jean discovered that she had lied to them. Lied to them both. To break them up. She supposes she did, though she believed what she told them at the time. She thought, then, that she saw the truth about what drew them together, and they were too dumb, too young, too lovestruck to see it for themselves. So, she hadn't lied so much as pointed out the obvious. The only lie was that she led each of them to believe the other had confessed to what she assumed were their unconscious motives. Sometimes, others can see what a person can't see for themselves. Like now. Luis can't see that he needs protecting. She's right about this. She knows she is. She can handle Gabe. Get him to butt out. Toby? Toby can't be handled, but she's decent. In the end, she'll want what's best for Luis.

By the time she's brought her thinking round, she's standing in a pool of water. Stomping her feet in the grass, she turns off the spigot. She removes her wet shoes, leaves them outside on the steps to the trailer. Pastes a smile on her face, takes a breath to quiet her quivering spirit, and goes inside to pretend that everything is all right.

Josie

IN NOLA JEAN'S ABSENCE, JOSIE ROLLS AND UNROLLS THE CORNER of her paper napkin, shredding it in the process. She had no way of knowing. Did she? Had she missed something in Nola Jean's letter? Should she go and check on Nola Jean? She's been gone a long time. Josie looks at her watch. Can't have been that long, five minutes, ten. She has no idea what to do. She pulls out her phone to call Dan when Nola Jean emerges from the lobby. She looks, what, resolute? Not shattered.

Josie waits until she sits. Then, she blurts, "I'm so sorry. I had no idea. Maybe I should have."

Nola Jean raises one hand. "You couldn't have known."

Josie clamps her mouth. The urge to apologize again and again is overwhelming, but she knows that is not what Nola Jean came to hear. She takes a deep breath. She looks over Nola Jean's shoulder, this corner, that, casting about for a place to start. She leans her arms on the table, removes them, leans again. Through all this, Nola Jean waits. Silent. Josie is conscious of the blower from the air conditioner. The sweat on the glasses of Arnie Palmer. Her mouth tastes metallic, which she read somewhere has to do with adrenaline, her body calculating that she's in a high-risk situation. Her heart thumps so hard she looks down at her chest to see if her shirt is moving.

"Please," Nola Jean says. "I'd like to know what happened."

Nola Jean's voice is calm. Almost soothing. How does she do it? Josie's nerves clang like a Salvation Army band. She opens her mouth. The words are tremulous, at first, but she gains confidence from Nola Jean's direct gaze. And it feels good, too, to let the words tumble out at last.

"Cecile was six years younger than me. Our parents were very strict. Our dad was a minister of a small Christian sect, house churches mostly. We lived in a small town in eastern Nebraska." She stops to take a drink. Gather herself. Takes a ragged breath. "I'm sorry. This is going to take a while."

"I'm not going anywhere."

Josie sighs. "Do you want any food?"

Nola Jean shakes her head.

Of course not. She just wants Josie to get on with it. She licks her lips and begins.

"I went to college at the university in Lincoln. Math major. And when I graduated, I got a job teaching math at Lincoln High School. I had a small apartment. Cecile was a senior in high school, 1961. Your father, Tom Brickman, was her boyfriend."

Josie pauses and leafs through her photos until she finds one of a young couple. Cecile, wearing a long, full-skirted, strapless pink gown; Tom, a tuxedo with a ruffled shirt front. They smile at the camera as only young people can, as if a benevolent world is wide open and waiting for them. She places the photo in front of Nola Jean who picks it up, studies it, traces her finger across the teen faces of her parents. Josie watches with a lump in her throat. She sees, now, how like Cecile this woman is, those striking blue eyes, the way she pays attention.

"That's them?" Nola Jean says. "Was this a prom?"

Josie smiles. "Yeah. Senior year. Anyone could see they were crazy for each other. Tom was good-looking, athletic. An only child of an older couple." Before Nola Jean can think to ask, Josie adds, "His parents are dead. Cecile, your mother, was everybody's friend. She loved to make beautiful things. Out of nothing, really: rocks, bird feathers, fabric, little bits of this and that. Of course, our father didn't consider that important."

Nola Jean makes a small sound, a yelp. Some recognition, Josie guesses, but there's time for that later. Right now, she needs to finish this story. The whole story. Then it will be up to Nola Jean to decide what she wants to do.

"Tom decided to enlist in the army. He was from a farm family. Not much money. He thought he could serve his term, then go to college on the GI bill. But he didn't make it out of basic training. Some kind of accident on the firing range."

"Wow," Nola Jean says. Just wow. The impossible. The improbable. What else is there to say?

Josie stops, drinks from her glass. Her hand flutters at her neck until her fingers land on the delicate heart necklace she's wearing. She rests her hand there, drawing strength.

"Did he know Cecile was pregnant?"

"No. They knew they wanted to spend their lives together. We were taught that sex outside of marriage is a sin, but my parents wouldn't give permission for them to be married. Cecile was seventeen. My father said she was too young to know what she wanted. But the real reason was that Tom was Catholic. In 1961 the Catholic Church required non-Catholics to pledge that any children would be raised in the Catholic faith, and to my father, this was tantamount to forcing Cecile to become a communist. Worse, even. Since it involved her immortal soul. My parents thought the separation would break them up."

"Would that have worked?"

"I doubt it. In their hearts, they were already married. When we received word of Tom's death, Cecile was devastated. She was attending a small college in Fremont, but she stopped going to class. Stopped, well, everything. We were very worried about her. Eventually she dropped out. Went home. I don't think she knew she was pregnant yet. And when she found out, she was glad. She thought she'd have a piece of Tom to keep. But our parents . . . well, they were outraged. And ashamed. The idea that one of their daughters . . . they just couldn't cope with it. So, they stuck Cecile in the car and drove her to Lincoln. To me. And my instructions were to take her to an unwed mothers' home. Our parents wanted nothing to do with her; my father thought it would taint his ministry."

"So, that's what you did?"

"Not exactly. Cecile wanted desperately to keep the baby. You. She talked me into letting her stay at my apartment. We lied to our parents. That was a sin, too, but we'd already committed that one many times. We had to, to have any semblance of normal life."

She watches Nola Jean to see if there's a flicker of understanding. She thinks Nola Jean could say something—all kids lie to their parents, or you did what you had to do—but Nola Jean just looks at her with that steady gaze. Says nothing. Josie shifts her weight in her seat and continues.

"Cecile concocted a plan, how she'd have the baby, get a job. I thought she was, to put it kindly, unrealistic. In 1962 there weren't a lot of options for unwed mothers. But Cecile could be very persuasive. She said we'd trade shifts; she'd work nights. Eventually, maybe we could find an older woman, some church lady, to take care of the baby while we worked."

"How would you keep your parents from finding out?"

Relieved to hear Nola Jean speak, Josie leans into her story. "Cecile had that figured out too. She thought once they met the baby, they'd fall in love with the child and all would be forgiven."

"So, you went along with it?"

Josie nods. "We bought a crib. Read baby books. Those are some of my happiest memories. The thought of raising Tom's baby restored my broken sister to life again. How could I not go along with that?"

"Didn't your parents check with the unwed mothers' home?"

"Oh, no. They wanted nothing to do with it. They wanted to keep themselves removed. And pure. They never came to Lincoln. I went home for the holidays, like always. Cecile stayed at the apartment."

"I see."

Josie bites her lip, knots and unknots her hands. "Now, the story gets harder."

"Please. Go on," Nola Jean says.

"We did go to a doctor. But neither of us knew what to expect. So, in the later stages of her pregnancy, when Cecile began to get headaches, and her feet and ankles swelled, we just thought that was a natural part of pregnancy."

"Preeclampsia," Nola Jean guesses. Her face clouds, hard to read. Pain, maybe.

Josie nods. "I was at school that day. Cecile was home alone, and her water broke. Early. Her due date wasn't for a couple of weeks. She called the principal's office, but I didn't get the message. By the time I got home, she was in a bad way. I took her to the hospital ER. You were born an hour and a half later, but by then, it was clear that Cecile was in serious trouble. Her blood pressure skyrocketed; they couldn't get it under control. You were beautiful, we both thought that. She had time to tell me that."

Josie looks down. Tears fall on the tabletop. She fishes in her purse for a tissue.

"Did she . . . did she give me a name?"

Josie wipes at her face with the tissue. "Rachel," she whispers. "She wanted to call you Rachel."

Nola Jean looks away, then back. "The birth certificate just said baby girl. No name."

"I know," Josie says. "That's because—I thought it would be harder."

"You thought?"

Josie's hands tremble. She clasps them together hard in her lap, but she can't keep the tremor from her voice. "Before Cecile . . . your mother, died, she made me promise." Josie looks away, toward the empty room, anywhere but at Nola Jean's face. Then, steeling herself, she looks back, and with a shaky breath says, "She made me promise that I would raise you. She insisted. She was so agitated. I was half out of my mind. I would have said anything to give her peace. And so, I did. I promised. I promised my dying sister that I would give her newborn infant a home."

Josie openly sobs. The waitress starts toward their table. Nola Jean notices, raises her hand, and signals that they're okay. Please don't disturb.

"Anyone might have done that," Nola Jean says.

"We weren't anyone. We were religious. I had never lied to my sister. And when I made the promise, I honestly thought I could do it. I intended to." Josie's eyes roam wildly, looking back at 1962, reliving those awful hours. "I went home that night. I couldn't sleep. I looked at your crib. I tried to imagine my life. The man I hoped to meet. The children I hoped to have. I didn't see how . . . how could I manage? I wept. And in the morning, when I went back to the hospital, I held you in my arms while the chaplain helped me make plans for my sister's burial. And then I asked a nurse to call the orphanage. Someone came that afternoon. I signed papers. And then, I walked out of your life. I called my parents and told them Cecile had died in childbirth. And I told them . . . I told them the baby died too."

Josie stops to blow her nose.

"I think . . . I think they were relieved," she says.

"Relieved?" Nola Jean sounds stunned.

"Well, the wages of sin . . ."

"I'm sorry. I don't understand."

"The wages of sin is death. I think my father thought Cecile got what she deserved. And her death solved a lot of problems for him. They told everyone she died of pneumonia."

"But the baby? Why did you tell them that the baby died?"

Josie shrugs. "I'm not sure I know. It just seemed, at the time, I didn't know what else to do. I was ashamed of the role I had played. I didn't want them to have any hold on you, to even know about you. I thought you'd be freer away from our family. Maybe, maybe I wanted to punish them. I was angry. So angry."

"Maybe you just wanted to remove another complication. That's why you didn't give the orphanage the name my mother chose for me. Because you thought it'd be easier to forget me. No name. No baby. Poof. Gone."

Nola Jean's tone is hard. Cold. Josie expected it, and still it hurts. Josie balls her fists on the tabletop. "They thought all along the baby would be adopted. That was what they wanted. I didn't . . . I guess . . . you're right, it did get me off the hook."

"You've played the dutiful daughter all this time?"

The sneer in Nola Jean's voice is marked. Josie works hard to keep her feet from carrying her out of the room.

"I married. Moved away. Had little contact with either of them until my father died. Twenty-five years ago. My mother stayed in Weston, where my father's last church was. We moved to Colorado eight years ago when Dan, my husband, retired. My mother's here now, in Fort Collins. In assisted living. She's ninety-four."

"You never told her?"

"No, I wanted to. I thought maybe, after my father died, I could. Because then, when he was gone, my mother got her ears pierced."

Nola Jean collects her bag. Shifts her weight to the edge of the booth and stands. "I need to go," she says.

"Wait. Please, wait. I don't know anything about you. Your life. I was hoping . . ." but Nola Jean walks away. Just like that. Josie is left staring at a vacant spot at the table and a gaping hole in her life.

Nola Jean

AFTER LEAVING JOSEPHINE KLINGMAN IN THE CONESTOGA RESTAURANT, Nola Jean walks blindly to her car. She knows she's in no shape to drive, but she doesn't want to be a spectacle in a coffee shop or bar either. She drives aimlessly until she discovers a city park with a playground, lake, a full-sized Union Pacific locomotive displayed. Not too many people. She parks, walks purposely to a metal bench, plops down, hides her face in her hands, and gives in to shudders and sobs.

What the hell is the matter with her? What did she expect? A living mother, for one thing. She is an utter fool. Entertaining fantasies of someone missing her, loving her in absentia all her life. Instead, she had been erased. Not even a memory or flutter in someone's mind. Nameless. Gotten rid of. Expunged. No one has been thinking of her.

God. Damn. Josephine. How could she live with such a lie? And to what end?

She wipes her eyes and nose on her shirtsleeve. Doesn't care if it's gauche. Nobody's watching. Nobody cares. That's the theme of her life. Nobody. Nobody.

Well, not nobody. Toby.

She sits for a long while, trying not to think. Dusk happens, unremarkable in a city. A couple walks by hand in hand, heedless of her existence. A goose explores the ground beneath her feet, hoping for crumbs. Squirrels sit on their haunches to beg until she shoos them away. No stars. Not even Venus on the low horizon.

She stands. Certain of only one thing. She wants to go home.

Josie

EXHAUSTED AFTER HER MEETING WITH NOLA JEAN, JOSIE CAN BARELY remember where she left the car. Luckily, the fob has a button that sounds a signal. She manages to buckle herself in. She sits and stares so long, attempting to calm herself, that a passerby taps on the car window and mimes, Are you all right? Josie tries to lower the window, but of course, she can't without starting the engine, these new-fangled cars, everything electronic. She forces a smile and waves, and the woman walks away.

After that, she does start the car. She herds it onto the freeway. The traffic is heavy this time of day, people going back and forth to work. She's happy to drive slowly. She turns on NPR, the classics station, but the music jangles her nerves further.

She should have called Dan. He'll be worried. But what could she say? The day had not gone at all the way she'd imagined. She had worried, there's that. She felt terrible all her life about not keeping the baby as she had promised. She thought that was worse than the lie she told her parents. Either way—adoption or dead—the baby was out of their lives. She hadn't thought it would matter to Nola Jean, but it did. Somehow. Nola Jean came thinking her mother was alive; that was a terrible shock. But even that, she seemed to take in. But what was it Nola Jean accused her of? Wanting to remove a complication. Had she? Is that what she had done?

At the time, she wanted her parents to feel bad. She wanted them to suffer. She thought the double loss, their daughter and any possible trace of her, would be harder for them to bear. But now, only now, she sees that it might have made things easier. They didn't have to wonder, as she always had, whether the infant found a good home, whether she took after Cecile in any way, whether she liked school or music or beautiful things. Watching her sons grow up, passing through every age and stage, she'd think about Cecile's baby: Did she throw tantrums when she got too tired? Did she like to hear *Goodnight Moon*? Did she mush her ice cream into soup in a bowl before eating it? She walked through her whole adult life with that child on her mind, while her parents mourned and moved on.

When she reaches the outskirts of Fort Collins, she does not head home. Dan will be waiting. And he can wait a little longer. She pulls into the parking lot of her mother's assisted living facility.

Think about this now, she says to herself. Be kind. What are your motives? Do you want to bring suffering to your ninety-four-year-old mother? Do you want to rub her face in your lie? Do you need atonement and expect it unfairly?

She shakes her head, but it doesn't help. Nothing falls into place. She doesn't have a clear sense of herself or her motives. She only knows that she has lived with this lie too long, and if she doesn't do something now, she never will.

Her mother is in her room. Evelyn keeps the door locked, so she's frightened when Josie knocks since she hardly ever calls on her mother in the evening. "Mom," Josie says. "It's me."

Evelyn unlocks the door. Takes one look at Josie's face. Says, "Oh, my dear, what has happened?"

"Mom, let's sit down."

She tells her the story, leaving nothing out. Their plan for keeping the baby. Her broken promise to Cecile. Her lie about the baby's death. She tells it in as few sentences as possible while looking straight into her mother's face. Evelyn doesn't flinch. She keeps her eyes glued on Josie's. At one point, Josie is not even sure that her mother is breathing.

She finishes and waits for the recriminations. She closes her eyes, blindfolded in front of a firing squad. When she opens them, tears are streaming down her mother's face, falling on the front of her shirt leaving dark blobs in the cotton fabric, but she is silent.

"Mom?"

Terrified that her mother has had a heart attack or a stroke, Josie grabs a tissue, kneels in front of her mother and wipes her face. Her mother grabs her by the wrist, clutches like an eagle with prey.

"Cecile's child is alive?" she says at last. Her voice filled with wonder.

Josie nods.

"Your father . . . your father would never let me speak of her. Cecile."

"I'm sorry, Mom. So sorry."

"Does she . . . does the girl look like Cecile?"

"I guess . . . maybe, the eyes. Something in her manner. She's fifty years old."

They laugh, then. Laugh and cry. Josie sits again across from her mother. She's been as tense as a stretched rubber band. Everything aches, her neck, her back, her shoulders.

"Mom, aren't you . . . I lied to you."

"Do you think I can meet her?"

"I don't know. She was very upset."

"Maybe, after a little time. Maybe then?"

"Do you want to?"

"She's the lamb in the thicket, don't you see?"

That terrible story. The one where God asks Abraham to sacrifice his son, Isaac, on an altar, and at the last minute, provides a lamb in the thicket instead. Josie's always hated that story. What kind of god would require such a test of obedience? And Isaac, going along willingly? It's supposed to be a story of God's provision, trust in the impossible and redemption. So, yes, she understands that to her mother Nola Jean's existence is a second chance. But can she possibly believe that their renouncement of Cecile was an act of obedience? She pulls back from her mother, chilled. She's ice. No, no, no, not this, not after all this time.

Her mother watches her. Evelyn's eyes narrow. Josie knows that look. Sanctimonious. "We did what we thought was right," she says. Her gaze does not falter, but her voice pleads.

Josie needs to know. She's afraid of the answer, but she leans forward, arms rested on her knees. "Do you still think it was right, Mom?"

Her mother looks down at her hands in lap. She turns them palm up, supplication, and whispers, "No."

Josie covers her mother's hands with hers. Both their hands tremble, but they don't let go.

Toby

IT'S GROWING LATE AND NEARLY DARK WHEN LUIS KNOCKS ON TOBY'S door. She's gone inside to avoid the night bugs but left the door open, so she spies him through the screen door before she rises from the couch.

"Luis, c'mon in," she calls.

He stands, just inside the door.

"I'm surprised to see you," she says. "Sit down." She waves him to the rocking chair. "You want anything? Tea? Water?"

"No, no." Luis sits. His hands play on his knees.

Toby sits on the couch. "I'm surprised Anita let you out of her sight," she says.

Luis chuckles. "She's having a word with Gabe. Sounds pretty heated. I thought I'd slip away while I had the chance."

Toby nods. "I see. Well. What's on your mind?" She can see this is hard for him. Tries to figure out how to help him say what he has to say, but mind-reading has never been her strong suit.

"If it's about the work, don't worry," she says.

"No. No, it's not that. Well, not only that. Anita'll have my hide if I don't take it easy, at least the rest of this summer. Until we get the medication figured out."

"That makes sense."

"I expect you'll need to hire somebody else."

"There's not all that much left to do." Toby's racing through her mind. She wants to tell him Gabe offered to fill in, but she's pretty sure that's what Anita is giving Gabe an earful about. Plus, maybe Luis is here to tell her they're moving into town, so she won't have to fabricate some excuse nobody would believe. So, she waits.

"It's just . . . well, I've come to think of the Bluestem as our home. Of sorts. I mean, I know we don't own it, but . . ."

"You belong here. Of course. You do." Toby's touched. She wants to say, you can come back any time. Or stay all the time you want. But, dammit it all, what's she supposed to do?

"I was just wondering . . . if it would matter . . . I mean, you wouldn't need to pay us or anything, but if we could just stay on . . . where we're used to. I'd miss the meadowlarks. Even the damn magpies. And the stars at night. You can't even see the Milky Way in town. I think I could rest better here than anywhere else. Do you know what I mean?"

"Oh, Luis," she manages to say before Anita bursts through the door without knocking. Close behind her is Gabe.

Anita heads straight to Luis. "C'mon, old man. Let's go home."

"Now, hold on, Anita," Luis says.

Anita turns to Toby. "Tell him. Tell him what you told me today."

Toby looks from Anita to Gabe. Gabe raises his hands, shakes his head.

Luis stands. "What's this about, Anita? You talked to Toby today?"

"Go on," Anita says. She looks exactly like Rita Winehart in third grade when she dared Toby to spit in their teacher's food. None of them liked the teacher, but Rita knew Toby couldn't resist a dare. And she was right. But it was Toby and not Rita who got in trouble.

Toby stands too. She looks from one face to another, these three people, all waiting for her to pronounce judgment on their lives. How can she? She loves all of them, can't they see that? She scrambles about for something useful to say when headlights cut across the room through the screen door.

"Oh, now what?" she cries.

All of them hear the slam of a car door. They're tuned to the steps on the porch when they hear Nola Jean's voice.

"What's going on in here? Some sort of convention?"

"Might as well join us," Toby calls.

Nola Jean steps into the room. She takes a stance beside Gabe, who pauses long to look at her. Quietly, he asks, "You alright?"

"Not really," Nola Jean says, intended only for him, but Toby hears and sees she is clearly not all right. Her eyes are red. Her hair disheveled.

"What's going on?" Nola Jean asks.

"Your mother has something to say," Anita states.

"Mom?"

Toby looks at their expectant faces. She shakes her head, full of sorrow. "I can't do it, Anita. I'm sorry."

"Oh, hell," Anita says.

"Do what?" Luis asks.

Anita turns to Luis, her eyes brimming with tears. "I asked Toby to tell you that we can't stay out here."

"Why the Sam Hill would you do that?"

"Delia and I . . . we think you'd be better off in town."

"So, you went behind my back?" His voice is incredulous. Anita takes hold of his arm, and Luis shakes it off.

"I knew you wouldn't listen to me," she says. "And besides, they went behind my back. And yours."

"Who did? What are you talking about?"

Anita points an accusing finger. "Them. Toby and Gabe."

"Nobody went behind anybody's back," Gabe says.

"You did too. You sure didn't talk to me first."

"Would somebody please tell me what the hell you are talking about?" Luis says. He so rarely raises his voice that the whole room stops cold.

"Take it easy," Anita says.

Toby, also fearful that Luis may have another heart attack, blurts, "Gabe talked to me about filling in for you over the summer."

"You did?" Luis says to Gabe. "Why didn't you say something?"

"I would have. I wanted to make sure it was doable first," Gabe answers.

Nola Jean chimes in, "Did anybody think to ask Luis what he wants?"

That's the last straw for Toby. "You're a fine one to talk. You didn't bother to ask me what I wanted when you went to Dr. Penny behind my back."

Suddenly, Nola Jean's face collapses. A jack-o-lantern left on the porch too long. She puts her face in her hands and sobs.

Horrified, Toby, along with the rest of them, stands frozen. Gabe puts his arm around Nola Jean. "Here, now," he says.

Nola Jean looks up from her tear-stained face, wipes her nose on her shirtsleeve. "I found out today that my birth mother is dead. She died in childbirth. My birth. And her sister told everybody that I died too. So, yeah, I talked to Dr. Penny. And you know why? Because I didn't think you'd listen to me. And because . . ." her voice pitches an octave higher, straining through tears, "I don't want to lose you too."

Toby opens her mouth, but no words come out. A river runs through her, washing all thoughts aside. Her throat aches. She reaches a hand toward Nola Jean; it flutters and falls at her side. Gabe has taken Nola Jean into his arms; she cries against his shoulder. Anita has grabbed hold of Luis's hand, for once not steamed up about Gabe and Nola Jean. Small mercies, Toby thinks, relieved to entertain an actual thought. Small mercies, how they need them.

"Everybody, calm down," she manages to say. Her voice sounds forced, squeaky, but somehow it takes effect. The room quiets. "Let's all sit down."

They do sit. Luis, in the rocking chair. Anita, on a stool at his feet. Nola Jean joins Toby on the couch, though on the opposite end. Gabe pulls a chair in from the kitchen and places it beside Nola Jean.

Toby realizes that she is in charge. It's up to her now. First, she turns to Nola Jean.

"I'm so sorry to hear about your mother. That must have been a terrible blow."

The others nod and murmur. Toby feels like she's conducting a group therapy session, not that she's ever been to a group therapy session. What the hell should she say next?

Nola Jean helps her out. "It's quite a story," she says. "For another time." She manages a quavering smile. Again, she wipes her nose on her sleeve. The sleeve is damp and streaked by now, and the incongruity of that sleeve on her fashion-minded, appearance-conscious, sometimes fastidious daughter nearly turns Toby into a quivering gelatinous mass.

Toby takes a deep breath, leans toward Nola Jean, and pats her arm. Nola Jean does not shy away as Toby expected she might. Toby shifts her weight nearer to make touching Nola Jean less awkward. Then, she turns to Anita and Luis.

"Now, I think you know, Luis, that Anita is only thinking of you." Luis grunts. Anita grabs his arm, and he nods.

"The two of you have some talking to do. But as for me, I would like nothing better than to have you stay on out here. For the rest of the summer. None of us knows what might happen after that. I'll continue to pay you, as I have, because Anita can help me out, and Luis, most of the fencing and heavy work is already done. Think of it as prorated wages."

Luis starts to protest, but Anita squeezes his arm, and he withdraws.

"Gabe has offered to fill in for you, especially with the horses. We've worked out an arrangement that we think is satisfactory, but the three of you can talk about that too. If you decide to move into town, I understand. But I would miss you. It gets lonesome."

Toby knows Nola Jean is looking at her, probably amazed to hear this admission. The silence stretches.

"Okay," Luis says.

"Okay?" Anita says.

Luis looks at her. "Okay, the three of us have some talking to do. Together."

"As for the rest, that's between me and Nola Jean," Toby says. She stands, dismissing them, and they know it. Luis, Anita, and Gabe all stand. Gabe turns to look at Nola Jean, and she stands too. Gives him a small smile.

Toby sees the three of them out the door. Then, she turns to her daughter. "Now," she says. "Do you want coffee, tea, or whiskey?"

Nola Jean looks down, silent, arms limp at her side. "I'm so tired. Do you think . . . ?"

Toby nods. "Tomorrow, then. Or the next day. Whenever you're ready."

Nola Jean moves toward the door where Toby is standing. "Tomorrow," she says. "For sure."

Toby steps out onto the porch with her daughter. They stand together silently, taking in the night.

"Look at that," Toby says. "You can see the Milky Way. You can't see that in town."

"I know," Nola Jean says. She's gazing up, but then she says, "I do know, Mom."

Toby nods, not trusting herself to speak. They stand like that, side by side. Nola Jean must be exhausted, but she makes no move to leave the porch. Somewhere out there, in the dark, Toby hears an owl asking whoo—who? Beyond the picket fence lie the things Toby knows, sage and yucca, the creak of windmills, the buzz of insects. She knows the meadowlark's song, the killdeer's cry. She knows the name of every blade of grass, the smell of coming rain, every hill and contour of her land, but she doesn't know what to do in this moment. Still, Nola Jean lingers, and Toby stands beside her, grateful and suffused with love. Bewildered, no more certain of tomorrow than the rest of us, Toby stands with her aching daughter, and, by god, she hopes it is enough.

THE END

ACKNOWLEDGMENTS

I AM A LUCKY WOMAN TO HAVE A CADRE OF FAMILY AND FRIENDS WHO love me, whether I am writing or not, and, at the same time, instill in me their value for my work. "Are you writing, Pam?" I hear when I walk in my neighborhood, attend Judson Church, meet friends for tea, participate in a Mundt family reunion. To all of you, I give my sincere thanks. Without you, I could not sustain this precarious work.

Seeds of this novel were planted when I had the good fortune to attend a Wishin' Jupiter Ranch Writing Retreat, hosted by Suzanne and Karl Kehm in the Sandhills of Nebraska. Inspired by other artists in attendance and reminded of the beauty of that fierce landscape, I sat on a bench in a cottonwood grove and began to dream this story. There, too, the original Cottonwood Leaf Band took form.

Thanks to Beth Waterhouse and the Oberholtzer Foundation for a writing week on Mallard Island, a week of cool weather, one wild storm, tons of camaraderie with other artists, and the blessed gift of time and space.

I have published four books now with the University of Nebraska Press. I graduated from the University of Nebraska–Lincoln a while ago, and it's especially sweet to have my work bear the Bison Books imprint. Thanks to Courtney Ochsner for choosing the book, to the anonymous reader who suggested I dump an ill-conceived epilogue, to Abigail Goodwin, Joeth Zucco, and all the staff at the press. It's a great comfort to me that I can rely on your professionalism and artistry.

Thank you to MOCA (Minnesota Ovarian Cancer Alliance) and the brave women I have met there for your commitment to honor life in all its various forms. Your ongoing work to educate and fund research is inspiring.

For my family—Shannon, Nadine, Henry, Raegan, Jacob, Elijah, Tyson, and Brad—you are the reason for everything. I love you.

Lamb Bright Saviors
Robert Vivian

The Mover of Bones
Robert Vivian

Water and Abandon
Robert Vivian

The Sacred White Turkey
Frances Washburn

Skin
Kellie Wells

The Leave-Takers: A Novel
Steven Wingate

Of Fathers and Fire: A Novel
Steven Wingate

To order or obtain more information on these or other University of Nebraska Press titles, visit nebraskapress.unl.edu.

CPSIA information can be obtained
at www.ICGtesting.com
Printed in the USA
LVHW111404110123
736566LV00003B/4